Aug 10.19

The
Fairy's Return
and
Other Princess Tales

ILLUSTRATED BY MARK ELLIOTT

GAIL CARSON LEVINE

The
Fairy's Return

and
Other Princess Tales

HARPERCOLLINSPUBLISHERS

Library of Congress Catalog Card Number: 2006929894
ISBN-10: 0-06-113061-3 (trade bdg.) — ISBN-13: 978-0-06-113061-8 (trade bdg.)

Typography by Al Cetta /   9 10 / ❖ First Edition

CONTENTS

The
Fairy's Mistake

All my thanks

to my wonderful editor, Alix Reid.

Without you, The Princess Tales

would never have been told.

—G.C.L.

One

Once upon a time, in the village of Snettering-on-Snoakes in the kingdom of Biddle, Rosella fetched water from the well for the four thousand and eighty-eighth time.

Rosella always fetched the water because her identical twin sister, Myrtle, always refused to go. And their mother, the widow Pickering, never made Myrtle do anything. Instead, she made Rosella do everything.

At the well the fairy Ethelinda was having a drink. When she saw Rosella coming, she changed herself into an old lady. Then she made herself look thirsty.

"Would you like a drink, Grandmother?" Rosella said.

"That would be lovely, dearie."

Rosella lowered her wooden bucket into the well. When she lifted it out, she held the dipper so the old lady could drink.

Ethelinda slurped the water. "Thank you. Your kindness merits a reward. From now—"

"You don't have . . ." Rosella stopped. Something

"She spat delicately into her hand."

funny was happening in her mouth. Had she lost a tooth? There was something hard under her tongue. And something hard in her cheek. "Excuse me." Now there was something in her other cheek. She spat delicately into her hand.

They weren't teeth. She was holding a diamond and two opals.

"There, dearie." Ethelinda smiled. "Isn't that nice?"

Two

"What took you so long?" Myrtle said when Rosella got home.

"Your sister almost perished from thirst, you lazybones," their mother said.

"I gave a drink to . . ." Something was in Rosella's mouth again. It was between her lip and her front teeth this time. "I gave a drink to an old lady." An emerald and another diamond fell out of her mouth. They landed on the dirt floor of the cottage.

"It was more important— What's that?" Myrtle said.

"What's that?" the widow said.

They both dove for the jewels, but Myrtle got there first.

"Rosella darling," the widow said, "sit down. Make yourself comfortable. Now tell us all about it. Don't leave anything out."

There wasn't much to tell, only enough to cover the bottom of Myrtle's teacup with gems.

"Which way did the old lady go?" Myrtle asked.

Rosella was puzzled. "She didn't go anywhere." An amethyst dropped into the teacup.

Myrtle grabbed the bucket and ran.

When she saw Myrtle in the distance, Ethelinda thought Rosella had come back. Only this time she wasn't tripping lightly down the path, smelling the flowers and humming a tune. She was hurtling along, head down, arms swinging, bucket flying. And then Ethelinda's fairy powers told her that this was Rosella's twin sister. Ethelinda got ready by turning herself into a knight.

"Where did the old lady go?" Myrtle said when she reached the well.

"I haven't seen anyone. I've been alone, hoping some kind maiden would come by and give me a drink. I can't do it myself with all this armor."

"What's in it for me if I do?"

The fairy tilted her head. Her armor clanked. "The happiness of helping someone in need."

"Well, in that case, get your page to do it." Myrtle stomped off.

Ethelinda turned herself back into a fairy. "Your rudeness merits a punishment," she said. But Myrtle was too far away to hear.

Myrtle went through the whole village of Snettering-on-Snoakes, searching for the old lady. The villagers knew she was Myrtle and not Rosella by her scowl and by the way she acted. Myrtle marched into shops and right into people's houses. She opened doors to rooms and even closets. Whenever anyone yelled at her, her only answer was to slam the door on her way out.

While Myrtle was in the village, Rosella went out to her garden to pick peas for dinner. As she worked, she sang.

"Oh, May is the lovely month.
Sing hey nonny May-o!
Oh, June is the flower month.
Sing hey nonny June-o!
Oh, July is the hot month.
Sing hey nonny July-o!"

And so on. While she sang, gems dropped from her mouth. It still felt funny, but she was getting used to it. Except once she popped a pea into her mouth as she sang, and she almost broke a tooth on a ruby.

Rosella had a sweet voice, but Prince Harold, who happened to be riding by, wasn't musical. He wouldn't have stopped, except he spotted the sapphire trembling on Rosella's lip. He watched it tumble into the vegetables.

He tied his horse up at the widow Pickering's picket fence.

Rosella didn't see him, and she went on singing.

"Oh, November is the harvest month.
Sing hey nonny November-o!
Oh, December is the last month.
Sing hey . . ."

Prince Harold went into the garden. "Maiden . . ."

Rosella looked up from her peas. A man! A noble-man! She blushed prettily.

She wasn't bad-looking, Prince Harold thought. "Pardon me," he said. "You've dropped some jewels. Allow me."

"Oh! Don't trouble yourself, Sir." Another sapphire and a moonstone fell out of Rosella's mouth.

Harold had a terrible thought. Maybe they were just glass. He picked up a stone. "May I examine this?"

Rosella nodded.

It didn't look like glass. It looked like a perfect dia-mond, five carats at least. But if the gems were real, why was she leaving them on the ground? He held up a jewel. "Maiden, is this really a diamond?"

"I don't know, Sir. It might be."

A topaz hit Prince Harold in the forehead. He caught it as it bounced off his chin. "Maiden, have jew-els always come out of your mouth?"

Rosella laughed, a lovely tinkling sound. "Oh no, Sir. It only began this afternoon when an old lady—I think she may have been a fairy—"

They *were* real then! Harold knelt before her. "Maiden, I am Prince Harold. I love you madly. Will you marry me?"

"HE ASKED HER ABOUT HER GARDEN, ABOUT
THE WEATHER . . . ABOUT ANYTHING."

Three

osella didn't love the prince madly, but she liked him. He was so polite. And she thought it might be pleasanter to be a princess than to be the widow Pickering's daughter and Myrtle's sister. Besides, it could be against the law to say no to a prince. So she said yes, and dropped a garnet into his hand.

"I'm sorry, sweetheart. I didn't hear you."

"Yes, Your Highness."

Clink. Clink. Two more garnets joined Harold's collection. "You must say, 'Yes, Harold,' now that we're betrothed."

"Yes, Harold."

Clink.

The fairy Ethelinda was delighted that Rosella was going to be a princess. She deserves it, the fairy thought. Ethelinda was pleased with herself for having given Rosella the perfect reward.

The widow Pickering agreed to the marriage. But she insisted that Harold give her all the gems Rosella had produced before their engagement. The widow was careful not to mention Myrtle. She didn't want the prince to know that Rosella had a twin sister who would also have a jewel mine in her mouth. After all, what if he took Myrtle away too?

Prince Harold swung Rosella up on his horse. He asked her to hold an open saddlebag on her lap. Then he mounted in front of her. As they rode off, he asked her about her garden, about the weather, about fly fishing, about anything.

The widow stood at the fence and waved her handkerchief. As she turned to go back into the cottage, she saw her favorite daughter in the distance. Myrtle was loping along, swinging the bucket. The widow opened the gate and followed her daughter into the house. "Darling, speak to me."

Myrtle sank into their only comfortable chair. "Hi, Mom. The stupid old lady wasn't—" There was a tickle in the back of her throat. What was going on? It felt like her tongue had gotten loose and was flopping around in her mouth. Could she be making jewels too? Did it happen just by going to the well? Whatever it was—diamond or pearl or emerald—it wanted to get out. Myrtle opened her mouth.

A garter snake slithered out.

The widow screamed and jumped onto their other chair. "Eeeeek! Get that thing out of here! Myrtle!" She pointed a shaking finger. "There it is! Get it! Eeeeek!"

Myrtle didn't budge. She stared at the snake

coiling itself around a bedpost. How had this happened if the old lady wasn't at the well? The knight? The knight! The old lady had turned herself into a knight.

Myrtle jumped up and raced out, taking the bucket with her. "'Bye, Mom," she called over her shoulder. "See you later." Two mosquitoes and a dragonfly flew out of her mouth.

The fairy Ethelinda watched Myrtle scurry down the road. She patted herself on the back for having given Myrtle the perfect punishment.

Four

P rince Harold and Rosella reached the court-yard in front of the prince's palace. He lifted Rosella down from the horse.

"I'm too madly in love to wait," he said. "Let's announce our engagement first thing tomorrow morning, dear heart."

"All right," Rosella said.

Harold only got a measly seed pearl. "Princesses speak in complete sentences, darling."

Rosella took a deep breath for courage. "I'm tired, Your High—I mean Harold. May I rest for a day first?"

But Harold didn't listen. He was too interested in the green diamond in his hand. "I've never seen one of these before, honey bun. We can have the betrothal ceremony at nine o'clock sharp. Your Royal Ladies-in-Waiting will find you something to wear."

Harold snapped his fingers, and a Royal Lady-in-Waiting led Rosella away. They were on the castle doorstep when Harold ran after them.

"Angel, I almost forgot. What would you like served at our betrothal feast?"

Nobody had ever asked Rosella this kind of question before. She'd always had to eat scraps from her mother's and her sister's plates. Nobody had ever asked her what she liked to eat. Nobody had ever asked her opinion about anything.

She smiled happily. "Your—I mean, Harold . . . uh . . . dear, I'd like poached quail eggs and roasted chestnuts for our betrothal feast." Six identical emeralds the color of maple leaves in May dropped from Rosella's mouth.

The Royal Lady-in-Waiting, who was at Rosella's elbow, gasped.

"Look at these!" Harold said. "They're gorgeous. So you want wild boar for dinner?" He didn't give Rosella time to say she hated wild boar. "What do you know? It's my favorite too. I'll go tell the cook." He rushed off.

Rosella sighed.

The fairy Ethelinda, who was keeping an eye on things, sighed too.

Myrtle returned to the well, determined to give a drink to anybody who was there. But nobody was. She lowered the bucket into the well anyway.

Nobody showed up.

She had an idea. It was worth a try. She watered the plants that grew around the well. "Dear plants," she began. "You look thirsty. Perhaps a little water would please you. It's no trouble. I don't mind, dear sweet plants."

Whatever was in her mouth was too big to be a jewel, unless it was the biggest one in the world. And a jewel wouldn't feel slimy on her tongue. She opened her mouth. A water bug crawled out. She closed her mouth, but there was more. More slime. She opened her mouth again. Two more water bugs padded out, followed by a black snake.

Giving the plants a drink hadn't done any good. Myrtle dumped the rest of the water on a rose bush. "Drown, you stupid plant," she muttered. A grass-hopper landed on a rose.

Myrtle filled her bucket one more time. Then—without saying a single word—she scoured the village again for the rotten fairy who'd done this to her. She swore to herself that she'd pour water down the throat of any stranger she found.

But there were no strangers, so Myrtle threw the bucket into the well and headed for home.

The widow was in the garden. She had dug up the peas and the radishes and the tomato plants. Now she was pawing through the roots, hoping to find some jewels that Prince Harold had missed. When she heard the gate slam shut, she stood up. "Don't say a word if you didn't find that old lady."

Myrtle closed her mouth with a snap. She picked up a stick and scratched in the dirt, "Where's Rosella?"

"She rode off to marry a prince. And like a fool, I

let her go, because I thought I had you. You bungler, you idiot, you . . ."

That made Myrtle furious. How could she have known the fairy would turn herself into a knight in so much armor you couldn't even see her—his—face? And hadn't she searched the village twice? And hadn't she watered those useless plants? Myrtle opened her mouth to give her mother what-for.

But the widow held up her hands and jumped back three feet. "Hush! Shh! Hush, my love. Perhaps I was hasty. We've both had a bad . . ."

Her mother's pleas gave Myrtle a new idea. She picked up the stick again and wrote, "Things are looking up, Mom. It will all be better tomorrow." She dropped the stick and started whistling—and wondering if whistling made snakes and insects too.

It didn't. Too bad, she thought.

Five

osella was used to sleeping on the floor, because Myrtle and the widow had always taken the bed. In the palace she got her own bed. It had a canopy and three mattresses piled on top of each other and satin sheets and ermine blankets and pillows filled with swans' feathers.

So she should have gotten a fine night's sleep—except that three Royal Guards stood at attention around her bed all night. One stood at each side of the bed, and one stood at the foot. If she talked in her sleep, they were supposed to catch the jewels and keep them safe for Prince Harold.

Rosella didn't talk in her sleep because she couldn't sleep with people watching her. By morning her throat felt scratchy. She thought she might be coming down with a cold.

Her twelve Royal Ladies-in-Waiting brought breakfast to her at seven o'clock. Scrambled eggs and wild-boar sausages. They shared the sausages while she ate the eggs. Rosella said "please" six times and "thank you" eight times. Each Royal Lady-in-Waiting got one jewel, and they fought over the remaining two.

"Nobody deserves that but me!" yelled one Royal Lady-in-Waiting.

"I work harder than any of you!" yelled another.

"I'm worth ten of each of you, so I should get everything!" shouted a third.

"You have some nerve, thinking . . ."

Rosella put her hands over her ears. She wished she could have ten minutes to herself.

Prince Harold came in. He coughed to get the attention of the Royal Ladies-in-Waiting. Nobody noticed except Rosella, who smiled at him. He'd be handsome, she thought, if he weren't so greedy.

The Royal Ladies-in-Waiting went on arguing.

"How dare you—"

"What do you mean—"

"The first person who—"

"SHUT UP!" Harold roared.

They did.

"You mustn't upset my bride." He went to Rosella, who was eating her breakfast in bed. He put his arm around her shoulder. "Are you all right, sugar plum?"

Rosella nodded. She liked the pet names he called her. But she hoped he wouldn't make her say anything.

"Tell me so I'm sure, lovey-dove."

The fairy Ethelinda was worried.

Myrtle, on the other hand, had a great night's sleep. When she woke up, she put paper, a quill pen, and a

"HE SCOWLED RIGHT BACK."

bottle of ink in a pouch. Then she set out for the village. She'd have a fine breakfast when she got there, and she wouldn't pay a penny for it. As for the bucket she'd thrown down the well, why, she'd have her choice of buckets.

Her first stop was the baker's shop. She's scowling, the baker thought, so it's Myrtle. He scowled right back.

"Give me three of your freshest muffins," Myrtle said.

She has some nerve, the baker thought. Bossing me— What was coming out of her mouth? Ants! He grabbed his broom and swept them out of his store. He tried to sweep Myrtle out too.

"Cut that out!" Myrtle said. A horsefly flew out of her mouth. A bedbug climbed over the edge of her lip and started down her chin.

The baker swatted the fly. He kept an eye on the bedbug, so he could kill it as soon as it touched the floor.

Myrtle took the pen and paper out of her pouch. "Give me the muffins and I won't say another word," she wrote. "I also want a fourteen-layer cake. It's for my party tomorrow, to celebrate my fourteen-year-and-six-weeks birthday. You're invited. Bring the whole family."

The baker swallowed hard and nodded. "I'll come. We'll all come. We'll be, uh, overjoyed to come." He wrapped up his most delicious muffins. When he handed them to Myrtle, he bowed.

The fairy Ethelinda was getting anxious. Punishments weren't supposed to work this way.

Rosella tried not to talk while she got ready for her betrothal, but her Royal Ladies-in-Waiting ignored her if she just pointed at things. They didn't yell at each other anymore, because they didn't want Prince Harold to hear, but that didn't stop them from fighting quietly.

When Rosella said, "I'll wear that gown," two amazon stones and an opal fell to the carpet. And the twelve Royal Ladies-in-Waiting went for the jewels, hitting and shoving each other.

So Rosella took the gown out of the closet herself and laid it out on her bed. Then she stood over it, marveling. It was silk, with an embroidered bodice. Its gathered sleeves ended in lace that would tickle her fingers delightfully. And the train was lace over silk, yards and yards of it.

"It's so pretty," she whispered. "It belongs in the sky with the moon and the stars."

Two pearls and a starstone fell into the deep folds of the gown's skirt. They were seen by a Royal Lady-in-Waiting who had taken a break from the fight on the carpet. She pounced on the gown.

The other Royal Ladies-in-Waiting heard the silk rustle. They pounced too. In less time than it takes to sew on a button, the gown lay in tatters on the bed.

Rosella wanted to scream, but she was afraid to. Screaming might make bigger and better gems. Then she'd have to scream all the time. Besides, her throat was really starting to hurt. She cried instead.

The fairy Ethelinda was getting angry. Rewards weren't supposed to work this way.

Six

osella didn't mean to, but she dropped jewels on every gown in her princess wardrobe except one. And her Royal Ladies-in-Waiting ruined each of them. The one that was left was made of burlap and it was a size and a half too big. It didn't have a real train, but it did trail on the floor, because it was four inches too long.

Harold met Rosella in the palace's great hall, where the Chief Royal Councillor was going to perform the betrothal ceremony. The prince thought she looked pretty, with her brown wavy hair and her big gray eyes. But why had she picked the ugliest gown in the kingdom? It was big enough for her and a gorilla. All he said, though, was, "You look beautiful, honey bunch. Are you glad to be engaged?"

Rosella didn't know how to answer. Being engaged wasn't the problem, although marrying Harold might have its drawbacks. The problem was the jewels.

"Did you hear me, hon? I asked you a question." He raised his voice. "Are you happy, sweetheart?" He cupped his hand under her chin.

Rosella spoke through her teeth so the jewels wouldn't get out. "Everybody wants me to talk, but nobody listens to what I say."

"I'm listening, angel. Spit it out."

"I hate wild boar, and I don't want guards to stand around. . . ." There were so many jewels in her mouth that one popped out, a hyacinth.

Harold put it in his pocket. The orchestra started to play.

She couldn't keep all these stones in her mouth. She spit them into her hand and made a fist.

"We're supposed to hold hands," Harold whispered. "Give them to me. I'll take good care of them."

What difference did it make? She let him have them.

The ceremony began.

Myrtle sat on the edge of the well to eat her muffins. After she ate them and licked her fingers, she headed for the stationer's shop. When she got there, an earwig and a spider bought her enough party invitations for everyone in the village. At the bottom of each invitation she wrote, "Bring presents."

She gave out all the invitations, and everyone promised to come. Then she stopped at the tailor's shop, where she picked out a gown for the party. It was white silk with an embroidered bodice and a lace train.

She was in such a good mood, she even bought a gown for her mother.

The fairy Ethelinda was furious.

⚓ ⚓ ⚓

At the end of the betrothal ceremony, the First Chancellor placed a golden tiara on Rosella's head. She wondered if she was a princess yet, or still just a princess-to-be.

"Some people want to meet you, honey," Harold said.

After a Royal Engagement, the kingdom's loyal subjects were always allowed into the palace to meet their future princess.

The Royal Guards opened the huge wooden doors to the great hall. Rosella saw a line that stretched for three quarters of a mile outside the palace. Everyone in it had something to catch the jewels as they cascaded out of her mouth. Pessimists brought thimbles and egg cups. Optimists brought sacks and pillowcases and lobster pots.

The first subject Rosella met was a farmer. "How are you?" he said.

"Fine." A ruby chip fell into his pail.

That was all? His shoulders slumped.

Rosella took pity on him. She said, "Actually, my throat hurts, and this crown is giving me a headache."

He grinned as stones clattered against the bottom of his pail. Rosella asked him what he planned to do with the jewels.

"My old plow is worn out," he said. "I need a new one."

"Do you have enough now?" she said.

"Oh yes, Your Princess-ship. Thank you." He bowed and shook her hand.

Next in line was a woman whose skirt and blouse

were as ragged as Rosella's had been yesterday. The woman wanted to buy a warm coat for the winter. Something about her made Rosella want to give her diamonds.

Rosella said, "Make sure your new coat is lined with fur. I think beaver is best." Diamond, she thought. Diamond, diamond.

But only one diamond came out, along with a topaz, some aquamarine stones, and some garnets. Thinking the name of the jewel didn't seem to make much difference. Anyway, the woman caught the stones in a threadbare sack and left happy.

A shoemaker came next, carrying a boot to catch the jewels. "What's your favorite flower?" he asked.

"Lilacs and carnations and daffodils." Rosella sang, wondering if singing would affect what came out—a diamond, a ruby, and a turquoise on the large side.

The shoemaker said he had been too poor to buy leather to make any more shoes. "But now," he said, "I can buy enough to fill my shop window."

Rosella smiled. "And peonies and poppies and black-eyed Susans and marigolds and—"

She was starting to get the hang of it. Long vowels usually made precious jewels, while short vowels often made semiprecious stones. The softer she spoke, the smaller the jewels, and the louder the bigger. It really was a good thing she hadn't screamed at her Royal Ladies-in-Waiting.

"That's enough. Don't use them all up on me."

Rosella wished Harold would listen to this shoe-maker. He could learn something.

Even though her throat hurt, she enjoyed talking to everybody. She liked her subjects! But why were so many of them poor?

Next was a boy who asked her to tell him a story. She made up a fable about a talkative parrot who lived with a deaf mouse. The boy listened and laughed in all the right places, and caught the jewels in his cap.

She smiled bravely and said hello to the next subject. Her throat hurt terribly.

Seven

The widow Pickering loved her new gown. She tried it on while Myrtle tried on her own new gown. The widow told Myrtle that she looked fantastic. Myrtle wrote that the new gown made her mother look twenty years younger.

They took off the gowns and hung them up so they wouldn't wrinkle. Then Myrtle went out into the yard to experiment. She hummed softly. A line of ants pushed between her lips. She hummed louder, and the ants got bigger. Even louder, and the ants got even bigger. She'd had no idea there were such big ants. These were as big as her big toe.

Enough ants. Myrtle opened her mouth wide and sang, "La, la, la, la. Tra lee tra la tra loo." Moths, fireflies, and ladybugs flew out.

She hummed again. This time worms and caterpillars wriggled out. Hmmm. So she didn't always get ants by humming.

She tried speaking. "Nasty. Mean. Smelly. Rotten.

"THEY WERE CROWDING OUT—CRAWLING,
FLITTING, SLITHERING."

Stupid. Loathsome." She giggled. "Vile. Putrid. Scabby. Mangy . . ."

They were crowding out—crawling, flitting, slithering, darting, wriggling, whizzing, oozing, flying, marching—escaping from Myrtle's mouth every way they could.

There were aphids, butterflies, mambas, lacewings, lynx spiders, midges, wolf snakes, gnats, mayflies, rhinoceros vipers, audacious jumping spiders, bandy-bandy snakes, wasps, locusts, fleas, thrips, ticks, and every other bug and spider and snake you could think of.

Myrtle kept experimenting. She had a wonderful time, but she didn't figure out how to make a particular snake or insect come out. All she learned was that the louder she got, the bigger the creature that came out.

After about an hour, she had worked up quite an appetite. So she and her mother went to the village to have dinner at the inn. Dinner was free, because the innkeeper wanted to keep Myrtle from saying one single solitary word.

The fairy Ethelinda was scandalized.

During the betrothal banquet Harold noticed that Rosella's voice was fading. He noticed because all he got were tiny gems, hardly more than shavings. So he didn't make her say much. But he did make her drink wild-boar broth.

"It's the best thing for you, tootsie," he said when she made a face.

She gulped it down and hoped it would stay there. She picked at her string beans. "Why are your subjects so poor?" she whispered. A tiny sapphire and bits of amber fell onto the tablecloth.

Harold brushed the jewels into his hand. His betrothed was sweet, but she didn't know much. Subjects were always poor. "I wish they were richer too, cutie pie. Then I could tax them more."

"Maybe we can help them." A pearl fell into Rosella's mashed potatoes.

Harold dug it out with his fork and rinsed it off in his mulled wine. "Honey, you'll wear yourself out worrying about them. Take it easy. Relax a little."

She fell asleep over dessert. Royal Servants carried her to her bedchamber. But she woke up when the three Royal Guards took their places around her bed. Then she couldn't fall back to sleep.

Eight

yrtle and the widow Pickering slept late the next morning. When they woke up, they strolled to the village. They stopped at the toymaker's shop for favors for the party guests. From the potter they ordered serving platters. The butcher promised them sausages and meat pies. By noon they had picked out everything for the party. Then they linked arms and sauntered home.

The fairy Ethelinda gnashed her teeth.

By morning Rosella's throat hurt worse than ever. She thought she had a fever, too. But her voice was stronger.

Breakfast was wild-boar steak and eggs. Before her Royal Ladies-in-Waiting had taken ten bites, Harold sent for her.

He was waiting in the library. As soon as she went in, she became very scared. There were thousands of books, but they weren't what scared her. She liked books. There were four desks. That was fine, too.

There were a dozen upholstered leather chairs, and they looked comfortable enough. A Royal Manservant and a Royal Maid were dusting. They were all right.

The terrifying sight was the fifteen empty chests lined up in front of one of the leather chairs.

"Sweetie pie," Harold said. "Am I glad to see you." He led her to the chair behind the empty chests. "Wait till I tell you my idea."

Rosella sat down.

"Did you have a good breakfast, cuddle bunch?"

It hurt too much to talk. She shook her head.

Harold was too excited to pay attention. "Good. Here's my idea. You've noticed how old and moldy this palace is?"

She shook her head.

"You haven't? Well, it is. The drawbridge creaks. The rooms are drafty. The cellars are full of rats. The place should be condemned."

She didn't say anything. The palace looked fine to her.

"So I had a brainstorm. You didn't know you were marrying a genius, did you?"

She shook her head.

"This is brilliant. Listen. We're going to build a new castle. That's my idea. Picture it. Cream-colored stone. Marble everywhere. Hundreds of fountains. Taller towers than anybody ever heard of. Crocodiles *and* serpents in the moat. People will travel thousands of miles to see it. You'll be famous, sweetheart."

"Me?"

Harold caught the tiny ruby. "Yes, you. I can't build a palace on current revenues. We need your voice. The kingdom needs you. So just make sure they land in the chests, will you, sugar?"

She was silent.

"I know. You're wondering how you'll ever think of things to say to fill fifteen chests. That's why we're in the library. All you have to do is read out loud. Here." He pulled a book off a shelf. "This looks interesting. *The History of the Monarchy in the Kingdom of Biddle.* That's us, love." He put the book in her lap. "You can read about our family."

She didn't open it. What could he do to her if she didn't talk? He could throw her in a dungeon. She wouldn't mind if he did. Bread and water would be better than wild boar. Then again, he could chop off her head, which would hurt her throat even more than it was hurting now.

"I know you're tired, darling. But after you fill these chests, you can take a vacation. You won't have to say a word." He got down on one knee. "Please, sweetheart. Pretty please."

He has his heart set on a new palace, Rosella thought. He'll be miserable if he doesn't get one, and it will be because of me. Rosella opened the book to the middle. I'm too kindhearted, she thought. She started reading, trying to speak around her sore throat. "The fourth son of King Beauregard the Hairy weighed seven pounds and eleven ounces at birth. He had a noodle-shaped birthmark on his left shoulder. He wailed for . . ."

A stream of jewels fell into the chest. Harold tip-toed out of the room.

Rosella went on reading. "The infant was named Durward. His first word, 'More,' proved him to be . . ." She was freezing. She looked up. The fire looked hot. ". . . proved him to be a true royal son. His tutors reported . . ." The room was spinning. ". . . reported that he excelled at archery, hunting . . ." What was wrong with this book? The letters were getting bigger and smaller. The lines of print were wavy. ". . . hunting, and milit—"

Rosella fainted and fell off her chair.

The Royal Manservant and Royal Maid rushed to the partly filled chest. They each grabbed a handful of jewels. Then the Royal Manservant ran to find Harold, while the Royal Maid used her apron to fan Rosella.

"Wake up, Your Highness. Please wake up," she cried.

Nine

The fairy Ethelinda was appalled. This was the last straw. She had to do something.

Harold was in the courtyard, practicing his swordplay. She materialized in front of him. She didn't bother to disguise herself, hoping he'd be terrified when he saw the works—all seven feet three inches of her, her fleshy pink wings, the shimmer in the air around her, the purple light she was always bathed in, her flashing wand.

"You're a fairy, right?" Harold said when he saw her. He didn't seem frightened.

"I am the fairy Ethelinda," she said, lowering her voice to a roar.

Harold grinned. "Pretty good guessing on my part, considering I've never met a fairy before."

"I am the one who made the jewels come out of Rosella's mouth."

Harold almost jumped up and down, he was so excited. "That was you? Really? Uh, say, Ethel . . . tell me, what did my sweetie pie do to make you do it?"

"HAROLD WAS IN THE COURTYARD PRACTICING
HIS SWORDPLAY."

"My name is *Ethelinda*," the fairy boomed. "I rewarded her after she gave me a drink of well water."

"I can do that. That's a—"

"I'm not thirsty. Do you know that you're making poor Rosella miserable?"

"She's not miserable. She's a princess. She's deliriously happy."

Ethelinda tried a different approach. "Why do you want jewels so much?"

"You wouldn't want them?"

"Not if it was making my betrothed unhappy."

"How could she be unhappy? If I were in her shoes, I'd be delighted. She wouldn't be a princess today if I hadn't come along. She gets to wear a crown. She has nice gowns, Royal Ladies-in-Waiting. And me."

"You have to stop making her talk."

"But she has to talk. That's what makes *me* happy."

Ethelinda raised her wand. Prince Harold was one second away from becoming a frog. Then she lowered it. Her self-confidence was gone. If she turned him into a frog, he might figure out a way to make it better than being a prince. She certainly didn't want to reward him the way she'd rewarded Myrtle.

She didn't know what to do.

The Royal Manservant who'd seen Rosella faint finally reached the courtyard. He ran to Harold.

Ethelinda vanished.

Myrtle's party started at two o'clock. The schoolteacher arrived first. His present was a slate and ten boxes of colored chalk.

Myrtle opened one of the boxes. She wrote on the slate in green and orange letters, "Thank you. I'll let you know when I run out of chalk."

The baker came next. His cake was so big that it barely fit through the cottage doorway. The icing was chocolate. The decorations were pink and blue whipped cream. The writing on top said, "Happy Fourteen-and-Six-Weeks Birthday, Myrtle! Please Keep Quiet!"

The whole village came. Nobody wanted to take a chance on making Myrtle mad. The guests filled the cottage and the yard and the yards of the surrounding cottages. The widow thanked them all for coming. Myrtle collected her presents. She smiled when anyone handed her an especially big box.

The food was the finest anybody could remember. Myrtle ate so many poached quail eggs and roasted chestnuts that she almost got sick. After everybody ate, she opened her presents. There were hundreds of them. Her favorites were:

The framed sampler that read, "Speak to me only with thine eyes."

The bouquet of mums.

The music box that played "Hush, Little Baby."

The silver quill pen, engraved with the motto "The pen is mightier than the voice."

The parrot that sat on Myrtle's shoulder and repeated over and over, "Shut your trap. Shut your trap. Shut your trap."

The charm bracelet with the golden letters S, I, L, E, N, C, and E.

After all the presents were opened, everybody sang "Happy Birthday." Myrtle was so thrilled that she smiled and clapped her hands.

Rosella was gravely ill, and Harold was seriously frightened. Even under mounds of swansdown quilts, she couldn't stop shivering. She felt as if a vulture's claws were scratching at her throat and a carpenter hammering at her temples.

The Royal Physician was called in to examine her. When he was finished, he told Harold that she was very sick. He said her only hope of recovery lay in bed rest and complete silence. His fee for the visit was the jewels he collected when he listened to her chest and made her say "Aah" sixteen times.

Ten

yrtle had a birthday party every week. She and the widow laughed and laughed at their silliness in wishing for jewels to come out of Myrtle's mouth. When Myrtle got bored between parties, she would speak into a big jar. Then she'd let the bugs and the snakes loose in the yard and make them race. She and her mother would have a grand time betting on the winners.

Rosella got better so slowly that Ethelinda's patience snapped. The evening after Myrtle's fourth party, Ethelinda materialized as herself in the widow's cottage. "I am the fairy Ethelinda, who rewarded your sister and punished you. You have to help Rosella," she thundered.

Myrtle sneered. "I do? I have to?"

A bull snake slithered under Ethelinda's gown. A gnat bit her wing.

"Ouch!" Ethelinda yelped.

"Be careful, dear," the widow told Myrtle. "You might make a poisonous snake."

"Yes, you have to help her," Ethelinda said. "Or I'll punish you severely."

Myrtle wrote on her slate, "I like your punishments."

"I can take your punishment away," Ethelinda said.

As fast as she could, Myrtle wrote, "What do I have to do?"

Ethelinda explained the problem.

"I can fix that," Myrtle wrote.

Ethelinda transported Myrtle to the palace, where Rosella was staring up at her lace bed canopy and wondering when her nighttime guards would arrive. As Ethelinda and Myrtle materialized, Ethelinda turned herself back into the old lady.

"I've brought your sister to help you, my dear," Ethelinda said.

Rosella stared at them. Myrtle would never help her.

Myrtle had brought her slate with her. She wrote, "Change clothes with me and hide under the covers."

Rosella didn't move. She wondered if she was delirious.

"Go ahead. Do it," Ethelinda said. "She won't hurt you."

Rosella nodded. She put on Myrtle's silk nightdress with the gold embroidery and slipped deep under the blankets. Myrtle got into Rosella's silk nightdress with the silver embroidery.

Myrtle climbed into Rosella's bed. She sat up and yodeled, long and loud. A hognose snake wriggled out of her mouth.

Harold heard her, even though he was at the other end of the palace. He started running, leaping, and skipping toward the sound. "She's better! She's well again!" he yelled. And how many jewels did that yodel make? he wondered.

Ethelinda made the snake disappear. Then she made herself invisible.

"Precious!" Harold said, coming through the door. He dashed to the bed. "The roses are back in your cheeks. Speak to me!"

"What roses?" Myrtle yelled as loud as she could. "I feel terrible." The head of a boa constrictor filled her mouth.

Harold jumped back. "Aaaa! What's that?"

Rosella lifted a tiny corner of blanket so she could watch. The snake slithered out and wound itself around Myrtle's waist.

Myrtle grinned at Harold. "Do you like him? Should I name him after you?" Three hornets flew straight at him. One of them stung him on the nose. The other two buzzed around his head.

"Ouch! Wh-what's going on . . . h-honey pie? Th-that's a s-snake. Wh-where did the j-jewels go? Why are b-bugs and snakes coming out?"

This is fun, Myrtle thought. Who'd have thought I could scare a prince?

Poor Harold, Rosella thought. But it serves him right. He looks so silly. She fought back a giggle and wished she could make a bug come out of her mouth once in a while.

"I'm angry. This is what happens when I get angry." A scorpion stuck its head out of Myrtle's mouth.

"Yow! Why are you angry? At me? What did I do?"

"It's not so great being a princess," Myrtle yelled. "Nobody listens to me. All they care about are the jewels. You're the worst. It's all you care about, too. And I don't want to eat wild boar ever again. I hate wild boar."

The air was so thick with insects that Harold could hardly see. Snakes wriggled across the carpets. Snakes slithered up the sconces. Snakes oozed down the tapestries. A gigantic one hung from the chandelier, its head swaying slowly.

A milk snake slipped under the covers. It settled its clammy body next to Rosella. She wanted to scream and run. Instead, she bit her lip and stayed very, very still.

"Sweetheart, I'm sorry. Forgive me. Ouch! That hurt."

Myrtle screamed, "I'M NOT GOING TO TALK UNLESS I WANT TO!"

"All right. All right! You won't have to. And I'll listen to you. I promise." Something bit his foot all the way through his boot. He hopped and kicked to get rid of it. "Everyone will listen. By order of Prince Harold."

"AND PRINCESS ROSELLA," Myrtle yelled.

"And Princess Rosella," Harold echoed.

Myrtle lowered her voice. "Now leave me. I need my rest."

Eleven

fter Harold left, Ethelinda made the snakes and bugs disappear. Rosella came out from under the covers.

"Thank you," Rosella told her sister. An emerald fell on the counterpane.

Myrtle snatched the jewel and said, "You're welcome." She snagged the fly before it got to Rosella's face. Then she crushed it in her fist.

"You've done a good deed," Ethelinda began.

Myrtle shook her head. "Don't reward me. Thanks, but no thanks." She let two cockroaches fall into the bed.

Ethelinda asked if Myrtle would help Rosella again if she needed it.

"Why should I?" Myrtle asked.

"I'll pay you," Rosella said.

Myrtle pocketed the two diamonds. Not bad. She'd get to frighten the prince again and get jewels for it, too. "Okay."

Myrtle and Rosella switched clothes again. Then

Ethelinda sent Myrtle back home. When Myrtle was gone, Ethelinda said she had to leave too. She vanished.

Rosella sank back into her pillows. She didn't want Myrtle to help again, or even Ethelinda. She wanted to solve the problem of Harold and his poor subjects all by herself.

Harold didn't dare visit Rosella again that day. But he did command the Royal Servants to listen to her. So Rosella got rid of her nighttime guards. And she had her meal of poached quail eggs and roasted chestnuts at last.

She also ordered the Royal Ladies-in-Waiting to bring her a slate and chalk. From then on, she wrote instead of talking to them. She was tired of having them dive into her lap whenever she said anything.

And she had them bring her a box with a lock and a key. She kept the box and the slate by her side so she'd be ready when Harold came.

He showed up a week after Myrtle's visit. Rosella felt fine by then. She was sitting at her window, watching a juggler in the courtyard.

"Honey?" He poked his head in. He was ready to run if the room was full of creepy-crawlies. But the coast seemed clear, so he stepped in all the way. He was carrying a bouquet of daisies and a box of taffy. "All better, sweetheart?" He held the daisies in front of his face—in case any hornets started flying.

He looks so scared, Rosella thought. She smiled to

"THEY SAT THERE NOT SAYING ANYTHING."

make him stop worrying.

He lowered the bouquet cautiously and placed it on a table. Then he sat next to her and looked her over. She seemed healthy. That silk nightdress was cute. Blue was a good color for her.

He hoped she wasn't feeling miserable anymore. Anyone who was going to marry him should be the happiest maiden in the kingdom. He still wanted her to talk up enough jewels for a new palace. Then, after that, he wouldn't mind a golden coach and a few other items. But he wanted her to be happy, too.

They sat there, not saying anything.

"Oh, here," Harold said finally. He held out the bouquet and the candy.

She took them. "Thank you."

An opal hovered on her lip and tumbled out. Harold reached for it, but Rosella was faster. She opened her box and dropped in the opal. It clinked against the stones already in there. She snapped the box shut.

That was pretty selfish of her, Harold thought. He started to get mad, but then he thought of boa constrictors and hornets. He calmed down. "What's the box for, darling?"

"My jewels." A pearl came out this time. A big one. It went into the box too.

"Honey . . . Sweetie pie . . . What are you going to do with them?"

"Give them away. Your subjects need them more than we do."

"NO YOU DON'T!" Harold hollered. She couldn't! It was all right to give jewels away for the engagement ceremony. That was once in a lifetime, but she wanted to make a habit of it. "You can't give them away. I won't allow it."

Rosella wrote on her slate, "I'm trying not to get angry."

"No, no, don't get mad!" Harold started backing away. "But don't you want a new palace? I'll tell you what—we'll name a wing after you. It'll be the Rosella Wing. How do you like that?"

She shook her head. "This palace is beautiful. Look at it! It's wonderful."

All those gems going into the box! thought Harold. Wasted! If she gave them away, soon his subjects would be richer than he was. "Tell you what," Harold said. "We'll split fifty-fifty."

"I won't read a million books out loud just to fill up your treasure chests."

He counted as they fell. Two diamonds, three bloodstones, one hyacinth, and one turquoise.

He sighed. "All right, my love."

"All right, my love. Fifty-fifty." Rosella wanted to be fair. He had made her a princess, after all.

They shook hands. Then they kissed.

Epilogue

Myrtle never had to come to her sister's rescue ever again. The fifty-fifty deal worked out perfectly. Harold got his new palace and golden coach, eventually. And Rosella was happy talking to her subjects and making sure they had enough plows and winter coats and leather for making shoes. Also, she built them a new school and a library and a swimming pool.

In time she and Harold grew to love each other very much. Harold even stopped trying to steal the jewels from Rosella's wooden box while she was sleeping. And Rosella stopped counting them every morning when she woke up.

Myrtle and her mother went into the bug-and-snake-racing business. People came from twenty kingdoms to watch Myrtle's races. They'd bet beetles against spiders or rattlers against pythons or grasshoppers against garter snakes. The widow would call the races, and Myrtle would take the bets. The whole village got rich from the tourist trade. And Myrtle became truly popular, which annoyed her.

Ethelinda grew more careful. Myrtle was her last mistake. Nowadays when she punishes people, they stay punished. And when she rewards them, they don't get sick.

And they all lived happily ever after.

Rosella's Song

Oh, January is the first month.
Sing hey nonny January-o!
Oh, February is the cold month.
Sing hey nonny February-o!
Oh, March is the windy month.
Sing hey nonny March-o!
Oh, April is the rainy month.
Sing hey nonny April-o!
Oh, May is the lovely month.
Sing hey nonny May-o!
Oh, June is the flower month.
Sing hey nonny June-o!
Oh, July is the hot month.
Sing hey nonny July-o!
Oh, August is the berry month.
Sing hey nonny August-o!
Oh, September is the red-leaf month.
Sing hey nonny September-o!
Oh, October is the scary month.
Sing hey nonny October-o!
Oh, November is the harvest month.
Sing hey nonny November-o!
Oh, December is the last month.
Sing hey nonny December-o!

The Princess Test

To Martha Garner,

who told me to be sweet.

—G.C.L.

One

Once upon a time, in the village of Snettering-on-Snoakes in the Kingdom of Biddle, a blacksmith's wife named Gussie gave birth to a baby girl. Gussie and her husband, Sam, named the baby Lorelei, and they loved her dearly.

Lorelei's smile was sweet and her laughter was music. But as an infant she smiled only four times and laughed twice. The rest of the time she cried.

She cried when her porridge was too hot or too cold or too salty or too bitter or too sweet. She cried when her bathwater was too hot or too cold or too wet or not wet enough. She cried when her diaper was scratchy or smelly or not folded exactly right. She cried when her cradle was messy or when her mother forgot to make it with hospital corners. She cried whenever anything was not perfectly perfect.

Sam and Gussie did their best to make her happy. Lorelei was the only village baby with satin sheets and velvet diapers. She was the only one whose milk came from high-mountain yaks. And she was the only one who ate porridge made from two parts millet mixed with one part buckwheat. But still she cried.

She cried less as she learned to talk.

Then one day Lorelei said, "Father dearest and Mother dearest, I'm terribly sorry for crying so much. You have been too good to me."

Gussie said, "Oh honey, it's all right."

Sam said, "Gosh, we thought you were the cutest, best baby in this or any other kingdom."

Lorelei shook her head. "No, I was difficult. But I shall try to make it up to you. And now that I can explain myself, everything will be much better." She smiled. Then she sneezed. And sneezed again. She smiled shakily. "I fear I have a cold."

From then on, Lorelei stopped crying. She didn't stop being a picky eater, and she didn't stop needing everything to be just so. She just stopped crying about it.

Instead, Lorelei started being sick and having accidents.

If a child in the village of Snettering-on-Snoakes had a single spot, Lorelei caught the measles. If a child two villages and a mountain away had the mumps, Lorelei caught them, and the flu besides.

She loved the other children, and they liked her well enough. But if she played tag with them, she was sure to trip and skin her knee or her elbow or her chin. When they played hopscotch, she always twisted her ankle. Once, when she tried to jump rope, she got so tangled up that Gussie had to come and untie her.

"SHE SMILED SHAKILY. 'I FEAR I HAVE A COLD.'"

When Lorelei turned fourteen, Gussie died. Sam and Lorelei were heartbroken. Sam swore never to marry again because Gussie was the sweetest wife anybody could ever have.

"Besides," he added, "all the old tales say that stepmothers are mean to their stepdaughters. You'll never have to worry about that, Lorelei honey."

Two

Sam knew that Lorelei couldn't cook and clean for him and be her own nurse too. Besides, he'd be leaving soon for his annual trip to shoe the horses of the Earl of Pildenue, and someone would have to take care of Lorelei while he was gone. So he looked around for a housekeeper.

A wench named Trudy had helped the shoemaker's family when their twins were born. The shoemaker said that Trudy was a hard worker, so Sam hired her. Trudy wondered why a blacksmith with a grown daughter needed a housekeeper, but she took the job.

As soon as Trudy walked in the door, Lorelei ran to her, stumbled, and fell into Trudy's arms.

"Dear Trudy, I'll do anything to help you. To the outer limits of my meager ability."

Nobody had ever called Trudy "dear" before. So she thought this could be a pretty cushy spot, even if she understood only one word in ten that the lass said. But then again, if the girl wanted to help, why were the dirty dishes piled as high as a horse's rear end? Trudy shrugged and pumped water into the sink. "Here, lass. You can start on these."

"Oh, good!" Lorelei took the soap and started to scrub a plate.

Trudy looked around for a mop.

"Oh dear," Lorelei said.

"What's amiss?"

Lorelei raised her arms out of the soapy water. Trudy was horrified. The girl's arms and hands were covered with a bright-red rash.

"Does this happen whenever you wash a dish?" Trudy asked.

"I don't know. I've never washed one before."

Never washed a dish! Her poor dead mother had let her get away with that? Had the woman mistaken her daughter for a princess?

"Mother kept the unguents and the bandages in the hutch," Lorelei said.

Trudy opened the hutch door. There were enough potions and herbs and simples to set up shop as a wise-woman.

"That one. There." Lorelei pointed to a big jar.

Trudy spread the salve over Lorelei's rash.

"It has to be wrapped in clean linen." Lorelei pointed again.

Trudy wrapped up Lorelei's arms—three times. The first time the bandages were too tight. The next time they were too loose. An hour passed before Lorelei said they were just right.

At last! Trudy thought, Her majesty is satisfied.

"The dressing has to be changed every two hours," Lorelei said. "I'm sorry to be such a bother."

Trudy frowned. It wasn't exactly her highness's fault, but over an hour had gone by and the dishes were still dirty. The floor hadn't been mopped, and there was a mountain of laundry in the basket. She'd be working half the night to get it all done.

Trudy worked half the night that night and every night. For a month she took off bandages and put on bandages. When the rash was gone, Lorelei offered to help again.

Trudy hadn't been able to do any spinning because of all the bandaging. Surely, she thought, her majesty can't come to grief spinning. "Can you help me with the spinning?"

Lorelei smiled happily. Gussie had never let her near the spinning wheel. She knew exactly what to do, though, because she'd watched her mother so often. She sat down at the wheel and got started.

Trudy nodded. There. She began to dust.

"Oh dear."

Trudy turned around. Lorelei had stabbed herself in the hand with the spindle, and blood was pouring onto the cottage's wooden floor. Trudy ran for the bandages.

While Trudy bandaged her, Lorelei apologized at least a thousand times. After that, Trudy spent an hour scrubbing blood off the wooden floor and wondering what the bungling ninny was good for.

Not much, Trudy soon discovered. Lorelei could hang laundry on the line, and she could make a bed neatly. But the only thing she was really good at was embroidery. And Trudy had no need for embroidery. What she needed was to scream, long and loud.

Every day Trudy got madder and madder. While she washed Lorelei's satin sheets, her ladyship would be sitting at her ease, embroidering by the window. As Trudy kneaded Lorelei's special millet-buckwheat bread, the lazy thing would be lying in bed because her poor little throat hurt. Or her poor little left eyebrow. Or her poor little big toe.

Then came the joyous moment when Trudy thought of doing Lorelei in. Cooking her highness's goose. Rubbing her pampered self o-u-t. *Out!* Trudy started whistling.

Lorelei looked up from embroidering the outline of a potato on one of Sam's breeches. She smiled. "I'm so glad you're happy here, Trudy."

"Oh, I am, lass, I am. Happier every minute."

Three

t was lunchtime in the nearby court of the king and queen of Biddle. Queen Hermione rang her little bell to let the Royal Servants know they could bring out the first course.

The Chief Royal Lunchtime Serving Maid carried a platter heaped with crab cakes into the royal dining room. King Humphrey helped himself to a tiny crab cake. Queen Hermione helped herself to a tiny crab cake. Prince Nicholas took a dozen or so crab cakes and started eating.

King Humphrey tasted his crab cake. Queen Hermione tasted her crab cake. They shook their heads. Queen Hermione rang her bell again. The Chief Royal Lunchtime Serving Maid stepped up to the royal table.

"I'm so sorry," Queen Hermione said. "These crab cakes taste a bit too fishy to me."

"We beg to differ or disagree," the king boomed. "They're not fishy enough."

"Crab isn't a fish," Prince Nicholas said, chewing

happily. "My compliments to the chef."

"Please bring grapefruit instead," the queen said.

The Chief Royal Lunchtime Serving Maid removed the platter. On her way into the kitchen she passed a counter where the royal lunch was laid out. There were platters of crusty beef Wellington, creamed potatoes, and asparagus in mustard sauce, and there was a basket of poppy seed popovers. And two plates of grapefruit sections, poached eggs, and dry toast.

At a long table the Royal Servants waited for their lunch. The Chief Royal Lunchtime Serving Maid handed the platter of crab cakes to the Chief Royal Steward at the head of the table. He took four or five cakes and passed the plate to the Chief Royal House-keeper on his right.

"There would be more for us if the prince didn't eat so much," the Chief Royal Undergardener complained.

"Hush," the Chief Royal Housekeeper said. "We're lucky to serve two such finicky rulers. My cousin Mabel doesn't fare half so well at the Earl of Pildenue's castle. The earl and his family adore their food, adore their clothes, adore their furniture. She never gets anything."

Back in Snettering-on-Snoakes, Lorelei ate her lunch of grapefruit, poached eggs, and dry toast, and patted her mouth with an embroidered napkin. Then she went out to hang embroidered laundry on the embroidered clothesline.

While she worked, she thought about her mother

and Trudy. Her mother had been so good to her. And Trudy was too. They both worked so hard. She hadn't helped her mother much, or Trudy, even though she always wanted to.

Trudy looked tired sometimes, although she never complained. Gussie must have been tired too. But no matter how tired she might have been, her mother had always had a kiss and a hug for Lorelei. And even if the hugs had made Lorelei a little black and blue, she would have given anything to have them back again.

She wiped away a tear with the embroidered toe of Sam's hose.

Prince Nicholas, riding by, saw the tear. He had gone out after lunch to get some fresh air. As soon as he had turned into the lane, he'd seen Lorelei. She looked pretty in the distance. As he got closer, she was still pretty. Not a raving beauty, but definitely pretty. Light-brown hair. Ordinary color, but thick and wavy. Nose a little too big. But her eyes were big too. Enormous. And she had roses in her cheeks. You didn't see roses in the cheeks of the noble and stuck-up ladies at court.

Then he saw she was crying! A corner of his heart that had never been touched before was touched. He leaped off his steed. "Maiden!" he cried. "You weep!"

Lorelei turned and knocked over the laundry basket. Embroidered petticoats and tunics and bodices danced across the small muddy yard.

Prince Nicholas vaulted over the low fence and helped Lorelei gather up the wash. He picked up one of Sam's shirts, embroidered with three-legged stools.

"Lorelei turned and knocked over the
laundry basket."

The stitchery was masterful. But why three-legged stools?

He asked, "Maiden, why were you crying? Perhaps I can be of service."

Lorelei blushed. He wasn't that handsome, but there was something regal about him. Who was he? "I was missing my mother, kind sir."

"Your mother is . . ."

"She died." Lorelei smiled bravely and gathered up the last item of laundry, a petticoat embroidered with tiny teakettles.

The poor maiden was an orphan, Nicholas thought. Or half of one if her father was alive. "You have my most sincere sympathy, maiden." He wanted to say more but couldn't think of anything else.

Lorelei smiled. "Thank you, kind sir." He was nice!

She had a wonderful smile. He found himself stammering. "Er . . . I am P-Prince N-Nicholas."

He was a prince! She swept him a curtsy. "I am Lorelei."

Inside, Trudy glanced up from her washtub. Look at her highness out there, she thought, passing the time with a young lord. Not for long, your ladyship. She hummed and danced a little jig. Not for long, hey-ho! Not for long, tra-la!

Four

When Nicholas got back to the castle, King Humphrey summoned him to the throne room. As usual it was full of courtiers and subjects. King Humphrey had just settled an argument between two farmers over a cow. When he saw Nicholas, the king ordered everyone to leave. The only ones left were the king, the queen, the prince, and the Chief Royal Window Washer, who was cleaning the stained-glass windows.

"Son," King Humphrey boomed. "We are growing old or advancing in years. We should like to abdicate. But before we do, you must wed or get married."

Nicholas thought of Lorelei and his heart started to race. "I just met—"

"We must find you a true princess," Queen Hermione interrupted. "The descendent of a long line of royalty. A noble maiden, with . . ."

That eliminates Lorelei, Nicholas thought. Her pretty, rosy cheeks alone would rule her out.

"We've devised a test," the king said. "Or an examination."

"But what if I don't love the true princess?"

"You'll love her," Queen Hermione said. "She'll be just right for you."

No she won't! thought Nicholas.

"You'll make yourself love or adore her," King Humphrey roared. "Or we'll abdicate in favor of Archduke Percival."

Nicholas hated the archduke. Percy threw his servants into the moat if they did something wrong or if he felt like it. He would be a terrible king.

"Would you like to hear the test, dear?" the queen asked.

Nicholas nodded.

"When a maiden arrives who claims to be a true princess," Queen Hermione said, "we shall give her a bouquet."

The king guffawed. "But amidst all the fragrant or sweet-smelling flowers, there will be a sprig or small bunch of parsley. And that's not a flower."

Nicholas wondered what parsley had to do with being a princess.

"The true princess will know," the queen said. "She will pluck that parsley right out of her bouquet."

"That's the test?"

"Certainly not," Queen Hermione said. "There's more. We shall serve her a salad. A beautiful salad."

"Except," King Humphrey said, chuckling, "right in the middle, there will be a bit—"

"A speck—" the queen interrupted.

"The merest fleck. We don't want to hurt or injure the maiden. There will be a fleck of uncooked or raw noodle."

"The true princess will find it!" Queen Hermione announced.

What did parsley and noodles have to do with being a kind and just ruler? Nicholas listened in amazement to the rest of the test. There would be a trial in every course of the banquet. Also, the poor princess would be given a gown with a skirt that was a tint lighter than the bodice. She'd have to notice. She'd be shown a tapestry and would have to find the single missing stitch.

Lorelei might pass that one, Nicholas thought.

Every inch of the princess would be measured. Her waist had to be tiny. Her hands and feet had to be small, although her fingers had to be long. Her big toe had to be longer than her index toe. She had to be tall, but not a giant. And so on.

"But the final test will be the most important one," Queen Hermione said.

"There's more?" Nicholas said.

King Humphrey nodded solemnly. Then he nodded again.

"She will sleep in a guest bedroom," the queen said. "Her bed will be piled with twenty soft mattresses."

"She'll fall off!" Nicholas said. "She'll hurt—"

"A princess does not fall," the queen said. She went on. "Each mattress will be filled with the finest swans' feathers. But under the bottom mattress we will place a pea. If she sleeps well, she is no true princess!"

King Humphrey agreed. "If she sleeps or slumbers well, she is no true princess!"

The Chief Royal Chambermaid heard about the pea test from the Chief Royal Window Washer. It made her curious, so she got a pea from the Chief Royal Cook. A dried pea, because they couldn't have meant a fresh one, which would just squoosh flat.

The Chief Royal Chambermaid made everything ready, just as it would be for the princess. One pea. Twenty mattresses. And a ladder.

She climbed up. The bed was sooo soft. It was delicious. Pea? She couldn't feel any pea. With twenty mattresses under her, she doubted she would feel a watermelon. She didn't think anybody could feel the pea—true princess, fake princess, or any other kind.

The Chief Royal Chambermaid climbed down and yanked off a few mattresses. Then she climbed back up. She still couldn't feel the pea. She pulled off more mattresses and tried again. Nothing.

She took off all the mattresses except the bottom one, but she still couldn't feel anything. She checked under the mattress. There it was. Well, she was no princess. Maybe a true princess could feel a pea under one or two mattresses. But under twenty? Not on your life.

Five

Sam got ready for his trip to the earldom of Pildenue. The earl was his only noble customer. Sam made enough from this one job to keep Lorelei in silk kirtles and embroidery thread for a year.

He said a long farewell to Lorelei in front of their cottage. "Be sure you wear your shawl at night, honey."

"I will, Father."

"Be sure she does, Trudy. I don't want her to get sick."

"Yes, Master," Trudy said. Would that be a good way to bump her off? Let her catch cold and die?

"And make her eat enough, Trudy. You have to keep your strength up, sweetie pie."

"Yes, Master," Trudy said. Should she starve Lorelei? No. It would take too long.

"Here, sweet. Give your old daddy a kiss."

Lorelei hugged him. "I'll miss you, Father. Hurry home."

Sam climbed up to the seat of his wagon. He flapped the reins, and the old mare started to trot.

Lorelei wiped away a tear. She turned to Trudy. "We'll just have to keep each other company." She sniffled. "We'll have a lovely time, won't we?"

"Yes, lass." Yes indeed!

King Humphrey wrote a proclamation to announce the search for a real princess.

"Hear ye! Hear ye! Or listen well! Insofar and Inasmuch as We, King Humphrey, Supreme Ruler and Monarch of the Kingdom and Monarchy of Biddle . . ."

The king paused here. But there was no synonym for Biddle, so he went on.

". . . Wish to Abdicate Our Throne in Favor of Our Son and Heir, the Noble and Royal Prince Nicholas. And Insofar and Inasmuch as We Stipulate and Require . . ."

And so on. The next important part came at the very end. ". . . and Said Princess Must Satisfy Us, King Humphrey, Supreme . . ." Blah blah blah. ". . . That She Is in Her Person and Her Self a Completely and Utterly True Princess. Our Judgment on This Matter or in This Respect Shall Be Final and Without Appeal."

Below that King Humphrey signed *King Humphrey or Supreme Ruler of Biddle*, as was his habit. The Royal Seal was affixed, and the proclamation was complete. And finished, too.

Except for one thing. The king wanted a portrait of Prince Nicholas to go with the proclamation. He sent for his Chief Royal Artist and Portrait Maker.

"My son or heir isn't a bad-looking boy, is he?" King Humphrey asked the artist. "There's nothing wrong with his looks, is there?"

"Oh no, Sire. Not in the slightest." The Chief Royal

Artist and Portrait Maker thought the prince was ordinary-looking. Nothing special.

"The prince has to look handsome in his portrait or picture," the king said. "That way a true princess will want and desire to come."

"I understand, sire." Smaller ears. Straighter mouth. Broader shoulders. He could do that.

Nicholas wanted to look as ugly as possible in his portrait. He wanted every princess who saw it to say, "Ugh. Who would want to marry *him?*" Because if no princesses showed up, he might be able to convince the king and queen to let him marry Lorelei.

So he squinted. He squirmed. He mussed his hair. He let his mouth hang open. He drooled. He borrowed Queen Hermione's makeup and drew a big black mole on his chin.

It made no difference. The Chief Royal Artist and Portrait Maker was a master craftsman. In the portrait Prince Nicholas' chin (without a mole) was lifted majestically. His eyes had a piercing look. A hint of a smile played around his mouth. His shoulders were broad. His mouth wasn't lopsided. His ears were perfect. Also, the Chief Royal Artist and Portrait Maker waved Nicholas' hair and thickened his eyelashes. Princesses would fall in love with those eyelashes. Guaranteed.

When all was ready, scribes copied the proclamation. Lesser Royal Artists and Portrait Makers copied the portrait. Messengers were dispatched to kingdoms near and far.

The search was on.

"THE SEARCH WAS ON."

Six

Trudy thought about how to do Lorelei in. She could hit her over the head with the frying pan. Or strangle her with the embroidered clothesline. Or drag her to the village square and push her out of the clock tower. Any one of those would be lots of fun. But she'd be caught. The dopey villagers liked Lorelei.

It should be easy to finish her off, Trudy reasoned. After all, her highness was in bed sick or hurt three times a week without anybody doing anything to her. Why, she could murder herself one of these days without Trudy's having to lift a finger! Hmm. Now that was an idea.

The morning after Sam left, Trudy announced that she didn't feel well. "You'll have to do the housework today, lass," Trudy said. "I'm not up to it."

Lorelei would wash the dishes and she'd get that rash again. But today Trudy would be too sick to put on the salve. So Lorelei would swell up like a balloon and *POP!* And nobody would think it was Trudy's fault.

"Oh dear. Does your stomach ache?"

Trudy nodded.

"Oh dear. Does your forehead pulse?"

Trudy nodded.

"Your throat. Is it hard to swallow?"

Trudy nodded.

Lorelei clapped her hands. "Then I know just what to do. You've been so good to me, dear Trudy. And now I can help you." She threw open the door to the hutch and pulled out strangely shaped bottles and odd bundles of herbs.

"I used to get what you have," Lorelei said. "Mother made me well in a jiffy." She dumped whatever was in the bottles and bundles into a pot. Then she hung the pot on a hook in the fireplace.

Soon a sharp odor filled the room. Trudy's eyes watered. The hairs in her nose felt like they were burning.

"Doesn't it smell wonderful?" Lorelei asked. "I always feel better when I smell the steam. In a few minutes you'll drink the broth and be well again, dear Trudy."

She was going to have to *drink* that slop? Trudy jumped up. "I feel much better. Fine. Really." She poured the disgusting brew on the fire. Stinky smoke billowed out. "You're a good wisewoman. You've cured me already." Trudy opened the cottage door and the windows. She could have been killed!

She started on the chores. What else could she do? Hmm. "Lass?"

"Yes, Trudy?"

"I'm off to the market. While I'm gone, would you like to try the spinning wheel again?"

"Oh yes!"

"I won't be long. Be careful with the spindle." Trudy shut the door behind her and sauntered down the lane. Her ladyship would stab herself again. By the time Trudy got back, Lorelei would have bled to death.

The market was busy. Trudy gossiped with the other shoppers. She told the peddlers what was wrong with their goods. She even bought herself a pink hair ribbon. Then she strolled back to the blacksmith's cottage. What a delightful day it was!

She opened the door. No, it was a terrible day! Lorelei wasn't bleeding. Not even a drop. The only thing that was hurt was the spinning wheel. It looked like a giant spider had spun a web all over it. It would take days to untangle the mess.

Lorelei was crying. "Oh, Trudy! I'm sorry. I wanted to have yards and yards of beautiful linen finished when you got back. You must be so disappointed in me."

Lorelei couldn't understand what Trudy was saying. It sounded something like "Argul! Gloog! Blub!" Trudy yanked open the cottage door and slammed it behind her. She stood on the doorstep, panting. She had to get a grip on herself. She couldn't let that little . . . that little good-for-nothing fancy *idiot* do this to her.

She had to plan it out better. She had plenty of time. Two months before Sam came home. Plenty of time.

Lorelei was as good as dead.

Seven

A month went by and no one arrived at the court of Biddle to take the princess test. Queen Hermione smiled knowingly. She said the young ladies were getting ready, having gowns made, making themselves beautiful for their prince.

Making themselves as princessy as possible, Nicholas thought. I want Lorelei! He wanted to cry.

Every day he rode to her lane in the village of Snettering-on-Snoakes. He spent hours watching the smoke curl out of her chimney. He didn't even have to see her. Just seeing the smoke was enough.

But sometimes he did see her, sitting at her window, embroidering. He'd wonder what she was sewing. Buckets? Doorknobs? Galoshes? He thought his heart would break in two pieces.

One day Lorelei was outside, picking roses from the bush outside the cottage door. She turned when she heard the clatter of his horse's hooves. It was that nice prince again, she thought. What was his name?

Nicholas. A nice name. She curtsied.

Nicholas jumped off his horse. He bowed. What could he say to her? "Er . . . hello. Er . . . hello, maid Lorelei."

She smiled. "Hello, Your Highness."

"Fine weather we're having." He wished he could think of something more interesting to say.

"I think the clouds mean rain." Why couldn't she think of something more interesting to say? He probably knew a hundred princesses who could make fascinating conversation.

"Those roses are pretty. Did you plant them?"

Inside the cottage Trudy was cleaning the stove. She saw Lorelei through the window and wished the sluggard would prick herself with a poisoned thorn. She wished that the young lord talking to Lorelei were a highwayman who would kidnap her. Then he'd have to clean up after her and bandage her. Then she'd be his problem.

Hmm . . . Trudy thought, that's it! That's the way to get rid of her, once and for all.

The very next day a princess showed up at King Humphrey's court. She was Princess Cordelia from the nearby kingdom of Kulornia.

King Humphrey himself helped her down from her carriage.

She was good-looking. The king didn't have his tape measure with him, but she seemed tall enough. And her hands looked the right size.

Queen Hermione smiled. The maiden looked promising.

Prince Nicholas frowned and bowed. He could tell already. He didn't like Cordelia.

"Thank you." She curtsied. "Well, well, well. Here I am. We made good time getting here. We only stopped three times on the road. Traffic wasn't bad. Dandy courtyard you have here, Humphrey. Hello, Nicky. I see they exaggerated on your portrait. I expected that, so don't worry about it. They always do it in the marriage game. Well, well. Dandy courtyard . . ."

Queen Hermione looked at her husband. They had forgotten to put in a test for the art of conversation.

King Humphrey looked at his wife. They had forgotten to put in a test for talking your head off or never shutting up.

Nicholas looked at the sky. Nicky! He mustn't scream. He didn't have to marry anybody yet.

The king snapped his fingers. The Chief Royal Bouquet Maker stepped forward. He presented a bouquet to Princess Cordelia.

Let her not find the parsley, Nicholas prayed.

Let her not find the parsley or herb, the king prayed.

Let her not find the parsley, the queen prayed.

"Well, well, well. You folks sure know how to roll out the red carpet. There's nothing like a bunch of flowers to brighten things up. Take a dull tower room and—"

"Would you like us to put them in water, my dear?"

Queen Hermione asked. If she said yes, it would be all over.

"Sure. Wouldn't want them to go limp and croak right in—"

"We're so glad you had a comfortable journey," King Humphrey interrupted firmly. "We hope or desire that it will be even better going the other way. Thank you so much for coming." He handed her back into the carriage and slapped the horses to get them moving quickly or rapidly.

Princess Cordelia stuck her head out the window. "Well! What did I do? I thought we were getting along just fine. When you issue a . . ."

The three of them went back into the castle. They could hear Cordelia yelling till the heavy doors thudded shut behind them.

Eight

On the same day that the talkative Princess Cordelia was thrown out of Biddle, Trudy perfected her plan. She would lose Lorelei, plain and simple. And whoever found her would have to keep her—finders keepers. Trudy giggled.

"Lass," Trudy said. "What's the name of that herb you like in your tea sometimes?"

"Hyssop?"

"That's the one. We're fresh out of it, and there's none in the market."

"That's all right." Lorelei smiled bravely. "I can do without."

"But I don't want you to, sweet. I want you to be happy, honey lamb."

"You're so good to me."

Hah! "Tim, the spice peddler, told me where it grows in the forest. I thought we could harness your dad's mule and go there tomorrow. We'll have a picnic."

"What fun!"

Hooray! Trudy thought. The bumbling ninny would never find her way home from the middle of the forest.

The next day princesses arrived at the castle in droves. They came in carriages drawn by horses, by camels, by oxen. One even came in a carriage drawn by crocodiles. And another arrived in a hot-air balloon. The courtyard was clogged with animals and carriages and princesses. The Royal Guards got tired of raising and lowering the drawbridge. They decided to leave it lowered till the prince announced his engagement.

There were too many princesses to test one by one. So the king and queen decided to test them all together.

Nicholas looked them over. Some were too short. Some were too tall. Some were too thin. Some were too fat. They'd all fail the measurement test. But the rest seemed about right. The most beautiful princess was the one who'd come in the carriage pulled by crocodiles. She had huge purple eyes and a slow smile. She gave Nicholas the shivers. He kept feeling she didn't want to marry him—she really wanted to roast him and eat him with cream sauce.

In the forest Lorelei finished weaving a daisy chain. She was in a small clearing, sitting on an embroidered blanket, a velvet embroidered blanket, of course. The only kind that didn't make her itchy.

"LORELEI FINISHED WEAVING A DAISY CHAIN."

Trudy was hunting for hyssop, the herb for Lorelei's tea.

"Do you see any?" Lorelei called.

"Not yet. Eat your lunch. I'll be there soon."

Lorelei opened the picnic basket. Trudy's voice sounded faraway. Lorelei bit into her cucumber sandwich with the crusts cut off. "Trudy!" she called. "Come back. You must be hungry."

"Soon. I think I see something."

Lorelei could hardly hear the words. It was too bad that Trudy couldn't enjoy this beautiful day. The spice peddler should have drawn a map showing exactly where the hyssop grew. Lorelei finished her lunch and leaned back on the blanket. Such sweet puffy white clouds. She closed her eyes. In a few minutes she was asleep.

Trudy led Leonard the mule along the trail next to the stream. Lorelei hadn't called in a while. It was safe to stop. Trudy tied Leonard to a tree and took the extra lunch out of his saddlebag. She kicked off her shoes and sat on a rock with her feet dangling in the cool water. She bit into her sandwich. Sausages and peppers. Her favorite. This was peace.

Prince Nicholas couldn't stand being around all these princesses for another minute. He saddled his horse and rode to Snettering-on-Snoakes. He had to see Lorelei.

But she wasn't there. Her cottage was empty.

⚓ ⚓ ⚓

The first drops of rain woke Lorelei. The sky was dark.

"Trudy?"

A roll of thunder drowned her out. The drops came down harder. They were huge.

"Trudy? Do you hear me?"

Had Trudy come back and eaten her lunch while she was asleep? Lorelei opened the basket. No. Trudy's sausage-and-peppers sandwich was still there. Trudy is lost! Lorelei thought. Poor Trudy. She must be terrified.

Lightning lit the sky. Were you supposed to get under a tree when there was lightning? Or stay away from trees?

At least she'd be drier under a tree. Lorelei jumped up and folded the blanket neatly. Then she took the picnic basket and ran under a tall maple.

She stayed under the tree for an hour. Every few minutes she called Trudy, but there was never an answer. The sky grew darker. Storm dark, but also night dark. Lorelei's stomach rumbled delicately. Time for dinner.

She had to find Trudy. It was her responsibility because she was Trudy's mistress. She had never felt so full of purpose before. She had to find Trudy and Leonard the mule and get them home safely. She'd go to the stream first. The last time she'd heard Trudy's voice, it had come from there.

The stream was across the clearing and straight ahead, through a stand of trees. Lorelei stepped into the clearing and was drenched instantly. Oh well, she thought. It was only water.

"Trudy! Stay where you are. I'm coming." She didn't want poor Trudy to have one second more of terror than she had to.

As the water soaked into them, Lorelei's skirts got heavier and heavier and dragged more and more. It was hard to walk, but she had to do it.

"Trudy! I'm coming!"

Where was the stream? She should have reached it by now.

"Leonard?" Maybe the mule would hee-haw and she'd find him. Then she could ride him and find Trudy more quickly. She pushed past bushes and over fallen logs.

Two hours passed. Lorelei still hadn't found Leonard, Trudy, or the stream. She was hungry and chilled. She sneezed almost as often as she took a breath. She couldn't get sick, not now when Trudy needed her.

Finally Lorelei sat on a tree stump and cried between sneezes. She had to admit it. Trudy was lost. Leonard was lost. And she was lost.

Nine

y dinnertime the flood of princesses had slowed to a trickle. Around ten o'clock it stopped. Seventy-nine princesses had come.

Queen Hermione set aside a wing of the castle just for them. Tonight they would sleep in ordinary beds with only one mattress and no pea. Tomorrow the tests would begin. Tomorrow night would be the final exam for those who had passed all the other tests. The mattress and pea test. The test that the Chief Royal Chambermaid was sure nobody could pass.

Prince Nicholas was beside himself. What was he going to do? And where was Lorelei?

Lorelei was flat on her face in the forest. She had tripped over a tree root, and she was too tired to get up. Too tired to do anything except sneeze.

But she had to get back to the village and form a search party. She stood and picked up the picnic basket and blanket. Her gown and face were covered with mud and dead leaves. Well, the rain would clean off her face. And the gown didn't matter, since she hadn't had a chance to embroider anything on it yet.

She heard something. She stood still and fought back a sneeze. There it was again. A snuffling noise. Trudy! She opened her mouth to yell. But wait. What if it wasn't Trudy. What if it was—

Lorelei had never climbed a tree in her life. But she climbed one now. One second she was on the ground. The next she was twelve feet up.

A bear crashed through the bushes. She sneezed. Oh no! He was going to find her!

But he passed right by, in a big hurry. He didn't even look up. He was probably going to his nice warm cave. Lucky bear.

Lorelei climbed down from the tree and stumbled on. "Achoo!" Hang on, Trudy, she thought. Hang on. I'm coming.

Nicholas couldn't sleep. He paced up and down in his room. He didn't want to marry anyone but Lorelei. He didn't care about having a princess for a bride. As soon as he married her, Lorelei would be a princess anyway. So what was the difference?

He wouldn't even care that much about becoming a king someday, if Archduke Percy wasn't such a monster.

The wind howled in the forest beyond the moat. He looked out his window. Sheets of rain poured down. Wherever Lorelei had been today, she'd have to be home by now. He wished he could peek in her window and see her, warm and dry and fast asleep, in an embroidered nightgown.

Had she seen a light? Way up ahead? So much water was coming down, it was hard to keep her eyes open. "Achoo!"

Lightning flashed, and Lorelei saw a castle. Towers and battlements, dark against the yellow-gray sky.

Who lived there? A royal family? A troll family? Ogres? An evil magician? Maybe she should stay in the forest. "Achoo!" No. She had to go on. For Trudy's sake.

She hurried across the drawbridge. "Achoo!" It would be dry inside. She'd be out of the wind. If the owner was an ogre and he decided to eat her, she'd warm up while she roasted. And if he was a decent ogre, he might even let her take a bath before he cooked her.

She knocked on the thick oak doors. The Chief Royal Night Watchman opened them. A dripping muddy maiden stood there. Another princess? She didn't look like much. But he had his orders, and he let her into the great hall. "Wait here," he barked.

Nicholas had seen the small figure cross the drawbridge. Another one, he thought. His parents weren't going to like having to get up in the middle of the night for her. He grinned sourly. They'd be sorry they hadn't put in a test for coming in the daytime.

He met his parents on the circular stairway to

"She knocked on the thick oak doors."

the great hall where the maiden stood shivering and sneezing.

He couldn't believe it. It was Lorelei! What was she doing here?

Lorelei watched them come down the stairs. They weren't ogres and trolls. One of them even looked familiar. It was that nice Prince Nicholas. Lorelei's heart lurched a little.

She curtsied deeply. She sneezed and wobbled and almost fell over.

They have kind faces, Lorelei thought, but they look annoyed. Except the prince. He looks glad to see me. She sent him a special smile. And then she sneezed.

"Who are you?" King Humphrey boomed. "Which one are you?"

"I am—achoo!—Lorelei. You see—achoo!—I got—"

"Another princess," Nicholas interrupted loudly. "There's always room for one more." He winked at Lorelei, hoping she'd see and go along. Hoping his parents wouldn't see. "Who knows?" he added. "She might be the one to pass the princess tests."

Lorelei saw the wink. He wanted her to pretend to be a princess? She could, if he wanted her to. But why?

She curtsied again. "I am Princess Lorelei. Achoo!"

Ten

"How did you get here?" Queen Hermione asked. "Where's your carriage?"

"Um . . . achoo! Um, I don't have a carriage. Um . . ." What could she say? "Um . . . I . . . I was bewitched." That was it! "Achoo! A fairy put a spell on our whole court. My father was turned into a blacksmith. I became a blacksmith's daughter. I was—achoo!—a baby when it happened."

Quick thinking, Nicholas thought. She was clever, too.

"Absurd! Ridiculous!" King Humphrey roared. "There hasn't been a case or example of a fairy spell in a hundred years. Not since Queen Rosella and King Harold's reign."

"Achoo!"

The lass is crazy, the queen thought.

"Suppose she is a true princess?" Prince Nicholas said. "She might be the only one of the eighty maidens here who is." He hoped Lorelei was paying attention. "If you don't give her the tests, you'll never know.

You won't be able to abdicate, Father. I'll never marry.
You'll never have grand—"

"Son or heir, you're right." The king put an arm
around Nicholas' shoulder. "The boy is correct or
accurate."

Lorelei listened between sneezes. Tests? Had they
said that if she passed some tests, she could marry
Nicholas? Really?

Queen Hermione shrugged. It couldn't do any
harm. A true blacksmith's daughter would certainly
fail the tests. She rang her bell for the Chief Royal
Chambermaid.

"Achoo! Excuse me. My Lady-in-Waiting was with
me when we got lost. Achoo! She's still under the
spell. She thinks she keeps house for a blacksmith."
Lorelei told them about Trudy.

She's so kind! Nicholas thought.

"And our black stallion got lost too. He looks like
a mule."

The king called for a groom to ride to the village of
Snettering-on-Snoakes to see if Trudy and Leonard
had gotten home safely.

Lorelei went upstairs with the Chief Royal
Chambermaid. Nicholas followed them. She'll pass
one test anyway, he thought, looking at her muddy
footprints. She has small feet. But what about the rest?

The tests began first thing in the morning.

Lorelei had slept well. Her sheets were satin. The
blankets were velvet. The mattress was stuffed with

swans' feathers. Just like home. When she woke up, she wasn't even sneezing anymore.

Someone had laid a gown out for her, and a Royal Chambermaid was there to dress her. The gown was pretty, with diamonds sewn into the skirt and pearls sewn into the bodice. But it wasn't embroidered, which was a shame. And look at that! "That's funny," she said out loud.

The Royal Chambermaid curtsied. "What's funny, your ladyship?"

"Well . . ." You'd think they'd get it right for a princess. "The skirt on the gown—I don't mean to criticize—but it's lighter than the bodice."

So Lorelei passed the first test.

Three princesses hadn't noticed. Seventy-seven maidens sat down to breakfast, which was a simple meal. Poached eggs, dry toast, and half a grapefruit—Lorelei's favorite food for breakfast, lunch, and dinner.

While they ate, King Humphrey welcomed them to the kingdom or monarchy of Biddle. Then he explained about the tests, but he didn't say what any of them were. "In closing," he concluded, "let the truest princess conquer or win."

After breakfast, the king and queen and Nicholas gave the princesses and Lorelei a tour of the castle. King Humphrey lectured about Biddle as they went. Nicholas stayed near Lorelei, wishing he could warn her about each test, but the princesses might hear.

When the tour was over, everyone returned to the royal banquet hall for lunch—the next round in the true-princess test (although the contestants didn't know it).

The queen rang her bell, and Royal Serving Maids entered the royal banquet hall.

A salad was placed in front of Lorelei. She picked up her fork.

Now why was a bit of uncooked noodle mixed in with the lettuce? Quietly, she pointed it out to a Royal Serving Maid. And passed the salad test. So that was it, Lorelei thought. You had to guess what was wrong with the food. Funny test.

Five maidens didn't find the noodle. They were escorted out immediately.

Seventy-one to go, Nicholas thought. He noticed that the crocodile princess was still in the running.

Lorelei found the toothpick under the flounder. It wasn't hard, now that she knew what to look for. Nicholas breathed a sigh of relief.

Only one princess didn't find the toothpick.

Lorelei fished the tiny marshmallow out of her ragout. Eight princesses didn't. One of them was dragged away, yelling, "It isn't fair! Mine melted!"

Nicholas thought he was going to die of worry before the meal ended.

Lorelei found the flake of tuna on the chocolate cake icing. Four princesses didn't. The meal was over. Lorelei and the crocodile princess and fifty-seven other princesses remained in the game.

Eleven

After lunch the measuring began in the queen's bedchamber.

Nicholas and the king weren't allowed to view this part of the test. They waited in the throne room. King Humphrey listened to petitions from his subjects while Nicholas paced up and down, chewing his nails.

In the bedchamber Royal Chambermaids with tape measures checked every inch of every princess. If a princess was too tall, she was out. If she was too short, she was out. If her ears were too big, they were out and she was out.

The measuring took the rest of the day. Lorelei worried about the size of her nose. It was her worst feature. She pulled in her nostrils. When she looked in the mirror, she always thought that made her nose seem a little smaller.

Her nose squeaked by. A hair bigger and she would have had it.

The measuring went on.

The waist of one of the princesses was too big by a sixty-fourth of an inch. Queen Hermione said she was sorry, but if she let this maiden slip by, she wouldn't know where to draw the line.

When the measuring was over, only ten princesses and Lorelei were left. The queen led them to the throne room.

The crocodile princess entered first. Nicholas bit his finger so hard it bled. She smiled at him. Her teeth looked pointy. Where was Lorelei? He held his breath.

Lorelei was the ninth to enter the room. Nicholas started breathing again. They looked at each other. This was scary.

The king gave bouquets to the princesses and congratulated or applauded them on getting so far.

Nicholas wanted to yell, It's another trick! It's a test!

Lorelei held her bouquet away from her to examine it. Some flowers made her sneeze and some made her eyes water. Roses were okay. Daffodils were okay too. Lilies made her sneeze. So did peonies. What was that? Parsley? That wasn't a flower. This was a test! She pulled out the parsley and sneezed.

The bouquet test fooled everyone except the crocodile princess and Lorelei. The best and the worst, Prince Nicholas thought. He was trembling.

Both of them passed the tapestry test. Lorelei spotted the missing thread from twenty feet away. Nicholas wished she could get extra credit.

King Humphrey announced that they would have a light supper and go to bed. The final test or examination, he lied, would be tomorrow, or the day after today.

Lorelei didn't have a moment to talk privately with Nicholas. She could tell he wanted her to be the one to pass the test, but she wanted to hear him say it. She also wanted him to give her a hint about the big test tomorrow.

He wanted to get near her, too. If he could whisper to her for just one second, he could tell her about the pea. But at supper she sat at the other end of the table, next to the king. Nicholas heard him telling her about his collection of unicorn horns or tusks.

The crocodile princess sat between the king and queen. Nicholas hated the way she ate. She seemed to swallow her food without chewing. And she kept looking at him and licking her lips.

Nicholas excused himself from the table. He went out to the garden and picked up a few large rocks. Then he slipped back into the castle and headed for Lorelei's bedchamber. He'd put the rocks under the top mattress, where she'd be sure to feel them.

But he couldn't get in. The Chief Royal Guard stood in front of the door. Nicholas tried to send him on an errand, but the fellow said that the king had told him not to budge for anyone or any person.

So then Nicholas said he'd leave a note for Princess Lorelei. But the Chief Royal Guard said, "Begging your pardon, Your Highness, no notes. I have my orders."

Nicholas couldn't do anything. By this time tomorrow either he'd be engaged to Lorelei, or Percival would be the future King of Biddle. Or he'd be engaged to the crocodile princess!

Twelve

Nicholas couldn't sleep. One second he was full of hope. She'd passed all the tests so far! The next second he was in despair. Nobody could feel a pea through all those mattresses. And the crocodile princess had a better chance than Lorelei. After all, the crocodile princess was a real princess, not a blacksmith's daughter.

But it didn't matter. If Lorelei failed, he'd marry her anyway. And his parents would have fits. And Percival would get the throne. He tossed. He turned. He finally slept, and he dreamed of being eaten by crocodiles and drowned in peas.

When Lorelei entered her room, she wondered why her bed had so many mattresses. Last night it had been an ordinary bed. She shrugged. Maybe they wanted her to have an extra-good night's sleep before the big test.

She climbed the ladder and slipped under the sheets. The bed was the softest she'd ever been in. She

"SHE WONDERED WHY HER BED HAD SO
MANY MATTRESSES."

stretched and wriggled her toes. Mmm. Lovely!

The prince was so nice! Even if he weren't a prince, even if he were a blacksmith, she'd love him. But he *was* a prince, and that was even better.

She rolled over. She couldn't get comfortable. The sheets felt all right. Satin. Satin was good. The blankets were velvet. Velvet was good.

She closed her eyes.

Something was wrong. Her nose itched and her back ached. She climbed down from the bed and looked at it.

It had to be the mattresses. Maybe there was a pigeon feather in one of them. But which one? There were so many.

She'd never fall asleep. She'd be up all night. Then she wouldn't be at her best for the big test tomorrow. Maybe she could stretch out in front of the fireplace.

She spread a blanket on the floor and laid another one on top of it. Then she got in between them and closed her eyes. The hours crawled by. The floor was hard, but you expected a floor to be uncomfortable. You didn't expect it from a bed piled with twenty mattresses.

Lorelei turned over on her stomach. No better. She rolled back. Could she, Lorelei, actually become a princess? She'd passed every test so far. If she married Prince Nicholas, she'd live in a castle. And so would her father. She giggled. Trudy would be a real lady-in-waiting.

Trudy! She sat up. She'd forgotten to find out if

Trudy had gotten home safely. What kind of queen would she make if she couldn't remember her subjects?

She lay down again. She'd ask first thing in the morning. What could the test tomorrow be like? Would they ask her questions? She didn't know anything about being a princess. She didn't know much about being a blacksmith's daughter either.

What if they asked her about laws! About geography! About how to sit on a throne! Lorelei was awake all night.

In the morning the Chief Royal Chambermaid led the two maidens to the throne room. Lorelei's bones ached, and the skin under her gown was black and blue.

King Humphrey and Queen Hermione and Prince Nicholas were sitting on their thrones. All the courtiers and subjects had been cleared out for the big moment.

The first thing Lorelei wanted to do was to find out about Trudy. Then she'd take whatever test they wanted. She'd probably fail it. But at least she'd know about Trudy.

The other maiden looked so rested and . . . Lorelei hated to admit it, but the other one was beautiful. Maybe by now Nicholas wanted her to win.

"Good morning, princesses or damsels," the king boomed.

"Did you sleep—" the queen began.

"Did you find out—" Lorelei began.

The doors to the throne room burst open. A man rushed in carrying a child in his arms. Lorelei thought the little boy didn't look right.

King Humphrey stood. "What or why—"

"Sire! I am a poor woodcutter! My son is sick, and I have no money to pay a wisewoman to cure him. I have nowhere to turn, except to you."

"Oh dear," Lorelei said. She ran to the child. "Does your forehead pulse?"

The boy nodded.

"Oh dear. Does it hurt to—"

Nicholas interrupted. "If you were a princess here," he asked the crocodile princess, "what would you do?"

This is the test! Lorelei thought. Maybe the boy wasn't really sick. But he looked sick.

The crocodile princess said, "They should be forbidden to trouble you with their problems. This man and his son must be put to death. That will cure the boy." And she smiled her slow smile.

"What would you do, Princess Lorelei?" Nicholas asked.

What was she supposed to say? Did that horrible one give the right answer? But if you couldn't help people—if you had to *kill* them to make them leave you alone—then she, Lorelei, didn't want to be a princess.

But then she'd have to give Nicholas up.

Well, it didn't matter what the right answer was. Somebody was sick! "Oh dear. I used to get sick when I was a little—uh—princess. I still do sometimes." She turned to the queen. "Do you have any betony?"

Lorelei was sure she was ruining everything, because the queen looked so upset. "I need the leaves of the chaste tree, too. If you don't have that, some bugloss will do. Where's the kitchen?"

Queen Hermione didn't know what to say. So she rang for the Chief Royal Serving Maid.

"Princess Lorelei would be kind to our subjects, Father," Nicholas said, while they waited for the serving maid. "Whether or not she can feel a pea under twenty mattresses." He dropped to his knees so hard, he thought he had broken a kneecap. "Ouch!"

"Oh dear," Lorelei said. A pea? What was he talking about?

"My darling princess." Nicholas took Lorelei's hand. "Will you marry me?"

"Oh dear. Yes, I'll marry you. We'll need hot water. Does your stomach ache?" she asked the boy.

He nodded.

"Did you sleep or rest well last night, Princess Lorelei?" the king asked. He had to know, even though everything had gotten confused or mixed up.

"No," Lorelei said. "I couldn't get comfortable. So I slept on the floor."

"The pea!" said the queen.

"The pea or bean," said the king.

"Darling!" said the prince.

Epilogue

orelei cured the woodcutter's son. King Humphrey and Queen Hermione gave their consent or permission to the marriage of Prince Nicholas and Princess Lorelei.

On their wedding day Nicholas wore a doublet embroidered with parsley, a shirt embroidered with tape measures, and hose embroidered with noodles. Lorelei's hood and veil were embroidered with tuna fish. Her bodice was embroidered with green peas, and her skirt and train were embroidered with tiny mattresses.

Trudy (who was perfectly safe, of course) was furious that she hadn't gotten rid of Lorelei. But when she moved into the castle, the other Royal Servants showed her the good side of serving a bunch of persnickety monarchs. She learned to agree with them over a dinner of cream of asparagus soup, venison crown roast, and twelve-layer mocha-raspberry cake.

When Sam returned from the earldom of Pildenue, he moved into the palace too. He never understood exactly how Lorelei had become a princess. And he couldn't for the life of him understand why everyone called him Lord Blacksmith. But he liked living in a palace and shoeing the king's wonderful horses.

So they all lived happily ever after.

Princess Sonora
and the
Long Sleep

To Sylvia,

my real fairy godmother.

—G.C.L.

One

hat a hideous baby, the fairy Arabella thought. She said, "My gift to Sonora is beauty." She touched the baby's yellow squooshed-up face with her wand.

The baby began to change. Her scrawny arms and legs became plump, and her blotchy yellow skin turned pink. Her pointy head became round. Honey-colored ringlets appeared on her scalp.

Ouch! It hurt to have your body change shape and to grow hair on your head in ten seconds. Sonora wailed.

King Humphrey II of Biddle thought, Why did the fairy do that? As his first-born child—as his lovey dovey oodle boodle baby—she had been fine the way she was. But he bowed low to the fairy. "Thank you, Arabella. What a wonderful gift." A person could get into a lot of trouble for failing to thank a fairy.

Queen Hermione II picked up the yowling baby and cuddled her. Then she curtsied deeply and thanked the fairy too, even though she wanted to wail along with her daughter. Sonora looks six months old, the queen thought. I wanted to watch her grow.

Gradually Sonora stopped crying, and her mother put her back into the gilded cradle. Time for the second fairy gift.

The fairy Allegra waved her wand over the baby. "I give Sonora the gift of a loving heart."

Something was happening again, Sonora realized. But this was better. This didn't hurt. She pictured the tall being and the soft being who fed her and held her and made noises to her. They were nice! She loved them! She said, "Goo," and blew a wet bubble.

Adorable! King Humphrey II thought.

Sweet! Queen Hermione II thought.

"My turn!" The fairy Adalissia stepped up to the cradle.

Adalissia gave Sonora gracefulness. Then the fairy Annadora gave her good health, and the fairy Antonetta made her the smartest human in the world.

Not much changed when Sonora got good health, since she was healthy already. And not much changed when she got gracefulness, because month-old babies don't have much opportunity to be graceful. But something did happen when Antonetta made her a smart person. Sonora listened more closely when the nice beings thanked the fairy. She noticed her own name and knew that she'd heard it before.

Aurora, the sixth fairy, was flustered. She had planned to make Sonora the smartest person in the world, but that miserable Antonetta had stolen her gift. Now what could she give the baby? She could make the child beautiful. But no, Arabella had already used that one. Adalissia had done gracefulness. What was left? They were all looking at her. They were laughing behind their sympathetic faces, glad they had been at the head of the line.

"Er . . ." Aurora waved her wand vaguely. Then she had it. It was so simple. It was much better than Antonetta's. She leaned over the cradle and touched Sonora on the nose with her wand. "My gift is brilliance. Sonora is ten times as smart as any human in the world." There.

Sonora felt something happen again, a tickle and a little shake inside her head. Then—it was done. She closed her eyes to think, really think, for the first time. She listened to the noise the tall being was making. She remembered all the noises people had made with their mouths since she'd been born. Some of the noises sounded alike. Some of them always went together.

Now the soft being was making noises. They were words! The noises were words. She was thanking the fairy for her gift. She was hoping that Sonora (that's me! that's me!) would use her extraordinary intelligence well.

Sonora opened her eyes. The soft being was her mother. She was beautiful, with her big brown eyes and those lips that liked to smile at Sonora. Of course she loved her mother, since the fairy had just given her a loving heart. Sonora wondered why the fairy had done that. Didn't she think Sonora might be naturally loving?

The fairy Adrianna came forward to the cradle. "My gift—"

The door to the royal nursery flew open. Adrianna gasped. The other fairies gasped. King Humphrey II gasped. Queen Hermione II gasped.

Sonora heard the gasps, but she could see only the things right above her, such as the pink dragon-shaped balloon that hung over the cradle. She thought, Why couldn't these fairies have given me something useful, like the ability to sit up and see what's going on?

A new fairy came in. She looked like all the others. Tall, with rubbery-looking wings, surrounded by a flickering rainbow of lights. Smiling like the others had been till a second ago.

Queen Hermione II rushed to the newcomer. "Belladonna! We're honored." In her mind she shouted, Don't hurt my baby! Don't hurt Sonora!

The fairy looked around the room. "Pretty nursery," she cooed in an extra-sweet voice. "Cuddly stuffed unicorn. Handsome dollcastle." She looked in the cradle. "Beautiful baby."

She looks angry, Sonora thought. You didn't have to be a genius to see that.

Belladonna continued. "You failed to invite me to the naming ceremony of your only child. I suppose you have a reason?"

"We didn't invite you because we thought you . . ." The king stopped. He had been about to say they thought she was dead, but he couldn't say that. "We . . . uh . . . thought you'd moved away. We're so glad you could come."

"Can I get you some refreshment?" the queen asked. "We have some deli—"

"I didn't move. Nobody thinks I moved." The fairy circled the cradle. "Some stupid people think I'm dead, but let me tell you, I'm very much alive."

"We have some delicious—"

"You can't buy me off with food. Maybe you figured the kid would get enough gifts from the seven of them." Belladonna waved her wand at the other fairies.

They drew back.

Belladonna went on. "You thought you'd economize—only buy seven gold plates, seven gold forks, seven gold . . ."

It's true, King Humphrey II thought unhappily. We do only have seven gold place settings, but because we thought she was dead. Not because we're stingy.

Queen Hermione II tried again. "There's plenty—"

"Maybe you thought I couldn't come up with a good gift. You thought I would run out of ideas, like Aurora here."

But I did think of a good gift, Aurora thought. How many people are ten times as smart as everybody else?

Belladonna roared, "You think I'm stupid like her? Is that what you think? Hump? Herm? Hmm?"

"Of course we don't think you're stupid," King Humphrey II said.

"I'll show you I can think of a new and special gift."

She leaned over the cradle. "Kitchy coo."

Oh no, Sonora thought, wincing at the furious face. Somebody stop her! Do something!

Everyone was silent, frozen.

I have to do it, Sonora thought. I have to talk her out of whatever she's going to do. "Excuse . . ." Her voice was too low. She'd never said anything before. She swallowed and tried again. "Excuse—"

Belladonna didn't hear. "Annadora gave the baby good health, which she will keep until my gift takes place. So my gift to the ootsy tootsy baby"—she waved her wand—"is that she will prick herself with a spindle and die!"

Two

hen? Sonora wondered. When will I prick myself? When I'm eighty? Or in the next five minutes?

"I can't stay," Belladonna cackled. "I must fly." She vanished.

Queen Hermione II snatched Sonora up and held her tight.

Tears ran down King Humphrey II's face in rivers. What good was it being king if fairies could do this to you?

"It won't happen," the queen shouted. "I won't let it. You're not going to prick yourself with anything, sweetheart, baby dove."

Sonora wondered if her mother could prevent it. Or did it have to happen? If it had to happen, it had to happen. She'd just enjoy everything until it did. Sonora breathed deeply. Her mother smelled so good.

The fairy Adrianna coughed. "Nobody seems to remember that I haven't given Sonora my gift yet."

King Humphrey II threw himself down on his knees and clutched the fairy's skirts. Queen Hermione II put Sonora back in her cradle and threw herself down on her knees too.

"Please save our baby," the king pleaded.

"I can't reverse another fairy's gift," Adrianna said, freeing her skirts from the king's grasp. "That would cause a fairy war, and believe me, you don't want that. I thought of making Sonora artistic. What do you think?"

"Can't you do anything to save her?" the queen sobbed.

"Tutors will teach her to draw and play the harp," the king said.

Adrianna went to the cradle. "Let me think." It was mean of Belladonna to kill the kid because of her parents' mistake. "I can change Belladonna's wish a little. She has to prick herself. I can't do anything about that. . . . I know." She waved the wand over the cradle. "Sonora will prick herself, but she will not die. My gift is that she will sleep for a hundred years instead of dying. Oh, this is brilliant!" The fairy beamed at the king and queen. "At the end of a hundred years a highly eligible prince will wake her by kissing her. How's that?"

Hmm, Sonora thought. A hundred years . . . her parents would be dead by the time she woke up! She started crying and howling and bawling. And wishing the fairy Allegra hadn't given her a loving heart.

King Humphrey II picked her up. "Funny baby."

"I CAN'T REVERSE ANOTHER FAIRY'S GIFT,"
ADRIANA SAID."

He bounced her up and down. "She doesn't cry when the fairy says she's going to die. But when Adrianna saves her . . ." He bowed to the fairy. "Then she cries."

"We can go to the banquet hall now," the queen said.

Sonora fought to catch her breath. She had to explain. "Wait," she said finally. "Wisten!" Talking was hard without teeth. She tried again. "Listen!" There. She'd done it.

The king's jaw dropped, and he almost dropped Sonora too.

"If I sleep for a hundred years, Mother and Father—" She started crying again. "Mother and Father will die before I wake up."

"She can talk!" the queen said.

"And what if I have a dog or—"

"You can talk!" King Humphrey II lifted Sonora way above his head. "The ibble bibble baby can talk!"

And Belladonna said I couldn't think of a good gift, the fairy Aurora thought, smirking. How many gifts make month-old babies talk?

"Don't let them die while I'm asleep," Sonora begged.

She's right, the queen thought. But we can't criticize Adrianna's gift. She could get mad and harm Sonora.

"Um . . ." Adrianna said. If she really wanted to help Sonora, she had to fix as much as she could. "Suppose I do it this way. Suppose, when Sonora falls asleep, everybody in the castle sleeps along with her."

"Excellent," the king said. "Except sometimes we're in the courtyard."

"All right." She waved her wand. "Everybody from the moat on in will fall asleep and sleep for a hundred years." She chuckled. "Sweet dreams."

When the fairies left, King Humphrey II and Queen Hermione II had a long talk about the hundred-year sleep. They should have included Sonora, who would have had lots of good ideas. But Sonora was in the nursery, being rocked in her cradle by a Royal Nursemaid.

"Maybe it doesn't have to happen," the queen said, brushing away a tear. "We'll be very groggy when we wake up."

"We'll issue a proclamation," King Humphrey II said. "No spindles inside the castle."

"No needles," Queen Hermione II added. "Nothing sharp. Maybe if *anything* pricks her she'll fall asleep."

"No knives. No swords. No toothpicks. We'll build a shed and keep everything in there."

"Belladonna didn't say when Sonora would prick herself," the queen said. "She could be fifty when she does it."

"No prince will marry her if he knows she's going to nap for a hundred years," the king said. "He could be out hunting, and when he comes home, nobody greets him. They're all fast asleep."

The queen agreed. "Besides, the servants would panic if they knew. The whole court would leave."

They decided to keep the hundred-year sleep a secret. They didn't think of telling Sonora to keep it a secret too, because they kept forgetting how smart she was. But they didn't need to tell her because she already knew. She'd figured it out ten seconds after Adrianna gave the gift. Now, while she lay in the darkened nursery, she was thinking it all over instead of sleeping. She'd save sleeping for her hundred-year snooze.

The fairy's gift would come true, Sonora decided. If her head could change shape and if she could become plump just because of a fairy, not to mention getting smart twice, then of course she'd prick herself and sleep for a hundred years.

Sonora also figured out that her parents would try to keep the gift from happening by hiding the spindles. But wherever they were hidden, she'd find them and take one. She wasn't going to prick herself by accident at the worst possible moment. No. She would do it on purpose when the time was exactly right.

Three

he Royal Nursemaids couldn't get used to Sonora. It was so strange to change the diaper of a baby who was reading a book, especially a baby who blushed and said, "I'm so sorry to bother you with my elimination."

In her bath, Sonora never played with her cute balsa mermaids and whales. Instead, she'd remind the Royal Nursemaids to wash behind her ears and between her toes. After the bath, she'd refuse to wear her adorable nightcap with the floppy donkey ears. She'd say it wasn't dignified.

The king and queen had trouble getting used to Sonora too. The king hated to watch her eat. It was unnatural to see a baby in a high chair manage a spoon and fork so perfectly. She never dribbled a drop on her yellow linen bib with the pink bunny rabbits scampering across it.

There were hundreds of things that the queen missed. Sonora never tried to fit her foot into her mouth. After her second word, "wisten," she never said another word of baby talk. She never drooled. She never gurgled. She refused to breastfeed. She admitted that it was good for her, but she said it was a barbaric, cannibalistic custom. Queen Hermione II wasn't certain what a cannibal was, but she was embarrassed to ask a little baby, even though she knew Sonora would be perfectly polite about it. Even though she knew Sonora would be delighted to be asked.

But then again, in some ways Sonora was exactly like other babies. She had to be burped like anybody else, although other babies didn't go on and on about how silly they felt waiting for the burp to come. And most babies didn't cry from shame when they spit up on someone.

Because of her loving heart, Sonora also cried whenever anybody stopped holding her. Queen Hermione II could explain that her lap was falling asleep from holding Sonora and the heavy volume on troll psychology Sonora was reading. It didn't matter. She cried anyway. It didn't matter either if King Humphrey II said he had to meet with his Royal Councillors. Sonora cried anyway. And when the king said she was too young to help decide matters of state, her loving heart and her brilliant mind were in complete agreement—she had a temper tantrum.

She learned to crawl at about the same time as other babies, although she was more of a perfectionist about it than most. She set daily distance goals for herself, and she only crawled in perfectly straight lines and perfectly round circles. After a day of crawling practice, she once told her father that she enjoyed watching "the miracle of child development" happening to her.

Although her overall health was excellent, sometimes she got sick just like other children. Except other children didn't diagnose their own diseases or tell the Chief Royal Physician what the treatment should be. And other children got well faster than Sonora, because other children listened when their parents told them to go to sleep. Sonora wouldn't listen and wouldn't sleep.

Most nights, sick or well, she'd crawl into the royal library. She could memorize five or six books in a typical night. Fairy tales were her favorites. The more she knew about fairies, she reasoned, the better off she'd be.

On nights when she didn't feel like reading, she'd lie in her crib and think up questions. Then she'd answer them. For example, why did bread rise? She knew about yeast, but yeast wasn't the whole answer— because why did yeast do what it did? The whole answer fit in with Sonora's Law of the Purposeful Behavior of Everything Everywhere. Bread's purpose, she knew, was to feed people. It rose so it could feed as many people as possible. The reason jumped out at you when you thought about it correctly.

She decided that when her hand was big enough to hold a pen comfortably, she'd write a monograph on the subject.

Sonora didn't learn everything by reading and thinking. She also learned from the people around her.

As soon as she could walk, she followed the Royal Dairymaids everywhere and asked them a million questions about milking. She watched the Chief Royal Blacksmith and asked him questions. She spent days in the kitchen with the Chief Royal Cook, until the Chief Royal Cook wanted to pound Sonora on her Royal Head with the Royal Frying Pan.

Once she found out everything the Royal Dairymaids knew about milking or the Chief Royal Blacksmith knew about smithing or the Chief Royal Cook knew about cooking, Sonora would get to work. She'd read every book there was on the subject. Then she'd think, and soon she'd come up with a better or faster way to milk or smith or cook or do anything else.

She'd be very excited. If it was the middle of the night, she wouldn't be able to wait until morning to talk about her discovery, so she'd wake her parents up. This was always a disappointment. The king and queen were too sleepy to listen, and sometimes they were grumpy about being awakened. The king even raised his voice once, when she woke him to say she'd found a way to grow skinless potatoes, which would save hours of peeling.

Sonora would imagine the joy her improvements would bring the Chief Royal Farmer or the Chief Royal Cook or the Royal Dairymaids. But she'd be wrong—they were hardly ever pleased. They liked doing things the way they were used to, and they didn't like being told how to do their business by a Royal Pipsqueak no bigger than a mosquito bite.

"She followed the Royal Dairymaids everywhere
and asked them a million questions."

Sonora couldn't understand it. She knew that the purpose of dairymaids was more than to milk cows. They were people, and people had lots of purposes. If her brain hadn't told her that, her loving heart would have. But part of their purpose was to get milk from cows, so she couldn't understand why they didn't want to do it in the best way possible.

In fact, nobody was nearly as interested in what Sonora knew as she wanted them to be. Even her mother wasn't. Often, while the queen wrote out menu plans, Sonora would talk about her latest research.

And for the thousandth time the queen would wish that Aurora had thought of a different gift. A simple one would have been fine, Queen Hermione II would think. An excellent sense of smell would have been good, or a pretty singing voice, which didn't run in the family. She and Humphrey II both sounded like frogs.

Then the queen would try not to yawn. What was the child telling her now? How to build the fastest sailboat in the world? But Biddle was landlocked, and even its lakes were small. A *slow* sailboat could cross the biggest one pretty quickly. Queen Hermione II's eyes would close then, and her handwriting on the menu would wobble.

And Sonora would feel terrible, even though she'd know her mother didn't mean to hurt her feelings.

It would be the same with the king. He'd be deciding which squires were ready to be knighted, for example. Meanwhile, she'd start telling him about a book she'd read, a book that had been in his library forever without his ever wanting to read a word of it.

He'd say, "Sonora, sweet, we're not as smart as you are. We can't think about knights and dwindling—um, dwindling what? What's dwindling, cutie pie?"

"Dwindling unicorn habitats."

"That's right, darling. Tell us about it later when we're not so busy."

Sonora would leave then, knowing that her father hoped she'd never mention a unicorn to him again—with or without a dwindling habitat.

A new proverb sprang up in Biddle. Whenever a Biddler asked a question that nobody could answer, someone would say, "Princess Sonora knows." Then somebody else would say, "But don't ask her."

And everybody would laugh.

Four

When Sonora was six, she read every book she could find on the art of picking locks. Then, on a dark night, she stole out of the castle and went to the shed that held the spindles and the other sharp things. The moment had come for her to get her very own spindle so she'd be able to prick herself when the time was right.

She set to work, ignoring the sign on the door that said, "Keep out! Do not enter! Private property! Danger! Get out of here!" It took her exactly twelve minutes to pick all ten locks and another fifteen minutes to very carefully remove the spindle from the first spinning wheel she came to. When that was done, she picked the spindle up with the tongs from the nursery fireplace and carried it very carefully back to the nursery, where she dropped it in the bottom of her toy chest. She left it there, under the toys her parents had gotten for the child they expected to have—the one who wasn't ten times as smart as anybody else.

Every year King Humphrey II and Queen Hermione II made a birthday party for Sonora, which never turned out well. The party for Sonora's tenth birthday began like all the rest. The lads and lasses had come only because they had to. They stood around in the tournament field, feeling silly in their party caps. Sonora tried to be a good hostess and make them feel comfortable, but every subject she brought up fell flat. Nobody wanted to discuss whether fairies and elves should obey Biddle's laws, or who was happier, all things being equal, the knight or his horse.

Nobody wanted to play any games either. They had played hide-and-seek last year, and Sonora had told them how to play it better. It had taken months to forget her advice and get their good old game back. The year before that she had ruined blindman's buff.

They all sighed, including Sonora. It would be hours before she could return to her latest project, finding out why things had colors.

Then she had an inspiration. She called for ink, quill pens, and parchment for everyone. When the supplies came, she began to interview each guest in turn. Sonora listened and took notes while everybody who wasn't being interviewed grumbled about how stupid and boring this was.

When the last guest had been interviewed, Sonora cleared her throat nervously. This was the first time she had spoken before an assembly. She said, "Silence." Gradually everybody got quiet. "From my notes, I see that none of you enjoys doing chores."

The lads and lasses groaned. Now the know-it-all was going to tell them how to be better children.

"Here are seven good ways to avoid doing them."

The lads and lasses began to write as fast as they could. During the rest of that wonderful party, which flew by much too quickly for everybody, Sonora told them how to stay out late to play, how to get even with their enemies and not get caught, how not to eat food they didn't like, and how not to go to bed at bedtime (Sonora's specialty).

When the party was over, Sonora told the guests to bring their homework next year and she'd do it for them. As they left, everyone told the king and queen that it had been the best party ever. King Humphrey II and Queen Hermione II were delighted. They told Sonora she'd be a popular queen someday.

But Sonora knew better. When the lads and lasses grew up to be Royal Bakers or Royal Chimney Sweeps, they'd dislike her advice as much as their parents did. And they'd laugh and say the proverb to each other. "Princess Sonora knows, but don't ask her."

The evening after the party, Sonora moved out of the nursery to her own grown-up bedchamber, which had only one thing wrong with it—a bed. Sonora had argued that she didn't need a bed and didn't want a bed and disliked beds very much. It didn't matter, though. She was stuck with it.

Late that night, when everybody else was asleep, she used her new fireplace tongs to carry the spindle very carefully from the toy chest in the nursery to the floor of her new wardrobe. She shoved it all the way to the back and covered it with a pile of the nightdresses she refused to wear.

Then she tried to forget about the spindle and a hundred years of sleep.

The right time for Sonora to prick herself didn't come. And the more time passed, the less she wanted to do it. She was only a little frightened by the hundred years. What she was most afraid of was sleep.

She hadn't slept at all since the fairy Aurora made her so smart. She'd seen her mother sleep, usually when Sonora was trying to explain something. She'd seen her father fall asleep while listening to the Royal Minstrels after dinner. Sometimes Sonora yawned when they sang, but then she'd sit up extra straight and open her eyes extra wide. She'd stay awake because sleeping people were scary. They were right in the room with you, sort of. Their bodies were, but their minds weren't, which was creepy. Sonora loved her mind, and she wanted to know where it was at all times.

When Sonora was fourteen, King Humphrey II and Queen Hermione II decided on a husband for her, if she didn't prick herself before the wedding. They chose Prince Melvin XX, heir apparent to the throne of the neighboring kingdom of Kulornia. He was the ideal choice. Kulornia was even bigger and richer than

Biddle. Sonora would be queen over a vast empire.

King Humphrey II sent a dispatch to King Stanley CXLIV, the prince's father. He also sent a portrait of Sonora. King Stanley CXLIV sent back his answer.

King Humphrey II opened the dispatch and read it. "King Stanley CXLIV has agreed to the wedding," he told Sonora and Queen Hermione II. "The prince is coming for a visit." A piece of foolscap fell to the marble floor of the throne room. King Humphrey II picked it up. "Oh, look. Here's a letter from the prince." He started reading.

> *My dear Princess,*
>
> *My father, King Stanley CXLIV, says I'm going to marry you. I believe him. He always tells the truth, so I believe him. If he were a liar, I wouldn't.*

King Humphrey II nodded. "He sounds sensible."

He sounds like a fool, Sonora thought.

The king went on reading.

> *I believe in honesty. The fairies made me Honest when I was born. Besides, I do what my father tells me. If he says to marry someone, I marry her. I'm Traditional. The fairies made me that too when I was born. Below is a list of all the other things they made me.*
> 1. *Brave.*
> 2. *Handsome.*
> 3. *Strong.*

4. A Man of Action. (I used to be a Baby of Action.)

5. A Good Dancer.

6. Tall.

Plus Honest and Traditional, as shown above. I trust you will find me as described.

Honestly,

Prince Melvin XX

"Sweetheart!" Queen Hermione II said. "He's just right for you. He's handsome and you're beautiful. He's a good dancer and you're graceful." They would have so much to share. The queen felt weepy. Her baby was leaving her.

Sonora also felt weepy. They had nothing in common. Nothing important. The fairies hadn't made him smart. They hadn't given him a loving heart. Was it time to get out the spindle and prick herself?

Five

In her room, Sonora reached into her wardrobe. She touched the nightdresses that covered the spindle. Her heart raced. The moment had come.

But she didn't want to go to sleep.

Maybe the moment hadn't come. Maybe Prince Melvin XX wasn't so bad. His letter was so bad. But maybe he wasn't. Maybe he was just not a talented writer. He probably wasn't brilliant, but that might not matter. At least people wouldn't make up horrible proverbs about not asking him the things he knew. Besides, maybe he was really wonderful.

He couldn't be.

Maybe he was. If she went to sleep now, she'd never find out. He'd get old and die before she woke up. And she'd have missed the great romance of her life.

It wouldn't hurt to find out. He was coming soon. She could always prick herself after she met him.

Prince Melvin XX came, following forty pages blowing trumpets. Sonora met him in the courtyard as he stepped down from his carriage. Probably he was handsome, but he was so tall she could hardly see his face, because it was too far away. He had dark hair and broad shoulders. She couldn't tell what color his eyes were. She'd have to wait to see them when he sat down.

She curtsied.

He bowed. He thought, I guess she's pretty. She's puny though. The fairies didn't make her Tall.

They had no chance to talk because they had to hurry to a banquet in the prince's honor. Sonora sat at one end of the banquet table with her mother. Prince Melvin XX sat with her father at the other end.

The prince ate, chewing very slowly. Sonora watched his mouth. He ate more slowly than anyone she had ever seen before. While he ate, he talked to the king. The prince spoke so slowly that King Humphrey II forgot the beginning of each sentence by the time Prince Melvin XX got to the end. Prince Melvin XX told the king about every second of his journey to Biddle. He explained how he had decided on each item he had brought from Kulornia. He said what he had been doing when his father had agreed to the marriage.

King Humphrey II wished there weren't so many courses. Another half hour of this and he'd faint.

The meal finally ended. King Humphrey II stood up quickly. "Sonora, sweet, show your guest the garden." Get him out of here!

Sonora curtsied and led the prince away. Queen Hermione II headed for her daughter's bedchamber to see what Sonora needed for her trousseau. The king decided to take a nap.

⚓ ⚓ ⚓

Prince Melvin XX held the door to the garden open for Sonora. "My father says you're smart," he said slowly. "And I believe him. He always tells the truth. If he were a liar, I wouldn't believe him."

"That's reasonable." Sonora tried to smile, but she couldn't. I can't smile because I'm sad, she thought. If I were happy, I would be able to. Aaa! I'm thinking the way he talks. "Our roses are over here."

"I see them. The red ones are very red." He went on. "I'm glad you're smart. When I'm king, you can write my proclamations. I'll tell you what to say."

"If you tell me what to say, why—"

"Thinking gets in the way. People can be too smart. I'm a Man of Action. The fairies made me that way. I always know what to do. Father had to write a proclamation the other day . . ."

Sonora bent over to sniff a peony. Here was another person who would never want to listen to her.

The king couldn't fall asleep. His head hurt too much. Compared to the prince, Sonora was a pleasure to listen to. He rolled over onto his stomach.

In Sonora's room, Queen Hermione II began to take gowns out of the wardrobe and spread them across Sonora's bed. The child needed new ones for her trousseau. Five or ten new gowns. The prettiest gown Sonora had was blue, embroidered with seed pearls. Where was it? She turned back to the wardrobe.

⚓ ⚓ ⚓

Sonora and Prince Melvin XX stood next to the weeping cherry tree. He was talking as usual. She had stopped listening an hour ago. He was saying very slowly that he didn't see much use for flowers. Vegetables were different. He saw a use for them. He began to list all the vegetables he could think of.

Sonora wondered how bad sleep could be. A hundred years of sleep would be shorter than five minutes with the prince. As soon as she got away from him, she'd go to her room and prick herself.

No! If she did, he'd fall asleep too, and in a hundred years she'd still have to marry him. But then she wouldn't have a hundred years of sleep to look forward to. So she couldn't prick herself now. She'd have to wait and do it when he went back to Kulornia to get ready for the wedding.

"I especially like boiled corn in the . . ."

But meanwhile she didn't have to spend hours with him. She could think of an excuse to get away. She wasn't so smart for nothing.

"Do you like corn too?"

He'd stopped talking. He was looking at her, waiting. He must have asked her something.

"I'm sorry. What did you say?"

"I said do you like corn too?" Was she hard of hearing? That wouldn't be good. His own hearing was perfect.

"Not particularly." Maybe he wouldn't want to marry her if she didn't like corn.

"Oh." He shrugged. "I never met anybody who didn't like it before."

"Sir, I fear I must leave you for a while. The king likes me to use this hour for quiet meditation in my room. I will—"

"Corn might be my favorite—"

She fled.

The queen lifted the last gown off its hook. Where was the blue one? Was that it on the floor of the wardrobe? She bent down to see. But it wasn't the gown. It was a pile of old nightdresses. How could the Royal Chambermaids have left them in such a heap? They could have been there for years. Queen Hermione II started pulling them out. She'd fold them up and shame the wenches with them.

Something underneath. What—

"Aaaaa! Aaaaa! Aaaaa! Help! Treason! Aaaaa! Aaaaa!" Have to get it out of here! "Aaaaa!" Protect Sonora! "Aaaaa!" She grabbed the spindle. "Aaaaa!" Had to run! She ran around the room, not knowing where to go. "Aaaaa!" The shed! She had to get it to the shed! "Aaaaa!" She ran out of the room.

Sonora heard her mother's screams and thought, Spiders! She started running. Tarantulas! The screams sounded like they were coming from her own room. She thought, Black widows! I warned Father just last week. I have to reach Mother! I'm the only one who knows what to do if she's bitten.

The king sat up in bed. Was someone yelling?

The prince lifted his head. Someone was screaming. Was there a dragon? He looked up at the sky. He

"'Aaaa!' The queen turned the corner.
"'Coming! Don't wor–' Sonora turned the corner."

didn't see a dragon, so one couldn't be there.

"Aaaaa!" The queen raced down the north corridor, away from Sonora's room.

Sonora raced up the west corridor, toward her room. Let me reach her in time!

"Aaaaa!" The queen turned the corner.

"Coming! Don't wor—" Sonora turned the corner.

The spindle pierced Sonora's outstretched hand.

Six

In the meadow across the moat, Elbert watched his father's flock of sheep. It was a boring job. The only time it was interesting was when the castle drawbridge was lowered. Then Elbert could watch who was going in and coming out, and he could also see into the castle courtyard.

The drawbridge was lowered now. A team of oxen was crossing with a wagonload of peaches. Juicy, ripe peaches. Elbert's mouth watered. Inside the courtyard, a butcher was cutting up a spring lamb. Elbert's stomach rumbled. He could almost taste it—roast lamb followed by peach pie.

On the drawbridge, the oxen stopped, and the driver slumped forward.

Huh? Elbert stared.

The driver almost fell off his bench. The heads of the oxen drooped. In the courtyard, the butcher stopped cutting. His head lolled to one side.

Arrows! Had to be arrows! Elbert spun around. No arrows were flying. He spun back. No arrows were sticking out of the wagon driver. None stuck out of the oxen.

He jumped up. Maybe he could help! Maybe he could get a few peaches and that lamb.

What was that? Something was growing along the outer rim of the moat. He started running. Whatever it was, it was growing fast—as high as his knee already. But he didn't have far to go. He ran faster. The hedge was as high as his waist. He'd jump over, grab the wagon driver, and drag him to safety.

He reached the moat. But the hedge was now up to his neck. He could still climb it, but he'd never get the driver out, and he'd get caught inside too. He stood before the hedge, panting. In his last glimpse of the drawbridge, Elbert saw one of the oxen switch its tail to brush away a fly. The ox was alive! It was—it was— asleep!

The hedge zoomed up, taller than Elbert. Taller than twice his height. Tall as the old maple in front of his cottage. Tall as the church steeple.

Elbert turned back to his sheep. Now herding was going to be completely boring, without the draw- bridge and courtyard to watch.

The queen's last wide-awake thought was: The child will spend the next hundred years lying on a cold stone floor.

The king's last thoughts were: Our headache's gone. We feel sleepy. We could sleep for a hundred years.

The prince's last thought was: I could take a nap. Sleep is good for you. My father told me that . . .

Sonora's last thought was: Oh no, I'll have to marry him. Aaaaa!

The fairy Adrianna appeared in the courtyard. The hedge looked good. It was high and dense and prickly, with thorns as long as her wand.

In the castle she stood over the sleeping forms of Sonora and Queen Hermione II. I can't leave them on the floor, she thought. She waved her wand, and the queen floated to the bed in the royal bedchamber, next to the king. Then she moved Sonora to her room and arranged her gracefully on the bed. She placed a wooden sign on Sonora's stomach. In flowing script it said, *"I am Princess Sonora. Kiss me, prince, and I shall be yours forever."*

Sonora wouldn't have liked that, not one little bit.

Prince Melvin XX was sneezing in his sleep, stretched out in a bed of clover. The fairy moved him to a wooden bench. Then she left without making anybody else more comfortable. They weren't royal, and they could make the best of wherever they happened to be.

In the next hour she appeared here and there throughout Biddle. She told everyone she saw that the royal family had gone on a journey. She said she had created the hedge to keep things safe while they were away.

Everyone believed her—everyone except Elbert the shepherd.

That night Elbert started building a very tall ladder, the tallest one in Biddle. A week later, when the ladder was finished, he dragged it to the hedge and climbed up.

The peaches were brown and rotten. The dead lamb was covered with flies. But everything else was the same. The oxen stood on the drawbridge, their heads drooping. The butcher leaned over his chopping block, the knife still in his hand. While Elbert watched, the butcher lazily reached up with his other hand to scratch his nose. They were all still asleep!

But why? Elbert wondered. Princess Sonora knows, he thought, but don't ask her. He laughed. Don't ask her because she's sleeping.

Seven

Sonora dreamed it was her wedding day. The great hall was filled with guests. Prince Melvin XX stood next to her. The Chief Royal Councillor was reciting the wedding ceremony. The prince hadn't moved once the whole time. He's like a block of wood, Sonora thought.

The ceremony was almost over. The Chief Royal Councillor said, "Prince Melvin XX, will you say a few words?"

The prince began to speak. Sonora saw a hinge at the corner of his mouth. She looked at his arm next to her. It was carved of wood! He was a big wooden puppet.

"Weddings are good. Everybody has fun at a wedding. There's always . . ."

Everyone clapped. Prince Melvin XX kept right on talking. Sonora screamed, "Aaaaaaaaaaaaaaaaaaaaaaa . . ."

When Prince Melvin XX didn't return to Kulornia, King Stanley CXLIV sent a messenger to Biddle. The messenger came back and told the king about the journey the royal family was thought to have made. King Stanley CXLIV reasoned that the prince must have left with them. He wondered where they'd gone and hoped it was a good place for an Honest, Traditional, Brave, Handsome, Strong, and Tall Man of Action who was also a Good Dancer.

Five years passed. King Stanley CXLIV died, and Prince Melvin XX's younger brother, Prince Roger XCII, was crowned king of Kulornia. His first act as king was to annex the kingdom of Biddle, the kingdom without a king.

The saying "Princess Sonora knows, but don't ask her" spread from Biddle to Kulornia.

Queen Hermione II dreamed that Sonora was a little girl again. She was in the queen's lap, talking about the hissing turtle. Sonora said that the turtle hisses to fool people into thinking it's a whistling teakettle. Then why does the teakettle whistle? the queen asked. Because it doesn't know how to sing, Sonora explained. And Queen Hermione II thought, She's an extraordinary child.

Ten years passed. The shepherd Elbert's son Elmo was four years old. Elbert dragged his long ladder to the hedge again. He climbed the ladder with Elmo in his arms. "See," he whispered into his son's ear. "They're all asleep. Fast asleep."

King Humphrey II dreamed that he was writing a proclamation making the beaver the Royal Rodent of

"HE CLIMBED THE LADDER WITH ELMO IN HIS ARMS."

Biddle. He wrote each word as clearly as he could. But as soon as he finished a word and went on to the next, the letters in the last word changed. For instance, "beaver" changed to "molar," and "rodent" changed to "jerkin." It was very annoying.

Every few years, Elbert's sons and grandsons and great-grandsons climbed the ladder to look at the sleeping court of Biddle.

Fifty years passed. Prince Melvin XX's grandnephew, Prince Simon LXIX, heir apparent to the throne of Greater Kulornia, had a son. Prince Simon LXIX's wife, Bernardine LXI, the princess apparent, invited the fairies to her son Jasper CCX's naming ceremony. She invited all eight of them, including Belladonna, so no one would have hurt feelings.

There was trouble anyway. The fairies started arguing over who was the most powerful. Adrianna bellowed that she was the most powerful and she could prove it. So she turned the princess apparent into a shoehorn. Not to be outdone, Allegra changed the princess from a shoehorn into a baby troll. Then Antonetta turned her into a lady's wig. In the space of a half hour, poor Bernardine LXI became a piccolo, a crab apple tree, a quill pen, and a green peppercorn.

In the end they turned her back into a princess. But no one was certain if they had turned her into the same princess she was before. She was a little different from then on, maybe because one of the fairies had made an eensy teensy mistake, or maybe because the experience had been so terrifying.

Whatever the reason, when the princess apparent gave birth to a daughter two years later, no fairies were invited to the new baby's naming ceremony. Prince Simon LXIX worried about fairy revenge, but there was none. Each fairy blamed another fairy for the ban, so they didn't get mad at the prince, but they didn't give the child any gifts either.

And that was the end of the custom of having fairies at naming ceremonies.

Prince Melvin XX dreamed about armor. He was polishing all the parts of his armor. While he polished, he named each piece. "One polished helmet. One polished visor. One polished haute-piece. One polished pauldron." And so on.

Eighty-three years later, Prince Melvin XX's great-grandnephew, King Jasper CCX, had a son, Prince Christopher I, or plain Prince Christopher.

Even though the fairies didn't give him any gifts, Christopher had a loving heart. He was smart, but not ten times as smart as everybody else. And he was handsome, pretty handsome anyway. But mostly he was curious. When he started talking, his first word was "why." And most of his sentences from then on started with "Why."

Why is your nose above your lips and not somewhere else?

Why are diapers white?

Why do you have nails on your fingers and toes? Why don't you have them anywhere else?

Why are peas round?

Why do birds have so many feathers?

He'd ask anybody anytime. The noble children of Kulornia liked Christopher, but they hated playing with him. If they were playing ice hockey, for example, he'd stop the game to ask why ice is harder to see through than water. If they were racing, he'd halt right before the finish line and ask why grass doesn't have leaves. Once, Christopher and his best friend, the young Duke Thomas, were watching a tournament. Just as the two champion knights galloped at each other, Christopher nudged his friend and pointed at a flock of geese flying above the stadium. "Look." Thomas did while Christopher whispered, "Why don't they flap their tail feathers too?" By the time Thomas looked down again, one knight was lying in the dirt and the other was trotting out of the arena.

Occasionally Thomas could answer one of Christopher's questions, but not often. Christopher's page could answer a few more questions, but then he'd be stumped. Christopher's tutors could answer even more, but then they'd be stumped. His parents could answer yet more, but they'd finally be stumped too.

When they were stumped, they all said the same thing. They all said, "Princess Sonora knows, but don't ask her." And when he asked who Princess

Sonora was, they all told him it was just an expression. There was no such person.

It was the answer he hated most in the whole wide world.

Eight

s Prince Christopher grew older, he tried to answer his own questions. He read as much as he could in King Jasper CCX's library. He found some answers, but not enough, never enough.

Whenever his research got interesting, something always took him away from it. He'd have to practice his jousting. Or he'd have to try on a new suit of armor, or attend a banquet, where his father would forbid him to ask the guests even one single measly question.

A week after Christopher's seventeenth birthday, he was in the library, trying to find out if a dragon ever burns the roof of its mouth. A stack of books was piled next to him. He picked up the top one, *Where There's Dragon, There's Fire.* One of the chapters was about dragon skin. Did skin or something else cover the inside of a dragon's mouth? He opened to page 3,832.

A Royal Squire came into the library. "Majesty, the king wants you to come to the audience room."

Christopher slammed the book shut. It never failed.

Ten shepherds and one sheep faced the king in the audience room. As soon as Christopher took his place next to King Jasper CCX, the oldest shepherd began to speak.

"Highness, something terrible is happening to our sheep. See?" He pointed to the sheep. "She's going bald. They all are. In the spring, there won't be much fleece for us to sell."

Christopher saw big bald spots on the sheep's back.

Another shepherd said, "In the winter, they'll catch cold. It's only October, and they're already starting to sneeze."

The sheep sneezed.

King Jasper CCX said, "God bless you." Then he called for his Chief Royal Veterinarian.

The Chief Royal Veterinarian spread a smelly ointment all over the sheep's bald spots. Then she gave the shepherds a vat of the ointment to spread on all the sheep.

A week later the shepherds and the sheep were back in the audience room. The bald spots were bigger. The sheep sneezed twice.

The Chief Royal Veterinarian told the shepherds to keep putting the ointment on the sheep. She also gave them medicine for the sheep to drink.

Two weeks later the shepherds and the sheep were back. Now the sheep had no wool left, and she never stopped sneezing.

The Chief Royal Veterinarian shook her head. "I

"The Chief Royal Veterinarian spread a smelly
ointment all over the sheep's bald spots."

don't know the cure," she said. "Princess Sonora knows, but don't ask her."

King Jasper CCX asked Prince Christopher what he thought.

As usual, the prince had a question. "Could we send for all the shepherds in Greater Kulornia? Maybe one of them knows how to cure the balding disease."

It was done. Shepherds came from all over Kulornia and also from the land that used to be Biddle. Four hundred shepherds camped outside Kulornia castle. One of them was Elroy, Elbert's great-great-grandson.

King Jasper CCX talked to half of the shepherds, and Prince Christopher talked to the other half. The first one hundred and ninety-nine shepherds Christopher talked to said their sheep weren't getting bald and they didn't know how to cure the balding disease.

The last shepherd Christopher spoke to was Elroy.

"Are your sheep going bald?" the prince asked.

"No, your majesty."

"Do you know how to cure the balding disease?"

"I'm sorry, but I don't, your highness. Princess Sonora knows, but don't ask her . . ."

Christopher turned away.

". . . because she's asleep."

Christopher spun around. *"What? What do you mean, she's asleep?"*

Elroy told Christopher everything. He told about the ladder and the hedge and the sleeping oxen and the sleeping wagon driver and the sleeping butcher.

Halfway through the story, Christopher started jumping up and down, he was so excited. When Elroy was finished, Christopher ran to his father. King Jasper CCX was talking to his last shepherd.

"Sonora lives!" Christopher yelled. *"She sleeps! She lives! She can tell us about the sheep! She can answer all my questions!"* He shouted to a squire, *"Saddle my horse!"*

But Christopher was too excited to wait. He ran after the squire and saddled his own horse. Then he rode to his father.

"Sire! I'm off to old Biddle Castle." He galloped away, calling behind him, *"To wake the sleeping princess!"*

Nine

After two days of hard riding, Christopher and his horse saw the hedge. The horse reared up and wouldn't go a step closer. Christopher jumped off and walked the rest of the way.

The hedge looked wicked. It was taller than the castle back home, and it was full of thick, hairy vines and thorns like spikes and waxy red berries that practically screamed, *"Poison!"*

Christopher wondered what the name of the vine was and what the berries were like. He smiled. Sonora would tell him.

It was going to take days to get inside. His sword wouldn't cut more than one vine before he'd have to sharpen it. Well, he might as well get started. He pulled the sword out of its sheath and walked toward the hedge, pointing the sword ahead of him.

It didn't touch so much as a leaf. A hole opened in the hedge and grew bigger and bigger until it was big enough for Christopher to step through.

Was it a trap? Was there really a princess named

Sonora, or was a prince-eating ogress inside? Was Elroy the shepherd her messenger?

He had to go on. He had to find out—even if he died trying. He stepped through the hedge.

It snapped shut behind him. Oh no! It was as thick as before. He pointed his sword at it. Nothing happened. The hedge—or Sonora—wanted to keep him here.

He was at the edge of the moat. How was he supposed to get across? He could swim across if he was sure that the crocodiles were asleep, but he wasn't sure and he wasn't going to dive in to find out.

What? Lightning flashed out of the blue sky and struck a tree on the castle side of the moat. Whoa! The tree came down, making a rough bridge.

Christopher crossed slowly, stepping carefully between the branches. On the other side of the moat, he climbed a shoulder-high wall. Then he jumped down into a field of weeds so dense and tall that he didn't see Prince Melvin XX sleeping only a few feet away. The prince slept on the ground now. The bench he'd been lying on had rotted and fallen apart twenty years ago.

The weeds were brown and dying because it was November. Christopher wondered if this had once been the garden. He heard a rumbling. It stopped. There it was again. And again. Was it the breathing of the Sonora monster who lived in the castle?

He looked up. One of the castle's towers had crumbled, and an eagle perched atop another. Ivy climbed the walls. The pennants flying above the entrance archway were tattered rags.

Rumble. The earth trembled a little. *Rumble.*

Something rustled near Christopher's feet. Aaaa! A rat as big as a cat scampered across his boot. Christopher thought he should leave the garden. The bees were probably as big as pigeons.

Rumble.

The shepherd had said something about a wagon on the drawbridge and a butcher in the courtyard. He pushed through the weeds toward the entrance.

Rumble.

He reached the courtyard. There was the butcher! Possibly the Chief Royal Butcher, although you couldn't tell by the rags he was wearing. His shirt was so frayed and tattered that his belly showed through. He was slumped across his butcher block, next to a pile of bones. Fresh meat a hundred years ago, the prince thought.

And there was the carpenter, bent over a sawhorse, his saw at his feet. He was lucky he hadn't cut himself when he'd fallen asleep.

Rumble. Louder.

Or maybe the carpenter wasn't sleeping. Maybe they had all been turned to stone.

"Hey, wake up!" Christopher yelled. "Time to get up."

Nobody moved.

Rumble.

Christopher ran to the carpenter, who was closest. "Wake up!"

The man was filthy. His skin was coated with mud and dirt and dust and who-knew-what-else. Christopher wrapped a corner of his cloak around his hand. Then he pushed the carpenter's arm without letting his skin touch the carpenter's skin. The arm moved! It wasn't stone. He felt the carpenter's skin through the cloak. It was warm and soft—skin, not stone.

Christopher shook the arm. "Wake up! Listen! I command you, wake up!"

The carpenter slept on. He breathed in. His nostrils flared and his chest heaved. He breathed out, and the rumble started again.

It was the carpenter breathing! No, it couldn't be. One person couldn't breathe that loudly. Christopher backed up so he could watch the butcher and the carpenter at once.

The butcher breathed in and the carpenter breathed in. The butcher breathed out and the carpenter breathed out—at exactly the same time.

There were more people in the courtyard. Two men, possibly nobles, had been standing and talking when they'd fallen asleep. A cobbler had been shaping leather on a last. A laundress had been washing a mountain of clothes. Rags now.

They all breathed in and out at the same time. After a hundred years, they must have gotten into the habit of breathing together. That was what made the rumble.

Christopher went to each of them. He yelled in their ears. He shook them. He hollered, "Fire!" He yelled, "Food! Aren't you hungry?"

He yelled to the wagon driver and the oxen on the moat. But he was afraid to go to them. The drawbridge was rotting. If he stepped out on it, it might give way.

He tried to wake the dog, lying with his head on a bone. He tried to wake the cat. He told her about the huge rat that had run across his boot. The cat and the dog, Christopher decided, were sleeping because they were pets. The rats weren't pets, so they were awake.

Anyway, nothing worked. He couldn't wake anybody up.

What if Sonora wouldn't wake up either?

Ten

The castle doors were halfway off their hinges, so Christopher was able to open them only wide enough to slip through. Inside, he heard the flapping of wings. Bats. Birds too, from the droppings in the dust on the floor. He sneezed. He looked behind him, and there were his footsteps, sunk into a hundred years of dust. He took another step. His boots didn't make a sound because of the dust.

It was dim in here, in the great hall. The sunlight was weak through the grimy stained-glass windows. Even the broken windows didn't let in much light, because they were draped with cobwebs.

He crossed the hall. Where should he look first for Sonora, and how would he know her when he saw her?

People were everywhere, just as they would be on a busy day in Kulornia castle. "Wake up! Wake up!" he shouted. Nothing happened. He had stopped expecting anything, but he kept trying.

He shouted at everybody. But he shook only the women, and only women who looked like they might be a princess. He didn't bother with somebody who was making a bed or stirring an empty pot. He tried not to touch anybody with his hands. The people were all so filthy.

Nobody on the first floor would wake up, and it was probably useless to go upstairs and search the bed-chambers. They had fallen asleep in the middle of the day, so why would anyone be in bed? But he had come all this way, and he had waited all his life to get his questions answered. Besides, he couldn't leave even if he wanted to, because of the hedge. He returned to the great hall and climbed the staircase.

Most of the bedchambers were empty. But Christopher found King Humphrey II and Queen Hermione II on the bed in the royal bedchamber. It was sweet, Christopher thought. They were holding hands. The king snored so loudly that he probably made half the rumbling. What was left of the curtains fluttered whenever he breathed out.

Finally Christopher came to Sonora's bedchamber. Finally he came to Sonora.

Generations of spiders had spun webs from post to post of her four-poster bed. Sonora slept under hundreds of layers of spiderwebs. The prince didn't know she was Sonora. All he knew was she was disgusting.

But she was probably noble, since she was on such a grand bed, or what used to be a grand bed. She might even be a princess. He had to do something. He coughed. Ahem.

Nothing happened.

He pulled out his sword and cut through the webs, which was a mistake. They all fell on top of her. Ugh. He brushed them away as well as he could with his cloak.

What was that on her stomach? Hmm, a wooden sign. He picked it up with his cloak and brushed it off. Dust and cobwebs and peeling paint came off. Drat! I should have been more careful, he thought.

He carried the sign to the window, where a broken pane let in a bit of sunlight. The paint had flaked off, but the wood was lighter where the paint had been. He could read it.

I am Princess Sonora. Kiss me, prince, and I shall be yours forever.

He didn't want her *forever*! And he certainly didn't want to *kiss* her.

Maybe he could live without getting his questions answered. He could train himself not to care so much. He'd hack his way through the hedge even if it took a month. They could find some other way to cure the sheep.

But what about all the people in the castle? And Princess Sonora, as sickening as she was? If he left, would they sleep till the end of time?

Let some other prince kiss her. Somebody who didn't mind getting ook and yuck and vech all over his face.

Who would that be?

Maybe he didn't have to kiss her. He touched her lips with the hilt of his sword. "Princess? Wake up.

Your prince just kissed you."

Nothing happened.

He bent over her. He'd do it. But she wasn't going to be his forever.

What was that on her cheek and in the corner of her mouth? Spit? Bird droppings? Ugh!

He straightened up and turned to leave. He couldn't do it. He couldn't kiss her.

Eleven

"People float . . ."

Christopher whirled around. She was talking. She was awake!

Her eyes were closed. "People float because their essences . . ."

She was talking in her sleep. She had a sweet voice—a little hoarse, but sweet.

"People float because their essences are equal parts water and air. Stones sink . . ."

Even in her sleep she knew things! Sonora knows. And she was Sonora. And he was going to ask her everything.

He kissed her. He didn't think about it. He just did it. It wasn't so bad.

It was suddenly quiet. Oh, Christopher thought, they're all awake.

"Sleep is pleasant." Sonora's voice was thoughtful. "Hmm. The purpose of eyelids is to cover your eyes. If you didn't sleep, your eyelids would have little reason to close, except when the sun was too bright. But then you could just put your hands over your eyes. That's right. If you didn't have sleep, you wouldn't need eyelids, so you have to have sleep. I made a mistake before."

Christopher was thrilled. She was answering questions he'd never even thought of!

She raised her head. "It's hard to open my eyes. I knew this would happen. My eyelids are covered with cobwebs and worse, aren't they?" She sat up slowly. "Do you have any clean water?"

"No. I'm sorry."

She opened her eyes and smiled at him. "You're dirty too."

Her eyes were big and gray, and her teeth were white against her dirty skin. Her teeth looked clean. The inside of her mouth was probably clean too, so she wasn't dirty all over.

He looks nice, Sonora thought. There was something smiley about him. He was sort of handsome, but mostly he looked nice.

He bowed. "I'm Prince Christopher."

Through the broken window, they heard people calling to each other.

She stood and swept a graceful curtsy. "I am Sonora."

"The sheep of some of our shepherds are getting bald. Do you know why?"

"Baldness in sheep is caused by scissor ants."

She did know! "Really! What cures it?"

"String is their favorite food, not fleece. To get the

scissor ants off the sheep, the shepherds have to put big balls of string near where the sheep graze. The ants will leave the sheep and go to the string. Then the shepherds can take the string and the ants away and get rid of them."

This was wonderful! "Do you like to answer questions?"

She smiled again. "I love to answer questions." Then she looked sad. "Only nobody likes to listen. They don't even like to ask."

"I love to ask, and I love to listen."

They smiled at each other.

The sign says she's mine forever, Christopher thought. I like that.

Sonora read the sign in Christopher's hand. That fairy Adrianna! The nerve of her! Sonora was about to say something nasty, but being so smart came to her rescue. She'd never exactly *belong* to anyone anyway, so it would be all right if the sign gave Christopher a good idea.

It did. He knelt on the dusty, cobwebby, bird-dropping-covered floor. "Will you marry me?"

Sonora started to say yes. Her loving heart loved this prince.

There were footsteps in the corridor.

She remembered. Prince Melvin XX!

The door opened. King Humphrey II and Queen Hermione II rushed in.

"Are you all right, dear?" the queen asked.

"You're dirty too," the king said. "Who's this?"

"THE ANTS WILL LEAVE THE SHEEP AND GO
TO THE STRING."

"He's Prince Christopher," Sonora said. "The sheep in his country are going bald from scissor ants."

Christopher stood up and bowed. "I am Christopher, crown prince of Greater Kulornia, and I've just asked the princess to marry me."

"But Melvin XX is crown prince of Kulornia," Queen Hermione II said.

Prince Melvin XX? Christopher thought. But he disappeared ages ago. Oh! He fell asleep too.

"Our daughter is betrothed to him. He—" King Humphrey II stopped in confusion. What did this fellow say about Greater Kulornia? Where did the "greater" come from?

Sonora said to Christopher, "Since one of the purposes of sheep is to make wool, you might wonder if a bald sheep is still a sheep."

Christopher nodded eagerly. "Is it?"

She nodded. "It is, because its other purpose is to become mutton stew, and it can still do that."

"That hadn't occurred to me." He couldn't stop smiling at her.

There were slow, heavy steps in the corridor.

Here he comes! Sonora thought. What can I do?

Prince Melvin XX came in, ducking to get through the doorway. "I fell asleep," he said slowly. "I'm dirty. My hose are torn. So is my doublet. So is my crown. So are—" He saw Christopher. "Who is he?"

Christopher bowed. "I am Christopher, crown prince of Greater Kulornia." Did Sonora want to marry this guy?

Prince Melvin XX drew his sword—*fast!* "I'm crown prince of Kulornia." But he still spoke slowly.

Sonora thought, Put that sword away! Don't hurt Prince Christopher!

Christopher thought, He probably won't kill me if I don't draw my sword. "And I just asked Princess Sonora to marry me."

Prince Melvin XX thought, I can't kill him if he doesn't draw his sword. I'm not a Bully. I'm a Man of Action. I used to be a Baby of . . .

Nobody said anything. Prince Melvin XX lowered his sword.

Sonora felt a little better. At least it wasn't pointing straight at Prince Christopher anymore. She thought, I can think of a way out of this. I'm not ten times as smart as anybody else for nothing.

Prince Melvin XX said, "I'm betrothed to Princess Sonora—"

Sonora had it! "Sir Melvin XX—"

"I'm Prince Melvin XX. Not Sir."

Sonora shook her head. "We slept for a hundred years, so you're not a prince anymore and I'm not a princess. You were betrothed to Princess Sonora, not to just plain Sonora. Right?"

"I don't know," said Prince or just plain Melvin XX.

She doesn't want to marry that great big tree trunk, Christopher thought. But does she want to marry me?

The king wondered if he was still a king, if Sonora wasn't a princess.

Sonora smiled at Melvin XX. "Your nature is to be strong and courageous."

Melvin XX nodded. "And Traditional and—"

She went on. "You will be a wonderful, traditional knight. You can have adventures and be brave and strong—"

"And Tall."

"And tall. I'm sure Prince Christopher would make you a knight."

Christopher didn't wait for Melvin XX to say yes or no. Usually Christopher did his dubbing with his sword. But he was afraid to draw it, because Melvin XX still had his out. So Christopher reached way way up. With his naked, dirty hand he touched Melvin XX on his forehead.

"I, Prince Christopher, dub you Sir Melvin XX, knight of Greater Kulornia."

"Now you won't need me to write your proclamations," Sonora said.

Sir Melvin XX said, "I will be a good knight. A Brave knight. A Strong—"

Christopher knelt. "I've always been curious, but I've never wanted to know anything as much as this. Will you marry me, just plain Sonora?"

"Yes, I will." She nodded and took his hand. "In case you were wondering, sheep grow wool because of winter. The purpose of winter is to make ice, so people can have cherry or lemon ices in the summer. The purpose of wool is to keep sheep and then people warm while the ice is being made."

"Really? That makes so much sense."

She looks so happy, Queen Hermione II thought.

"Are we still a king?" King Humphrey II asked.

"Of course," Christopher said, standing up. He'd work it out somehow.

Then it's all right, King Humphrey II thought. "In that case, we approve of the marriage. An excellent match."

Epilogue

As soon as King Humphrey II said he approved of the marriage, a gust of wind blew through the bedchamber, and the fairy Adrianna appeared. She beamed at everyone and crowed, "My gift was the best!" Then she married Sonora and Christopher on the spot.

After they both said "I do," and after they kissed, Christopher turned to Sonora. "Do you know if dragons burn the roofs of their mouths?"

"Yes, I know. No part of a dragon burns. You see, the essence of a dragon is fire . . ."

And they all lived happily ever after.

Cinderellis
and the
Glass Hill

To Nedda,

zesty, kind, and true—

my dear friend.

—G.C.L.

One

Ellis was always lonely.

He lived with his older brothers, Ralph and Burt, on a farm that was across the moat from Biddle Castle. Ralph and Burt were best friends as well as brothers, but they wouldn't let Ellis be a best friend too.

When he was six years old, Ellis invented flying powder. He sprinkled the powder on his tin cup, and the cup began to rise up the chimney. He stuck his head into the fireplace to see how far up it would go. (The fire was out, of course.)

The cup didn't fly straight up. It zoomed from side to side instead, knocking soot and cinders down on Ellis' head.

Ralph and Burt came in from the farm. Ellis ducked out of the fireplace. "I made my cup fly!" he yelled. The cup fell back down the chimney and tumbled out into the parlor. "Look! It just landed."

Ralph didn't even turn his head. He said, "Rain tomorrow."

Burt said, "Barley needs it. You're covered with cinders, Ellis."

Ralph thought that was funny. "That's funny." He laughed. "That's what we should call him—Cinderellis."

Burt guffawed. "You have a new name, Ellis—I mean Cinderellis."

"All right," Cinderellis said. "Watch! I can make my cup fly again." He sprinkled more powder on the cup, and it rose up the chimney again.

Ralph said, "Beans need weeding."

Burt said, "Hay needs cutting."

Cinderellis thought, Maybe they'd be interested if the cup flew straight. What if I grind up my ruler and add it to the powder? That should do it.

But when the cup did fly straight, Ralph and Burt still wouldn't watch.

They weren't interested either when Cinderellis was seven and invented shrinking powder. Or when he was eight and invented growing powder and made his tin cup big enough to drink from again.

They wouldn't even try his warm-slipper powder, which Cinderellis had invented just for them—to keep their feet warm on cold winter nights.

"Don't want it," Ralph said.

"Don't like it," Burt said.

Cinderellis sighed. Being an inventor was great, but it wasn't everything.

In Biddle Castle Princess Marigold was lonely too. Her mother, Queen Hermione III, had died when

Marigold was two years old. And her father, King Humphrey III, was usually away from home, on a quest for some magical object or wondrous creature. And the castle children were too shy to be friendly.

When Marigold turned seven, King Humphrey III returned from his latest quest. He had been searching for a dog tiny enough to live in a walnut shell. But instead of the dog, he'd found a normal-size kitten and a flea big enough to fill a teacup. He gave the kitten to Marigold and sent the flea to the Royal Museum of Quest Souvenirs.

Marigold loved the kitten. His fur was stripes of honey and orange, and his nose was pink. She named him Apricot and played with him all day in the throne room, throwing a small wooden ball for him to chase. The kitten enjoyed the game and loved this gentle lass who'd rescued him from being cooped up with that disgusting, *hungry* flea.

King Humphrey III watched his daughter play. What an adorable, sweet child she was! Soon she'd be an adorable, sweet maiden, and someone would want to marry her.

The king sat up straighter on his throne. It couldn't be just anyone. The lad would have to be perfect, which didn't necessarily mean rich or handsome. Perfect meant perfect—courageous, determined, a brilliant horseman. In other words, perfect.

When the time was right, he, King Humphrey III, would go on a quest for the lad.

Two

When Cinderellis was old enough to start farming, his brothers gave him the rockiest acres to work, the acres that went halfway up Biddle Mountain, the acres with the caves he loved to explore.

"It's a small section," Burt said, "but you're no farmer, Cinderellis."

"Not like us," Ralph said. He smiled his special smile at Burt, the smile that made Cinderellis ache with longing.

"Do we have any popping corn?" Cinderellis asked, excited. This was his big chance to prove he *was* a farmer. Then Ralph and Burt would smile the special smile at him too.

He took the popping corn and mixed it with flying powder and extra-strength powder. Then he stuffed the mixture under the biggest rocks on his acres. He added twigs and lit them.

The corn popped extra high. The rocks burst out of the ground and rolled to the bottom of the mountain.

The soil became light and soft and ready for planting. Cinderellis mixed his seeds with growing powder and planted them. Then he set up an invention workshop in his biggest cave.

At harvesttime Cinderellis couldn't wait for his brothers to see his vegetables. His carrots were sweeter than maple syrup. His tomatoes were redder than red paint. And his potatoes were so beautiful, you could hardly look at them. Ralph and Burt would have to admit he was a farmer.

Cinderellis sprinkled balancing powder on his vegetables and loaded them on his wheelbarrow. Then he pushed the wheelbarrow to the barn without losing even a single ruby-red radish.

Ralph and Burt were still in the fields, so Cinderellis arranged his vegetables outside the barn door. Using more balancing powder and a pinch of extra-strength powder, he stacked the tomatoes in the shape of a giant tomato and the beets in the shape of a giant beet. His masterpiece was the carrots, rising like a ballerina from a tiny tiny tip.

Finally his brothers drove up in the wagon behind Thelma the mule.

Burt took one look and said, "Tomatoes are too red."

Ralph tasted a carrot and said, "Carrots are too sweet."

Burt added, "Potatoes are too pretty."

Cinderellis said, "But carrots should taste sweet, and tomatoes are supposed to be red." He shouted,

"His masterpiece was the carrots, rising
like a ballerina from a tiny tiny tip."

"And what's wrong with pretty potatoes?"

Ralph said, "Guess I'll load them on the wagon anyway."

Burt said, "Might as well take them to market."

Cinderellis left them there. He went to his workshop and screamed.

When Marigold was seven and a half, King Humphrey III left Biddle Castle again, to go on a quest for water from the well of youth and happiness. Marigold missed him terribly. She told Apricot how miserable she was. Apricot purred happily. He loved it when his dear lass talked to him, and he was sure it meant she was in a good mood.

Marigold patted the cat. Apricot was wonderful, but she wished for a human friend, someone who would understand her feelings, someone who would rather be home with her than be anywhere else in the world.

It was the end of the first day of fall, and Cinderellis was nine years old. He woke up exactly at midnight because his bed had begun to shake. On the bureau the jars of his wake-up powder and no-smell-hose powder jiggled and rattled.

But as soon as he got up to see what was going on, the shaking stopped. So he went back to sleep.

In the morning Ralph and Burt and Cinderellis discovered that the grass in their best hay field had vanished.

A tear trickled down Ralph's cheek. "Goblins did it," he said.

Burt nodded, wiping his eyes.

Cinderellis walked across the brown field. Huh! he thought. Look at that! Hoofprints! He picked up a golden hair. "It was a horse with a golden mane," he announced. "Not goblins."

His brothers didn't listen. Ralph knelt and poured dirt from his left hand into his right. Burt poured dirt from his right hand into his left. Cinderellis got down on his knees too. Although he didn't see what good it would do, he poured dirt from his left hand into his right. Then he poured it from his right hand into his left.

Ralph said, "Get up, Cinderellis. Don't be such a copycat."

Cinderellis stood, feeling silly. And lonelier than ever.

Three

uring the winter after the hay disappeared, King Humphrey III returned. He hadn't found the well of youth and happiness, but he'd brought home a flask of coconut milk that was supposed to be just as good.

The milk didn't make anyone a day younger or a smile happier, though. All it did was make people's toenails grow, a foot an hour. This kept the Chief Royal Manicurist busy for a week, till the effects wore off.

Marigold waited for her turn with the manicurist in the throne room with her father and all the nobles who'd had a sip of the milk. Everyone's boots and hose were off, and the smell made Apricot sneeze on his cushion next to Marigold's chair.

Marigold didn't mind the smell. She was too happy about seeing her father to mind anything—until he mentioned that he was planning a new quest, this time for a pair of seven-league boots.

Marigold would have left the room, if she had been able to walk with three-foot-long toenails. As it was, everybody saw her cry.

A year to the day after the hay vanished, Cinderellis' farmhouse shook again in the middle of the night. In the morning the hay was gone again from the same field, and Cinderellis picked up another horse hair, a copper one.

Every night for the next year, Ralph practiced a spell to scare away the goblins.

Goblins, go away NOW!
Go go go go GO!
Away away away away AWAY!
Now now now now NOW!

"The words are hard to remember," Ralph said.

Burt agreed. "Almost impossible."

Even though he knew that goblins had nothing to do with the disappearing hay, Cinderellis wanted to help. So he invented goblin-stay-away powder. It was made of dried vinegar and the claw of a dead eagle, the two things goblins fear most.

The first day of fall came. At night Ralph headed for the barn, which was right behind the hay field. He'd wait there for the goblins and say the spell.

"Let me come along," Cinderellis said. "I'll bring my goblin-stay-away powder."

"Don't need you," Ralph said. He smiled his special smile at Burt.

Burt smiled back. "What good would you be?" he asked.

In the middle of the night Cinderellis was still awake, because he was having imaginary conversations with his brothers, conversations in which they were amazed at how wonderful his inventions were. Conversations in which they begged him to be their friend.

At midnight the ground shook. Cinderellis smiled. Now Ralph would see that he, Cinderellis, had been right all along. Now Ralph would see the horse.

The next morning Ralph was already eating his oatmeal when Burt and Cinderellis sat down for breakfast.

"Hay all right?" Burt asked.

Ralph shook his head. "Rain today."

"Have to get the corn in," Burt said. "What happened?"

"Ground shook. Said the spell. Went to sleep. Hay was gone."

"Did you see the horse?" Cinderellis asked.

"What horse?"

"Didn't you look outside the barn?"

Ralph smiled at Burt. "What for?"

Burt guffawed.

Later that day Cinderellis found a silver horse's hair in the hay field.

The following year it was Burt's turn to spend the night in the barn. In the morning the hay was gone.

"My turn next," Cinderellis said, picking up a golden horse hair from the bare field.

Ralph and Burt roared with laughter.

"My turn next," Cinderellis insisted, turning red.

He'd save the hay. His brothers would admire him at last. And he'd never be lonely again.

A month after Burt's night in the barn, King Humphrey III returned to Biddle without finding seven-league boots. What he had found were three shoes that walked backward, very slowly. They went straight to the Royal Museum of Quest Souvenirs.

Marigold asked her father when he would go off on his next quest. He said he was leaving in three days to find the lark whose song is sweeter than harp music.

Marigold nodded sadly and went to her bedchamber, where she patted Apricot's head and thought gloomy thoughts. Apricot closed his eyes, glad that his dear lass was happy.

Cats are so loyal, Marigold thought, swallowing her tears. They never go off on quests. They never leave you alone and lonely.

Four

inderellis spent day after day in his workshop cave, getting ready for the horse's arrival. He needed something to keep it from grazing, so he invented horse treats. They were made of oats and molasses and a few other ingredients to make the treats particularly scrumptious to horses—ground horse chestnuts, minced horse mackerel, and chopped horse nettles.

And since horses are partial to apples, Cinderellis made the treats apple shaped. He tried them out on Thelma and she liked them, even though she was a mule. Horses would adore them.

After he'd perfected the treats, Cinderellis turned one of his caves into a stable—an unusual stable, where the water trough refilled itself from a rain barrel outside the cave, where the rock floor had been softened by fluffy powder, and where there were paintings of subjects that horses like. Cinderellis had done the paintings himself. One was a close-up of three blades of spring grass. Another was of the ground as it would look to a galloping horse. And the last was of trees as they'd look to a cantering horse.

It was a lot of effort for just one night—because after that Ralph and Burt would probably keep the horse in the barn with Thelma. But Cinderellis didn't mind. It would be worth everything if he could be friends with his brothers. A little extra work didn't matter compared to that.

In the middle of the summer King Humphrey III returned from his quest. But instead of the lark that sings more sweetly than a harp, he brought home a mule whose bray drowns out an orchestra.

A week later, the king left on a quest for the goose that lays golden eggs.

Marigold noticed that the other castle children were laughing at the latest quest souvenir. Whenever she and Apricot approached a group of them, they'd be braying as hard as they could. When they saw her, they'd run away, giggling.

Marigold wished she could be a part of their group and laugh along with them. The king's souvenirs *were* funny. They would make her laugh too, if she had someone to laugh with.

Late at night after the first day of fall, Cinderellis snuck out to the barn with a bucket of horse treats. A little before midnight he heard distant hoofbeats. He opened the barn door a crack. The grass was still there.

The hoofbeats grew louder. The floorboards

hummed. The hoofbeats grew even louder. The rafters hummed along with the floorboards. Cinderellis' hands shook and his teeth rattled.

Then the shaking stopped. A copper-colored mare stepped into the field. She was the biggest, most beautiful horse Cinderellis had ever seen. Across her back lay a knight in copper armor.

This was a surprise. Cinderellis hadn't expected anyone to be on the horse.

The mare lowered her head and started to graze.

She mustn't do that! Cinderellis thought. He grabbed the bucket of horse treats and left the barn.

The horse looked up and saw an ordinary farm lad, but she liked his face. He could rescue her from the evil magician who had put a spell on her and her two sisters. The lad only had to touch her bridle and she'd be safe. The spell would be broken, and she wouldn't have to return to the magician ever again. She let the lad come right up to her. Touch the bridle, she thought. Touch the bridle.

He held out the horse treats.

She sniffed the bucket. Mmm, pleasant. She put her head in the bucket and started to munch. Yum, delectable. And the treats were shaped like apples. Great combination!

Take the bridle, lad. Please!

Cinderellis grabbed the bridle. I've got you now, he thought.

Aah! The mare was so happy. She loved this lad. She would do anything for him.

"She was the biggest, most beautiful horse Cinderellis had ever seen. Across her back lay a knight in copper armor."

Cinderellis put the bucket down and tiptoed to the knight lying across the mare's back. "Sir, are you all right?"

The knight didn't move.

"Sir?" Cinderellis raised his voice. "Sir? Can you hear me?"

The knight didn't answer.

Cinderellis tapped the metal. "Excuse me, sir. I hope you don't mind . . ."

Nothing.

He tapped louder. It sounded hollow. He lifted the couter, which covered the knight's elbow. It felt too light. If an arm were in there, it would be heavier. The knight was just an empty suit of armor! And he'd been talking to it!

Five

Cinderellis led the mare to the stable cave. Inside, he lifted the armor off his back and dumped it behind a mound of hay. He took her saddle and bridle off too. Then he began to brush her.

It felt sooo good. She whinnied softly.

What should he call her? He wanted a name that meant something.

He had it. Chasam. It stood for Copper Horse Arrives Shortly After Midnight. He picked up a handful of oats and fed it to her. "Good night, Chasam."

In the morning Cinderellis led his brothers to the hay field.

"See," he said. "I saved it."

Burt said, "Goblin spell worked after all." He smiled the special smile at Ralph.

It wasn't the spell!

Ralph smiled back. He said, "Just took a while."

"It wasn't the spell," Cinderellis hollered. "I did it!"

"Time to gather the hay," Ralph said.

Cinderellis opened his mouth to tell them about

Chasam and then shut it again. What if he told them and they still wouldn't admit he'd done anything? What if they said a goblin had run away because of the spell, but his horse had stayed? That was probably what they would say! And once they saw Chasam, they'd keep her for themselves. They'd never let him have a turn riding her or plowing with her.

Well, he wasn't telling them. Chasam would be his secret. He'd let them have next year's horse—*if* they admitted that he had saved the field. He'd let them have all the horses if they'd be his friends. After all, friends don't hold out on each other.

To get his mind off his brothers, Cinderellis spent the day with Chasam. He rode her, which was nothing like riding Thelma the mule, or even like riding the horses at the yearly fair in Snettering-on-Snoakes. Those horses weren't as tall as Chasam was. So tall you were higher than anybody and felt more important too. And their gaits weren't silken like hers. She hardly jiggled, even when she trotted. And her gallop was completely thrilling. The trees whizzed by, and the breeze that had ruffled Cinderellis' hair when he started out—that breeze was miles behind. Why, he almost caught up to yesterday's thunderstorm.

After an hour Cinderellis dismounted and started tossing horse treats to Chasam. He'd throw them, and she'd run after them and gobble them up. Sometimes she'd catch them before they landed. As time went on she became better and better, till she could catch almost anything he could throw.

It was fun, but he couldn't spend every minute playing, so he stopped and got busy. His drying powder wasn't quite right, and there had been a lot of rain lately. His lettuces were drowning.

He let Chasam graze while he did his experiments. He added ingredients that kept out water—ground umbrella, diced hood of a poncho, and pulverized roof shingle.

Chasam came over and watched.

At least someone's interested in me and my inventions, Cinderellis thought. Even if it's only a horse.

Two days before Marigold's thirteenth birthday King Humphrey III returned from his latest quest, bringing with him the turkey that lays tin eggs.

A week later the king mounted his horse in the castle courtyard. He was leaving again, this time to search for the lamp that commands a genie. Marigold begged him not to go.

King Humphrey III reached down and stroked her forehead. "But sweetheart," he said, "wouldn't you like a genie who would make all your wishes come true?"

Apricot squirmed in Marigold's arms. That horse's head was bigger than his whole body. He wanted his dear lass to step away from the horse.

Marigold shrugged. Sure she'd like a genie, so she could wish for her father to stop going on quests. But if he'd just stop on his own, she wouldn't need a genie. Besides, the king would never actually bring back a genie, so what was the point of wanting one?

Six

ate at night, a year after Chasam's arrival, Cinderellis and the mare waited in the hay field. Cinderellis had a pail of horse treats with him. At a few minutes before midnight Chasam started neighing and running in circles.

At midnight the ground began to tremble. Cinderellis' hands shook. The earth shimmied and lurched. Cinderellis' teeth rattled. The trees swayed and twisted. The hay field churned and pitched. Cinderellis' stomach sloshed.

Then everything grew quiet. A silver mare stepped into the hay field. A suit of silver armor lay across her back. Cinderellis felt disloyal thinking it, but the silver horse was even more beautiful than Chasam. Bigger, stronger, and just a little prettier around her eyes.

Chasam galloped to the mare. They nuzzled. They raced together across the field. They reared up and batted each other playfully with their front hooves.

Then, at last, they trotted to Cinderellis and stood by him, their sides heaving.

Cinderellis grabbed the silver mare's bridle. The silver mare was overjoyed. She loved this farm lad and would do anything for him.

"Welcome, Shasam," Cinderellis said. Shasam stood for Silver Horse Arrives Shortly After Midnight. He led her to the stable cave. Inside, he lifted off her armor and tossed it on top of the copper armor.

In the morning Cinderellis showed Ralph and Burt that the hay field was all right.

Ralph said, "Goblins didn't come back."

Burt said, "Good year for turnips." He put his arm across Ralph's shoulder. They walked to the barn, leaving Cinderellis standing by himself.

He swallowed the lump in his throat. He wasn't going to give Shasam to his brothers either.

She was even more fun to ride than Chasam. Faster, smoother, *mightier*. She was better at catching horse treats too. But Cinderellis didn't want to hurt Chasam's feelings, so he pretended he never noticed the difference.

The following June King Humphrey III returned home. Instead of finding the lamp that commands a genie, he had stumbled over the candle that rouses an imp. The imp was so angry about being bothered that he put a curse on the king—King Humphrey III had to go home and stay there. No quests for five whole years.

The king was heartbroken. His next quest was going to be the most important one ever. Marigold was old enough to get married, and he'd planned to find the perfect lad for her. And now he couldn't.

Marigold was sorry her father was unhappy, but she was delighted that he was going to stay home. She was also delighted that he couldn't search for her husband. It would be awful to have to marry something he brought back from a quest.

Apricot noticed the king weeping, and he worried that his dear lass might be sad too.

The day after he returned, King Humphrey III sat in the throne room and tried to listen to his Royal Councillors, but he couldn't concentrate. Without a quest, how was he going to find the right husband for his darling daughter?

Then he had a brilliant thought. If he couldn't go searching for the right lad, he'd make lots of lads come to him! But how would he know which one was perfect? Hmm. He began to have an idea.

Exactly a year after Shasam's arrival, Chasam, Shasam, and Cinderellis waited in the hay meadow for Ghasam (Golden Horse Arrives Shortly After Midnight).

Half an hour before midnight, the wind picked up. Cinderellis felt a tremor. And another. The wind howled.

Midnight came. The ground rocked and bucked. The wind went wild, blowing from every direction. A tree was uprooted and sailed away into the east.

Cinderellis' hands shook, his teeth rattled, and his stomach sloshed.

The world went black. The moon had gone out! The stars had gone out! Cinderellis' heart bounced up and down.

Then the wind stopped. The ground steadied. The moon and stars reappeared.

A golden horse stepped into the hay field. A suit of golden armor lay across her back. Cinderellis gasped. She was gorgeous. You looked at her, and you heard trumpets playing and cymbals crashing.

Chasam and Shasam nickered. They cantered to their sister and nuzzled her. Then all three galloped joyously around the hay field, legs flying, necks stretched out, their manes and tails streaming.

Finally they stopped, and Ghasam trotted to Cinderellis. She whinnied as he took her bridle. She loved this farm lad already. She'd do anything for him.

The next morning Cinderellis told Burt and Ralph that the hay would never disappear again. He held his breath and waited. If they thanked him and smiled the special smile at him, then they could have Ghasam.

Ralph said, "Wet weather coming."

Burt said, "Maybe some hail."

Cinderellis breathed out. Nothing had changed. So he'd keep the horses, and he'd have three loyal and true animal friends. Who needed human friends anyway?

Seven

Ghasam was better than her sisters at catching horse treats. And she was faster than they were too. Once, when Cinderellis jumped on her back, he started to sneeze. "A—" he said. She took off. He finished the sneeze. "Choo!" They had gone two miles.

When they got back to the stable cave after that gallop, Cinderellis told Ghasam what a phenomenal horse she was. Then he told Chasam and Shasam what phenomenal horses they were, because he didn't want them to feel left out. He knew only too well what that was like.

Princess Marigold turned fifteen. There were banquets and balls and puppet shows in her honor. Everyone said she was the sweetest, kindest, least uppity princess in the world. And pretty to boot.

Nobody mentioned that she was also the most terrified princess, because she had told only Apricot about that, and he had misunderstood anyway.

She was scared because of her father and his—well, his crazy ideas. Since he couldn't go on a quest, he had devised a contest to find her future husband. He hadn't revealed the contest rules yet, but he had said that the winner would be courageous, determined, and a fine horseman. Considering the king's quest souvenirs, though, Marigold thought she'd probably wind up marrying a mean stubborn gnome who could ride kangaroos!

The final banquet was almost over when King Humphrey III stood and beamed at his guests. "Dear friends," he began. "Tomorrow our Royal Glassworkers will begin to create a giant hill in the shape of a pyramid. It will be made entirely of glass. When it is completed, our darling daughter will wait at the top with a basket of golden apples. The brave lad who rides his horse up to her and takes three apples will have her hand in marriage."

Marigold fainted. Her father was too excited to notice. Except for Apricot, nobody noticed. They were too astonished. Apricot was worried. Had his dear lass eaten something that disagreed with her?

King Humphrey III continued. "We will also give the provinces of Skiddle, Luddle, and Buffle to the winner to rule immediately. And he will be king of all of Biddle after I'm gone. Any lad can compete. All he needs is a horse and a suit of armor."

After she recovered from her faint, Marigold tried to persuade her father to change his mind. But he wouldn't listen. He said the winner of the contest would be perfect for her and perfect for Biddle.

Marigold disagreed. The man who won the contest would be cruel and evil. No kind person would make a horse climb a glass hill.

And she would have to marry him.

In a week the pyramid was built. Its glass was clearer than a drop of dew and slipperier than the sides of an ice cube. King Humphrey III wasn't completely satisfied, though, because it was level on top. But Marigold had flatly refused to sit on a point.

The pyramid's actual point was made by a cloth canopy that would be over the princess's head, giving her shade. King Humphrey III sighed. It would have to do.

The king announced the contest in a proclamation. Cinderellis heard about it from Ralph at breakfast. Not because Ralph told him. No. Ralph told Burt. Naturally.

"The contest starts tomorrow." Ralph laughed. "Burt, do you think Thelma wants to climb a glass hill?"

Burt laughed for five minutes straight. "That's funny," he said.

Ralph said, "Want to see it?"

Burt said, "Wouldn't miss it."

They didn't ask me if I want to see it with them, Cinderellis thought. Well, he didn't. He wanted to climb the pyramid. He wondered how slippery the glass was.

Cinderellis didn't want to become a prince and marry a princess he'd never even met. He just wanted to see if his sticky powder would take him and one of the mares up the glass hill. And then he wanted to show the golden apples to Ralph and Burt. They were giving up a day of farming to see the contest. That meant they cared about it. And they'd love the golden apples. They were farmers, after all. They loved fruit. When Cinderellis gave the apples to them, they'd love him too.

He took some sticky powder from his room and started walking toward Biddle Castle.

Dressed as a Royal Dairymaid, Princess Marigold wandered through the field around the pyramid. She passed gaily colored tents and neighing, stamping horses and shouting, striding knights and squires. There are hundreds of contestants, she thought. And not one of them had even asked to meet her. All they wanted was to rule Skiddle, Luddle, and Buffle. And to make their poor horses go up a stupid glass hill.

But perhaps there was one man among them who would be a good ruler, even if he didn't care about her. Maybe he had an extraordinary horse who didn't mind trying to climb glass, a horse so well treated that it would do anything for its rider.

If such a man was here, she had to find him and figure out how to get him to the top.

She squared her shoulders. To find him, she had to talk to all of them, all the horse torturers. That was why she had dressed as a Royal Dairymaid and left Apricot in the castle—so no one would suspect she was a princess.

Cinderellis saw the glass hill from a mile and a half away, sparkling in the sunlight. It was as high and almost as steep as the castle's highest tower. When he got close, he saw the Royal Guards surrounding the pyramid. He knew one of them—Farley, who used to sell candy apples at the yearly fair in Snettering-on-Snoakes.

Cinderellis asked Farley to let him touch the glass hill. Farley looked around to make sure nobody was watching. Then he nodded.

Cinderellis barely felt the hill because his hand slipped off so fast. For a second it felt lovely—cool and smoother than smooth. And then his hand was back at his side. He tried again. Mmm, pleasant. Whoops!

"A lot of people are here, aren't they?" Cinderellis said.

Farley turned to look at the crowd. Quickly, Cinderellis tossed a handful of sticky powder on the hill.

"Yup," Farley said.

Three quarters of the powder rolled off the hill! If sticky powder, which stuck to *everything*, rolled off, then that hill was the slipperiest thing Cinderellis had ever seen, felt, or imagined.

Eight

Princess Marigold hadn't talked to a single contestant who would be a good ruler. Some wanted to raise taxes. Some wanted to have hunting parties all the time. One even said he'd declare war and take over all of Biddle! Another said he'd drown Apricot, because he didn't want cat hair all over everything! If either of them reached the top of the hill, she'd kick him all the way to the bottom. She'd swallow the golden apples before she'd let either of them get his hands on them.

After talking to at least a hundred contestants, Marigold gave up. She just stared at the pyramid, trying not to bawl.

Cinderellis stared at it too. He imagined climbing it while Ralph and Burt watched.

He said good-bye to Farley and backed into a person behind him. "Oops! Excuse me." He turned around.

He'd bumped into a Royal Dairymaid. A pretty one, with a sweet face, a very sweet face.

Now here's someone with a kind face, Marigold

thought. Too bad he was a farm lad. It would be a waste of time to talk to him, since he wouldn't have a suit of armor. But she wanted to know what someone who looked so kind would say.

She smiled at him, feeling shy because he looked so nice. "Er, pardon me. What would you do if you won the contest and became prince of Skiddle and Luddle and Buffle?"

He liked her dimple. "What?" What had she said? "Sorry."

None of the others had apologized for anything. "That's all right." She repeated the question.

"I don't know." He wished he had a good answer. "I don't want to be a prince."

Ah. What a good answer. "But if you had to be?"

He wondered why she wanted to know. But why not? He was curious about lots of things too. "I guess if I were prince, I'd create inventions that would make my subjects' lives easier." That's right. That's what he *would* do. What could he invent for a Royal Dairymaid? "For example, I'd invent cow treats." He nodded, figuring it out. He'd leave out the special horse ingredients and add some ground cow parsnip and dried cow shark instead. "The cows would love the treats, and they'd love to be milked."

"That would be a great invention," the princess said. He wanted to do something that animals would like! This lad would never torture a horse.

Nobody had ever encouraged Cinderellis before. She was the nicest maiden in Biddle. "I already invented horse treats," he said, boasting a little.

"'I DON'T KNOW.' HE WISHED HE HAD A GOOD
ANSWER. 'I DON'T WANT TO BE A PRINCE.'"

"They must be delicious," Marigold said. Gosh! she thought, he's already done something to make horses happy. "Um," she added, "if you did become a prince, would you go on quests?"

Cinderellis shook his head. "When I want something, I invent it, or invent a way to get it." He added in a rush, "Most of my inventions are powders that do things." He stopped. "You're probably not interested."

"I am! Please tell me about them." If she knew him better, they might be friends—her first human friend.

"Well, my first invention was flying powder." He told her about the powders.

She listened and asked questions. Cinderellis had never had so much fun in his life. This Royal Dairymaid was splendid!

Marigold had never had so much fun either. She especially liked the idea of fluffy powder. You'd always have a soft place to sit, and—oh my! "Your fluffy powder could save lives. If a person—or, say, a cat—fell out of a window, you could sprinkle fluffy powder on the ground. And the cat wouldn't be hurt." She beamed at him.

He beamed back. "I'm thinking of using my sticky powder—"

"Oh no!" Marigold saw the king heading their way. "I'd better go. I have some milking to do." She curtsied and fled into the crowd.

"Where do you . . . When could I . . ."

But she was gone, and he didn't even know her name.

Nine

ack in his workshop cave, Cinderellis got to work. Sticky powder alone wouldn't get him up the glass hill, so he mixed in extra-strength powder and a few other ingredients. While he invented, he thought about the Royal Dairymaid. He wished he'd had a chance to tell her he was going to climb the pyramid. Then she could have watched and rooted for him.

But she might have thought he wanted to marry the princess. He didn't. He wanted— He stopped mixing. He wanted to marry the Royal Dairymaid! He hadn't felt lonely for a second while they'd talked.

But he didn't know her name, so how could he marry her? Well, she was a Royal Dairymaid, so he should be able to find her again. There couldn't be that many of them.

Suppose he didn't show the golden apples to Ralph and Burt. They might like the apples, but they probably wouldn't be interested in his special sticky powder, since they never cared about his inventions, not one bit. So suppose he hid the apples instead, till the princess married somebody else. Then suppose he sold them and used the money to set up an invention work-shop in Snettering-on-Snoakes. He'd do what he'd said a prince should do—invent things to make people's lives easier. He'd sell his inventions, and he'd marry the Royal Dairymaid.

He started mixing again. Yes, he'd marry her. That is, if she'd have him.

The powder was ready to try out. He spread it on Ghasam's front hoof.

She couldn't lift her foot. She strained. Finally she forced it up—with grass and dirt attached.

Too strong. He cleaned off her hoof. Then he added a pinch of this and a teaspoon of that and spread the mixture on Shasam's hooves.

Now the powder didn't work at all. Shasam could even gallop. He frowned. Maybe his on-off powder was in the "off" phase when her feet were on the ground and in the "on" phase when her feet were in the air. That would mean that the sticky powder was only active when there was nothing to stick to.

He could fix that. He tapped each hoof with a stick. That should reset the phases.

There. Each step was difficult, and Shasam had to strain a little to lift her hooves, but she could lift them and the grass and dirt didn't come up too. Good.

Now he needed to add his time-release powder, which would turn the stickiness on when they started

"THE POWDER WAS READY TO TRY OUT."

climbing the glass hill and turn it off when they got back to the bottom.

Marigold woke up in the middle of the night. She had dreamed of a secret weapon that would keep a horse and rider from getting to the top of the glass hill. With her secret weapon she wouldn't have to marry someone who was mean and nasty and cruel. She patted Apricot, who was curled up next to her, and fell back to sleep, smiling.

Early the next morning Royal Servants climbed a ladder to the top of the pyramid. They brought with them an outdoor throne, a picnic lunch for a princess and a cat, the basket of golden apples, and a water bowl for Apricot. When they came down, Marigold carried Apricot and the secret weapon to the top. As soon as she got there, the Royal Servants took the ladder away and the contest began.

After breakfast the same morning, Ralph said, "Good day to watch a glass hill." He guffawed.

Burt guffawed.

Ralph pushed back his chair and walked out of the farmhouse. Burt pushed back his chair and followed him. Cinderellis wondered if the Royal Dairymaid would be watching the contest.

At the workshop cave, he worked on his powder some more. Finally he thought it was ready.

At first Marigold had been ready with her secret weapon whenever a horse galloped at the pyramid. But rider after rider failed to climb up even one inch, so she relaxed and became interested in looking down on everything. The knights and squires seemed no bigger than her hand, and their cries and the neighing of their horses sounded muffled and thin. Only Biddle Mountain appeared as big as ever, looming in the distance, much higher than the glass hill.

The day grew warmer and Marigold grew hot—hot and bored. Apricot was hot too, but he knew his dear lass had brought him up there to show everyone how important he was to her. So he rubbed himself against her leg and purred.

Marigold wished she knew the name of the nice farm lad. Even if she never saw him again, though, she'd remember their conversation forever.

Cinderellis wanted to scream. He'd been putting the copper suit of armor on for hours. He'd finally gotten the tasset and the mail skirt on over his waist and hips. The cuisses and the poleyns and the greaves were on his legs. The sabatons were on his feet. The vambraces were on his arms. The couters were over his elbows.

But the breastplate kept popping off!

Over and over he'd hammered it here and bent it there. And it would hold—for about ten seconds. Then—*POP!*

At this rate he'd never get to the pyramid.

Ten

A knight on a black stallion prepared to climb the hill. The stallion looked bigger than any of the other horses. Marigold reached for her secret weapon.

But the stallion's hooves slipped off the pyramid as soon as they touched it. The knight made the horse try again—and the horse slipped again. The knight wanted to try a third time, but everybody yelled that he should let the rest of them take a turn.

Burt and Ralph laughed so hard, their sides hurt.

Marigold put her secret weapon down and started breathing again. It was three thirty. Only a few more hours till it would be too dark to see the hill and she could come down. Only a few more hours and it would be over forever.

But then her father would come up with another horrible plan.

Cinderellis had finally wedged the breastplate under the fauld. And he'd managed to mount Chasam, even though it had taken over an hour. He'd picked Chasam because she'd looked so disappointed when he'd tried the powder out on Ghasam.

He pulled the gauntlets over his hands. Now for the helmet. Uh-oh. He couldn't make his hands in the gauntlets do anything. He'd never get the helmet on. He took the gauntlets off again and put the helmet on.

Now he couldn't see to put on the gauntlets. He could only see through one chink in the visor, just enough to steer Chasam.

Well, he didn't need to see. He could feel. There. The gauntlets were on.

Now where were the reins? He couldn't tell through the gauntlets. Were these the reins? He hoped so.

He kicked Chasam, harder than he meant to. She didn't mind. They were off. It was five o'clock.

Two more horses to go. Marigold scratched under her tiara. She felt hot and sticky. Apricot was drinking from his water bowl. She was glad he was up here with her. She wished that kind farm lad were here too. She'd introduce him to Apricot, and he'd invent something nice for a cat.

One more horse to go.

Marigold wondered what her father would dream up next. Maybe he'd make her sit at the bottom of a glass hole, and the horse that didn't crash down and squash her would have her hand and Skiddle, Luddle, and Buffle.

The last horse, like the 213 before it, failed to climb the hill. Marigold stood up. At last. She hadn't needed her secret weapon. Wait! What was that? A cloud of dust coming from Biddle Mountain?

In the field below, King Humphrey III couldn't see the dust cloud. He decided that the contestants could all try again tomorrow. He didn't want to end the contest after just one day when it was so important.

Then he heard people shouting. There was another rider? Let him come, then. Maybe this one would be enough of a horseman to climb the pyramid. Maybe this one deserved Marigold.

Cinderellis saw the pyramid through the chink in the visor. They were almost there.

Everyone was astonished at the beauty and size of the copper-colored mare. Everyone was also amazed that such a glorious horse would let herself be ridden by that nutty knight or whatever he was. For one thing, his armor was tarnished and filthy. His posture was terrible. His hands and the reins were flopping around in his lap. He wasn't even really riding the mare. She was carrying him, like cargo.

Marigold's heart started pounding.

Chasam cantered up to the glass hill. Cinderellis sort of kicked her to keep going. She placed her front right hoof on the hill. She leaned her weight on it. It held!

She started to climb. The watching crowd grew silent.

Marigold didn't know what to do. If this mare climbed the hill, it would be because she wanted to. Any fool could see the mare's rider wasn't making her do anything. But the rider still could be mean and nasty. Marigold picked up her secret weapon.

But maybe he's nice, she thought, as nice as the farm lad. She had to find out. At least she had to see his face. "Sir!" she called. "Please take off your helmet."

Who was yelling? Cinderellis could see only the glass hill in front of him. He tried to look up, but all he saw was the inside of the helmet. Was something wrong? He tried to push his visor up. Nothing happened.

"I'd like to see your face," Marigold called.

Somebody was yelling again. Cinderellis decided to take the helmet completely off. He pushed up on it. Nothing happened.

Chasam was a tenth of the way up the hill. The crowd on the ground almost stopped breathing.

He's trying to do what I want, Marigold thought. That's something. And he didn't force the horse up the hill. She laughed. If he couldn't even get his helmet off, he'd never be able to pick up the apples—if he climbed all the way up.

She thought of tossing the apples into his lap. If nobody ever got to the top, the next contest could be worse than this one. Or her father might let this contest go on forever, and she'd spend the rest of her life up here.

She put the secret weapon down. The apples were

next to the throne. She took one, aimed carefully, and threw. The apple landed on Chasam's saddle, in the little valley between the saddle and Cinderellis' mail skirt.

Huh! Cinderellis thought. Did something hit me?

Marigold picked up another apple. She would have thrown it, but she got worried. She was taking an awful chance. She hadn't seen the knight and she hadn't talked to him. Maybe they could talk, even if she couldn't see him. "Sir," she called, "what would you do if you ruled Skiddle, Luddle, and Buffle?"

"What?" Cinderellis yelled. "What? Speak louder."

A roar came from the helmet. Marigold didn't hear words, just a roar. Whatever was in the armor didn't know how to talk. It could only roar. It was a monster! And she'd given it an apple!

Eleven

arigold reached for the pitcher that held her secret weapon. But she hesitated. She didn't want to hurt the horse.

Chasam was a third of the way up the hill. And climbing.

The monster would be up here in a minute. She had to do something! She'd try to use only enough to make the mare slide down slowly. She leaned over the edge of her platform and poured a thin stream of olive oil down toward Cinderellis.

Everyone watching wondered why the princess was leaning over the edge of the pyramid. They were too far away to see the pitcher of oil.

The powder wasn't made to withstand olive oil. Chasam started to slip.

Cinderellis thought, We're going down! Is Chasam hurt? What went wrong with the powder?

Chasam couldn't drop Cinderellis. She loved him

too much. She spread her legs so she wouldn't topple over and slid down slowly.

Ralph's and Burt's mouths dropped open. What a mare! Any other horse would have fallen on its head, or on top of its rider.

At the bottom of the pyramid Chasam turned around and took off at a gallop.

King Humphrey III issued a proclamation announcing that there would be a second and a third chance to climb the glass hill.

Cinderellis lay panting in the dirt in front of the workshop cave. Chasam, Ghasam, and Shasam were grazing nearby.

It had taken him a half hour to get his helmet off. Once it was off, he'd used his teeth to tear the gauntlets off his hands. And then he'd squirmed out of everything else.

His powder had failed. He had failed.

Shasam sniffed the golden apple, which had fallen into the parsley patch. Cinderellis picked it up, and Shasam cantered a little ways off, ready for a game of horse-treat catch. But Cinderellis was too depressed for games. Besides, Shasam might break a tooth on the stupid golden apple.

One apple wouldn't buy a workshop in Snettering-on-Snoakes. He wouldn't be able to marry the Royal Dairymaid on just one apple. He might as well not have it.

Still, he wondered how he'd gotten it. The only explanation he could think of was that the princess had thrown it to him. But why would she?

He stood up and carried the armor and the apple into the cave. He dumped the armor on the heap with the other armor and hid the apple behind an outcropping of rock. Then he headed to the farmhouse for dinner.

Ralph and Burt were just finishing up.

"Did anyone win the contest?" Cinderellis asked.

"Not today," Ralph said. He smiled his special smile at Burt.

Cinderellis didn't even notice.

"Maybe tomorrow," Burt said.

Tomorrow?

"Or the day after," Ralph said.

He had two more chances!

"There was a beautiful mare," Ralph added.

"Mare's rider was an idiot," Burt said.

"Real idiot," Ralph said.

They both laughed.

"Work to do," Cinderellis said. He ran out of the farmhouse. He had to find out what had gone wrong with his powder. And then he had to fix it.

He'd marry that Royal Dairymaid yet!

In the stable cave he lit a lantern and bent over Chasam's left front hoof. She whinnied and blew warm air across his forehead.

Hmm. The hoof looked greasy. Cinderellis touched the greasy spot. He tasted it.

Olive oil! They'd used olive oil to make the pyramid slipperier. How could they do that without telling? It wasn't fair.

What would repel olive oil? Drying powder might help, but drying powder worked best on water. Olive pits mixed with drying powder? Olive pits were surrounded by olive oil right there in the olive, and they never became soggy, so they must repel the oil. Yes, that should do it. He ran to the farmhouse pantry for olives and olive oil.

In the morning Marigold asked the Chief Royal Cook to refill her secret weapon pitcher. But the Chief Royal Cook was fresh out of olive oil. Marigold said walnut oil would be fine.

In the field around the glass hill the contestants prepared for the day's trial. A knight painted sticky honey on his horse's hooves. A squire scraped his stallion's shoes to make them rough. Another knight screwed hooks into his mare's shoes.

Outside the workshop cave Cinderellis poured olive oil down a rock that was about as steep as the glass hill. Then he dusted his new powder on Ghasam's hoofs. She started to climb and then slipped. Cinderellis added a little more olive-pit powder and told Ghasam to try again.

The knight who had painted honey on his horse's hooves galloped up to the glass hill. His horse tried to step onto the hill but slipped right off.

Marigold petted Apricot. It was going to be another long, hot day.

Ralph grinned at Burt. Burt grinned at Ralph. It was going to be another fun day.

It had taken all morning and almost all afternoon, but Cinderellis' new powder was ready. And Cinderellis was ready, in the silver armor. It had been easier to get into, because he'd learned a few tricks the day before. But being inside was as bad as ever. He could hardly see anything, and his hands were almost useless inside the gauntlets. Still, he was in it, and he was mounted on Shasam. Chasam had earned a rest. He'd ride Ghasam tomorrow if anything went wrong today.

But what could go wrong?

Twelve

The sun was setting behind Biddle Mountain. I didn't need the oil at all today, Marigold thought. But then she saw a dust cloud in the distance. Oh no! Could the mare be coming back? Could the monster be coming back?

People started yelling. "The mare! The mare!"

But it wasn't the copper mare. This horse was a mare, but she was silver and even bigger than the copper mare. One thing was the same, though: The same fool was riding as yesterday. Anyone could see that, even though the rider wore dirty banged-up silver armor instead of dirty banged-up copper armor.

Cinderellis and Shasam reached the pyramid. Shasam started to climb the hill. It wasn't hard. She began to trot.

Marigold was terrified. The mare was halfway up the hill. Where was the walnut oil? She put Apricot down and reached for it. The hem of her gown knocked into the basket that held the apples and sent an apple clattering down the pyramid.

Shasam saw the apple. *Horse treat!* She veered and caught it with her teeth. Then she started climbing again.

Marigold poured the walnut oil. Shasam was two thirds of the way up the glass hill, but when the oil touched her hooves, she started to slip. Oh nooo! She fought, and her hooves beat the glass.

At first Cinderellis thought Shasam was dancing. But no, she was falling. Was she all right? Was she hurt?

Shasam slid down the same way Chasam had. At the bottom she made sure Cinderellis was still in the saddle. Then she galloped away, still holding the golden apple between her teeth.

Cinderellis was furious. How could they have switched oils on him?

And what would they use tomorrow?

And how had Shasam gotten a golden apple? He couldn't even guess, and he didn't have time to think about it anyway. He had to figure out how to fix his powder. What he needed was an all-purpose oil repellent. On the farm they grew the nuts and grains for every kind of oil that Biddlers used. What if he ground up the hulls and pits of all of them and added that to the powder? It was a big job, but when he was done, he'd have an all-purpose oil-repellent extra-strength time-release on-off sticky powder that would climb any glass hill anywhere.

Inventing the new powder took all night and most

of the next day, but finally it was ready. Cinderellis started putting on the golden armor. It was too big, so he dusted it with shrinking powder. And made it too small. So he dusted it with growing powder. And made it too big. He wasn't used to working in such a rush, and he hated it. He sprinkled on just a little shrinking powder. And made it exactly the way it had been when he started. He was going to bounce around in it, but it would have to do. When the contest was over, he was going to invent better armor.

Marigold waited for the dust cloud. Everybody else was waiting too.

And there it was—the dust cloud.

The mare was golden this time, and so splendid she took Marigold's breath away. Why did such a marvelous horse let a monster ride her?

Cinderellis ached all over from crashing into a different part of the armor whenever Ghasam took a step. Not only that, his helmet kept bouncing around too. Sometimes he could see outside pretty well. Sometimes he could just see a little. And sometimes all he could see was the inside of the helmet. Whenever he could see, he pointed Ghasam toward the pyramid and hoped for the best.

They reached the glass hill. Ghasam started climbing. Cinderellis' helmet shifted. All he could see now was gray metal and three rivets.

Marigold didn't waste a second. She went right for her pitcher of oil, which was walnut again. She leaned over the edge of the pyramid and started pouring.

The oil flowed down the hill. It reached the mare, but it didn't stop her. She didn't slip a bit. She just kept climbing.

Marigold dropped the pitcher and picked Apricot up. She petted the cat and trembled. She was going to have to marry the monster.

Cinderellis felt Ghasam climb higher and higher. It's working! he thought. If only he could see.

Ghasam stepped onto the platform and stopped. She didn't like being so high up. She shifted from foot to foot.

Cinderellis wondered why Ghasam had stopped. Were they at the top? Had they made it? He tried to move the helmet so he could see. He banged on it, but it didn't budge. He tried to raise the visor, but it wouldn't budge either. How would he get the third apple if he couldn't see?

Marigold hugged Apricot even tighter. Too tight, the cat thought. He wished that she'd stop squeezing and that the horse would go away.

Marigold screamed, "Stay away from us! I won't marry you!"

Somebody was yelling again. "What?" Cinderellis yelled back.

That sounds like a word, Marigold thought. But what was it? What difference did it make? She yelled, "Go away! Leave us alone!"

"What?"

She got it! It had said, "Cat." It wanted Apricot!

The monster wanted Apricot! "I'll never give him up, not even if you torture me."

Ghasam wished her dear lad would tell her what to do. She took a step back and then a step forward. She hated it up here.

"What? What is it? What's happening?" Cinderellis shouted. If only he could see. If only he could hear. If only he could find the apple.

Marigold made out another word. The monster had said "cat" again, and "apple." It was saying she better give it the apple or it would take the cat! She jumped up and down with fear and anger. "You can't have them! Go away!"

Cinderellis shoved at the visor and banged the helmet. *Ping!* It sounded like a rivet popping out, but the visor still wouldn't budge.

Ghasam wanted to go home. She took two steps forward.

It's coming at me! Aaaaa! It's going to get us! It can have the apple. Marigold rushed to the basket and snatched up an apple. Then she darted forward and placed it on the saddle in front of Cinderellis.

Apricot hated being so near a horse. He hissed and shot out a paw.

Ghasam shied back. Cinderellis bounced in the saddle. His helmet snapped back, and he stared at the inside of it where his nose should have been.

The visor came off and fell onto the platform, but the visor opening was over his forehead, way above his eyes.

Ghasam shied again. Cinderellis' legs knocked into her sides. He wanted her to leave. At last. She started down the hill. At the bottom she began to gallop.

On top of the pyramid Marigold picked up the golden visor. The monster had gone at last.

But it had three apples.

Thirteen

very day Cinderellis walked to Biddle Castle. He asked all the Royal Dairymaids about his Royal Dairymaid. Nobody knew her. The Royal Dairymaids swore there was no such person.

What good was it to have the golden apples without his sweet, adorable Royal Dairymaid? No good at all.

King Humphrey III waited a week for someone to show up with the golden apples. When no one did, he and his Royal Pages went from house to house, looking for the lad whose armor matched the golden visor.

Marigold came along. She wanted to be there when they found the monster so she could do something. She didn't know what, but something. She left Apricot home to keep him safe for as long as possible.

Two weeks after the last day of the contest, the king reached Cinderellis' farm.

Ralph was weeding the alfalfa field.

King Humphrey III didn't think the fellow looked

brave or determined or at all like son-in-law material, but he asked anyway. "Did you climb the glass hill? And do you have a suit of golden armor and three of the princess' golden apples?" He gestured at Marigold.

Ralph bowed to the king. "Nope."

Burt said the same exact thing when they found him in the barley field.

"Are you two the only ones on the farm?" Marigold asked.

"Yup." Then he remembered. "I mean, nope. We have another brother, Cinderellis, but he didn't go to the contest."

"Where is he?" King Humphrey III asked. Burt pointed to Biddle Mountain.

Cinderellis was outside his workshop cave, inventing armor improvements, when Ghasam whinnied. He turned and saw the king and his attendants heading up the mountain.

Cinderellis picked up the pieces of armor and ran into the cave, shooing the horses in ahead of him. Then he rushed to his tomato patch and started weeding.

The king reached the tomatoes. Cinderellis stood and bowed. Then he stared. The Royal Dairymaid was with him. His heart started racing. What was she doing here?

It was the nice farm lad! Marigold smiled in delight.

Cinderellis wondered why there were jewels on her gown.

"Did you climb the glass hill?" King Humphrey III

"DID SHE SAY SHE'D MARRY HIM? HE PUSHED UPON
THE HELMET. IT WOULDN'T COME OFF. 'IT'S STUCK.'"

asked. "And do you have a suit of golden armor and three of the princess' golden apples?" He gestured at Marigold.

She was the princess? "Yes! Yes! I have them! I'll get them!" He ran into the workshop cave.

Marigold thought, He's the monster? How could he be?

Cinderellis came out of the cave, leading Chasam, Shasam, and Ghasam. In his arms were the golden helmet and the three golden apples. He put everything down and knelt before Marigold. "Will you marry me?"

He was smiling up at her. He still looked nice. But then why had he wanted Apricot? "Why did you try to take Apricot?"

What was she talking about? "What apricot?"

"My Apricot. My cat. I had him with me on top of the glass hill."

Cinderellis started laughing. He put on the helmet, jamming it hard over his head. The visor space was over his forehead again. "I can't see anything," he said.

Marigold laughed too. He sounded like the monster. "Take off the helmet," she said.

She was saying something, but he couldn't hear what it was. Did she say she'd marry him? He pushed up on the helmet. It wouldn't come off. "It's stuck."

"Yes, I'll marry you."

What did she say?

Epilogue

In three days Cinderellis and Marigold were married.

Ralph and Burt came to the ceremony. As soon as it was over, they smiled their special smile at each other and hurried home to harvest the corn.

Chasam, Shasam, and Ghasam became Marigold's pets, just as Apricot was. The only difference was that the horses couldn't fit on the princess' lap. Apricot got used to the horses and even became friends with them. He liked Cinderellis too, once he was convinced—after a few misunderstandings—that his dear lass was happy with the lad. And he loved Cinderellis' first invention as crown prince: cat treats.

Marigold loved all Cinderellis' inventions. She and Cinderellis celebrated their wedding anniversary every year with a demonstration of his all-purpose sticky powder on the glass hill, which they kept polished just for the purpose.

King Humphrey III resumed his questing when the imp's curse ended. He returned with so many souvenirs that an extra wing had to be added to the Museum of Quest Souvenirs.

Cinderellis never went on a single quest. His only trips were to Skiddle, Luddle, and Buffle, and Marigold always went along. While there, she made so many friends that she was never lonely again.

Cinderellis' wetting powder cured a drought in Skiddle, and his drying powder worked wonders on the floods of Buffle. What's more, he showed the Luddlites how to use growing powder on their wheat crop. Everyone was so grateful that Cinderellis became the most popular ruler in Biddle history. He was never lonely again either.

And they all lived happily ever after.

For
Biddle's Sake

All my love to Rani and Ronnie—

friend, fellow artist, sister.

—G.C.L.

One

When she was two years old, Patsy tasted a sprig of parsley at a traveling fair. She loved it, and from that moment on, the only food she would eat was parsley. After a while her parents, Nelly and Zeke, began to call her that, Parsley.

The trouble was that parsley grew in only one spot in the village of Snettering-on-Snoakes, and that spot was the garden of the fairy Bombina, who was renowned for turning people into toads.

Nelly said she couldn't let her daughter starve, and Zeke, who rarely spoke, nodded.

So every Thursday night, Zeke would head for Rosella Lane, where he'd climb the high wall that surrounded the fairy's garden. He'd stuff a sack full of fresh parsley and return home. His stealing went undetected for three years because Bombina was serving time in the dungeon of Anura, the fairy queen. Bombina's crime was failure to get along with humans.

Meanwhile, Parsley grew into a plump, happy child with a lovely smile, in spite of teeth that were stained a pale green.

Then Bombina returned.

That Thursday evening, she strolled in her garden and saw Zeke gathering armloads of parsley. Armloads! She would have turned him into a toad on the spot, but she had already reached Anura's legal limit of five human-to-toad transformations per fairy per year, and she didn't want to go back to jail.

"What are you doing?" she shrieked.

Zeke grabbed the parsley and ran. Bombina stood on her left foot and blinked twice. Zeke froze, unable to move a muscle. Bombina thought of turning him to stone, but stone wasn't her specialty. Her specialty was toads.

"Why are you stealing my parsley?" she thundered. Then she unfroze Zeke's mouth.

Zeke wasn't used to talking. So even though his mouth could move, it didn't.

Bombina dropped her voice to a sugary whisper. "I can turn you into a chicken . . ." She never ran out of legal chicken transformations. "A clucking—"

Zeke found his voice. "It's for m-my d-daughter."

His daughter? Anura always said that fairies should be kind to children. Fairies who were kind were her favorites. Bombina was on probation, and she was definitely not one of the fairy queen's favorites.

"Bring your daughter to me."

"B-but—"

"Bring your daughter to me!" Bombina unfroze all of Zeke.

He stumbled once, then started to run.

"And drop the parsley."

Back in their cottage Zeke told Nelly what Bombina had commanded. Nelly began to run around frantically, bumping into Zeke and shouting that she wasn't bringing her precious daughter to anybody. Zeke ran around frantically too, and he bumped into Nelly when she wasn't bumping into him.

Bombina materialized in the cottage, right next to Parsley's bed. "Is this your daughter?"

Parsley awoke and sat up, blinking in the bright light that flashed around Bombina's big pink wings.

"Hello, child," Bombina boomed.

Parsley was frightened. She'd never seen anyone so enormous or so grumpy-looking.

"What's your name, honey?"

Parsley said, "Parsley," in a small voice.

"Parsley!" Bombina whirled on Nelly and Zeke. "You dared to name your daughter after my parsley?"

Nelly held her ground. "We named her P-Patsy, Your G-Graciousness, but—"

"Silence!" Bombina leaned over the bed. "Why do you like parsley so much, Parsley?"

Parsley didn't know why. She just did. She stared at Bombina and didn't say anything.

"Answer the nice fairy," Nelly said. "Tell her why . . ."

She's a fairy? Parsley thought. She'd been taught

that fairies were gentle and good. Then this one was only pretending to be mean. She smiled up at Bombina.

Nothing was sweeter than Parsley's smile.

A tiny corner of Bombina's heart melted. "Harrumph." She cleared her throat. And had a brilliant idea. Anura would be delighted! "I will take the child home to live with me. Then Parsley can eat parsley whenever she likes."

Live with a fairy! Parsley was thrilled. Maybe she'd learn magic. "Can I, Mama?"

A tear trickled down Nelly's cheek.

A tear trickled down Zeke's cheek.

"Well?" Bombina yelled. "Can she?"

Nelly and Zeke couldn't refuse a fairy. Nelly said, "Yes, Parsley gumdrop, you can go."

Two

Nearby in Biddle Castle, Prince Tansy was in the throne room with his brothers, Prince Randolph and Prince Rudolph, who were arguing as usual. Randolph and Rudolph were twins, and they were nine years old, two years older than Tansy. No one else was in the room.

Tansy could tell the twins apart because Randolph's left nostril was slightly larger than his right nostril, and Rudolph's right nostril was slightly larger than his left.

"The right hand, fool!" Randolph held King Humphrey IV's gilded wooden scepter just beyond Rudolph's reach. "A king holds the scepter in his right hand."

"The left hand, numskull!" Rudolph twisted Randolph's nose and tried to grab the scepter.

With his free hand Randolph twisted Rudolph's nose.

Tansy removed Rudolph's fingers from Randolph's

nose and Randolph's fingers from Rudolph's nose. He said, "I think—"

"You don't have to think," Randolph said, trying to grab some part of Rudolph again.

"You'll never be king, Tansy," Rudolph said, lunging for the scepter and getting one hand on it.

Randolph tried to yank the scepter away from Rudolph.

Rudolph hung on and tried to yank it away from Randolph.

Tansy said, "Stop! You'll break it."

Crack! The scepter broke in half.

Randolph and Rudolph dropped their halves and ran out of the throne room. Tansy ran too, although he knew what was going to happen next. The Royal Guards were going to find the three of them. Randolph and Rudolph were going to tell King Humphrey IV that he, Tansy, had broken the scepter, and King Humphrey IV was going to believe them, no matter what Tansy said. Then the king was going to make him write *I will never again break a Royal Scepter* at least a hundred times.

While Tansy ran, he thought about the question his brothers had been arguing over. The solution was simple. A king should hold his scepter in his right hand on Sundays, Tuesdays, and Fridays, and in the left on Mondays, Thursdays, and Saturdays. That would show how fair he was. He should hold it with both hands on Wednesdays. That would show how stable his kingdom was.

Randolph and Rudolph hadn't thought the matter through. They never did.

But one of them would be king anyway, and Tansy never would be, even though he had hundreds of great ideas about how to rule the kingdom of Biddle. Youngest sons didn't become king.

Bombina liked having Parsley live with her. She especially liked having Parsley's smile live with her. She'd do anything to see that smile, and anything included some surprising things—smiling back at Parsley or occasionally smiling first, tucking Parsley in at night, and even letting Parsley touch her wings. Bombina had never let anyone do that before.

For her part, Parsley loved living in the fairy's palace, although she missed Nelly and Zeke. Bombina's cook knew dozens of parsley recipes. Parsley could have her parsley scrambled, steamed, stewed, barbecued, braised, broiled, fried, or liquefied. She could have parsley pesto, parsley pasta, parsley pizza, parsley pilaf, or parsley in puff pastry. And for dessert she could have parsley pie, parsley pudding, parsley penuche, parsley taffy, parsley upside-down cake, or, the one she liked best, parsley ice cream sundae with hot parsley sauce and parsley sprinkles on top.

But most of all Parsley loved watching Bombina make magic.

The fairy never used a wand. She began all her magic by standing on her left foot. To disappear, she'd make her chin jut forward and put her left pinky finger in her mouth. And *poof!* she'd be gone. To sink into the ground, she'd bend at the waist and hop twice. A hole would appear, and she'd slide into it till only her head showed.

But the magic that Bombina did most often was to turn objects into toads. The fairy queen's limit applied only to humans—Bombina could transform as many of anything else as she liked.

Parsley was astonished at the things Bombina turned into toads—a single thread in a bodice, an egg, a tile roof, a picture frame, an umbrella handle.

Once, when her footman Stanley failed to open the carriage door quickly enough, Bombina turned his bushy red beard into a purple Fury-Faced Trudy Toad. It looked funny, hanging upside down from Stanley's chin. Bombina laughed, and Parsley would have too if Stanley hadn't looked utterly shocked.

Parsley tried to cast spells too. For example, she'd let her hot parsley tea cool. Then she'd stand on her left foot, lick her index fingers, and grunt *ung huh tuh* exactly as Bombina would. But her tea never warmed up. She couldn't fly either, or make her slippers come to her from halfway across the bedchamber.

She never tried to turn anything into a toad. It didn't seem right. Maybe Stanley's beard was pleased to be a toad, but maybe it wasn't. Maybe it didn't like croaking and catching flies.

Once Parsley asked Bombina, "Why can't I make magic? It looks simple when you do it." She smiled.

As usual, Bombina was enchanted by the smile.

"BOMBINA TURNED HIS BUSHY RED BEARD
INTO A PURPLE FURY-FACED TRUDY TOAD."

That's another kind of magic, she thought, to be able to smile so charmingly with teeth as green as a green onion.

"You have to be magical to make magic, dear. I'm a magical creature, and you aren't."

Three

arsley had been living with Bombina for ten months when June 23, Midsummer's Eve, the fairies' New Year, came around. As always, Bombina attended the ball at Anura's palace, where she received, along with the other fairies, her new allotment of legal transformations.

During the ball Bombina told the fairy queen about adopting Parsley. Anura clapped her hands in joy. "Hurrah, Bombina! With your little Oregano you will—"

"Parsley," Bombina said.

"Ah, yes. You will usher in a golden age in your Snetting-Snooks. You and your Tarragon will—"

"Snettering-on-Snoakes. Parsley."

"Whatever. A river of love will flow from humans to you and from you to them. You won't want to turn a single one, not even the most aggravating, into a toad." Anura embraced Bombina and bathed her face in kisses.

When Parsley went into Bombina's bedroom the

next morning, Bombina sat up instantly. She couldn't wait to begin her new life of deep and abiding friendship with humans.

"Come here, child." And she kissed Parsley on the forehead.

Parsley didn't know about the fairies' New Year or what Anura had said, but she liked the kiss. She smiled and said, "How are you going to wear your hair today?" She thought Bombina's hairstyling magic was the best magic of all.

"We'll see." Bombina knew Parsley liked to watch, so she decided to try out a few new styles until the serving maid brought breakfast. She sat at her dressing table. Parsley came and stood next to her.

Bombina shook out her long red hair. Then she lifted her right foot, stuck out her front teeth, and said *arr arr arr*. Her hair shrank into her scalp until only a couple of inches were left, and those inches curled into ringlets. She knocked her fists together, and her hair turned blue with blond stripes.

Parsley giggled.

Bombina's stomach rumbled. She frowned. Where was that lazy serving maid?

Ah, well, Bombina thought. Perhaps Cook was preparing something special to please her. Bombina stuck out her chin and said *raa raa raa*. Her hair grew long again and piled itself on top of her head.

"Oooh!" Parsley said.

Bombina's stomach rumbled again. She didn't want something special. She wanted her ordinary breakfast at its ordinary time. But it was too late for that. I must calm myself, she thought. Perhaps the serving maid was carrying my breakfast to me when she fell and broke both her ankles. That would be nice.

Bombina stood up and started to pace.

Uh-oh! Parsley thought. She got out of the way and stood in the window alcove.

Bombina paced and thought. Perhaps Cook fell into the porridge and drowned. That would be nice too.

In fact, the serving maid had quit the night before. The servants knew that the fairies' New Year always brought new toad transformations. Bombina had been kinder lately, but they were still frightened. The year before Bombina had gone to jail, she had turned three gardeners, a manservant, and a seamstress into toads.

No one wanted to deliver Bombina's breakfast. After arguing for a half hour, the servants ganged up on the scullery wench, who had started her job only the week before. Cook carried the breakfast tray to Bombina's door, and two menservants carried the wench. When they got there, Cook put the tray into the scullery wench's hands. One manservant opened the door, and the other shoved her inside.

"There you are!" Bombina shouted while shifting her weight onto her left foot. Then she began to stare at the scullery wench. She lowered her chin to her chest and continued to stare.

Oh, no! Parsley thought. She's going to—

Bombina flapped her right wing once while singing

oople toople in a high scratchy voice.

The scullery wench looked startled. Parsley heard the beginning of a yelp. The breakfast tray clattered to the floor, and the scullery wench shrank. For a moment she stood there, an orange scullery wench two inches tall. Then she was a toad, an orange Christopher Inquisitive Toad.

Parsley wanted to scream, but she couldn't, or she might be turned into a toad too. She slipped behind the window drapes and peeked through them.

Bombina hiccuped twice, and the toad vanished. She noticed the smashed breakfast tray on the tile floor. Her yummy coddled eggs were a yellow puddle, and her lovely porridge with figs and raisins was hardening into a big brown lump.

She was so angry, she stamped her feet and shrieked *aargh* and accidentally turned a candlestick into a feathered bonnet. Then she stormed out of her bedchamber.

A minute later Parsley crept out too, gladder than ever before to still have two human legs and two human hands and no warts.

Within a quarter hour Cook was a mauve Sir Melvin Dancing Toad, the two menservants were both turquoise Belladonna Spinning Toads, and the laundress, who happened to be in the kitchen, was an ultramarine Ethelinda Bumbling Toad. Bombina had beaten her own record for using up toad transformations.

Four

Parsley felt terrible about the toads. She had liked all of them when they were human, and she had especially liked Cook. Parsley was almost certain that toads ate their food raw, and Cook would hate that.

Bombina did everything she could think of to cheer Parsley up and get her smiling again. The fairy found a new cook who knew a hundred parsley recipes, including one for parsley bubble gum.

Parsley blew big green bubbles, but she wouldn't smile.

Bombina invented fifteen new hairdos, but Parsley still wouldn't smile.

Bombina gave Parsley a magic spyglass that could see anything anywhere in Biddle, no matter what was in the way.

But Parsley still wouldn't smile.

Bombina was frantic. She begged Parsley to smile. She shouted. She wept.

But Parsley still wouldn't smile.

Finally, in desperation, Bombina said, "I won't turn people into toads anymore."

Parsley smiled.

Bombina was so happy that she hugged Parsley with both arms and both wings. But while she hugged, she thought, By next New Year, Parsley will have forgotten my promise.

Parsley loved her magic spyglass. She looked through it at Zeke and Nelly and the new baby. She looked over all of Biddle. She saw Elroy the shepherd's great-great-grandson herd sheep. She saw Ralph's and Burt's grandchildren do their farm chores, and once she even saw Ralph and Burt themselves, sitting on their porch, rocking back and forth, perfectly in time with each other.

Parsley watched the Royal Banquets in Biddle Castle, examining the plates for parsley dishes. She watched the Royal Balls, searching for ladies' hairdos that Bombina could try out. Once she saw a hair ornament atop an especially tall hairdo—a miniature sailing ship, with all sails billowing.

The first time Parsley saw the Royal Family was at a banquet. King Humphrey IV was bald, and his ears stuck out. The twins, Prince Randolph and Prince Rudolph, would have been handsome if they had ever stopped glaring at each other. The youngest prince, Prince Tansy, had freckles, a cowlick, and a serious expression. Parsley thought he looked exactly the way a prince should.

One twin sat on the king's right and the other sat

on his left, and they glared at each other around King Humphrey IV's belly. Tansy sat farther down the banquet table, between two Royal Councillors.

The twin on King Humphrey IV's left cut his baked potato the long way, but the twin on the right cut his potato the short way. The twin on the left ate in this order: roast hart, potato, lentils, watercress. The twin on the right ate in the reverse order.

All Tansy was eating was the watercress. Parsley was thrilled. He loved watercress and she loved parsley. They had something in common!

Actually, they didn't. Tansy never ate more than one dish at any meal, so he could give it his undivided attention. The watercress was pretty good, but he didn't love it.

The next time Parsley observed Tansy, he was in the Royal Wardrobe Room with his two brothers. The twins were both trying on King Humphrey IV's red satin Royal Ceremonial Robe. One twin had his arm in the left sleeve and the other had his arm in the right sleeve. Each was struggling to pull the robe away from the other.

They were caroming from one side of the room to the other—smashing into the shelves that held the king's breeches, corsets, codpieces, garters, jerkins, and undershirts. Tansy was dodging the flying Royal Wardrobe and saying something.

Oh no! The Royal Ceremonial Robe was ripping, up from the filigreed hem all the way to the ermine collar.

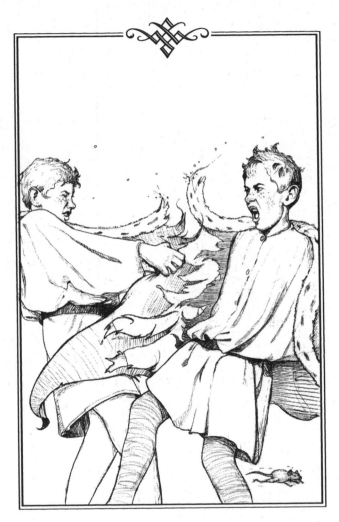

"OH NO! THE ROYAL CEREMONIAL ROBE
WAS RIPPING."

Now the twins were pulling off the robe and running out of the Royal Wardrobe Room, with Tansy right behind them. Parsley followed him in her spyglass. He dashed through the castle, out a first-floor window, along a cobblestone path, and into the Royal Museum of Quest Souvenirs, where he threw himself into the pile of straw under the turkey that lays tin eggs.

He wormed his way in so far that only the tippy toe of one boot stuck out, and Parsley feared he wouldn't get enough air to breathe.

She turned her spyglass back to the castle, where a search was in progress. A Royal Guard found one twin hiding under a bed in a Royal Bedchamber. Another guard found the other twin under a bed in a different Royal Bedchamber.

Randolph and Rudolph don't have much imagination, Parsley thought, feeling proud of Tansy for hiding in such a good spot. She watched the Royal Guards search Biddle Castle from the cellar to the towers. Then she joined Bombina for lunch.

After lunch Parsley watched the Royal Guards search the Royal Stable, the Royal Dairy, and Queen Sonora's old spindle shed. They searched the museum last and finally found Tansy, who emerged covered with straw and bits of tin. He looked sad and scared. Parsley's heart went out to him.

The Royal Guards marched him to the throne room, where his brothers and King Humphrey IV were waiting. Randolph and Rudolph pointed at

Tansy. Parsley saw their mouths shape the words *Tansy did it. He ripped the Royal Robe.*

But he didn't! Parsley thought. He didn't do anything.

King Humphrey IV yanked Tansy up by his ear and shook him. Then he dragged Tansy out of the throne room. Randolph and Rudolph watched him go. They were both grinning.

Royal Rats! Parsley thought.

With the spyglass she followed Tansy and King Humphrey IV along the Royal First Floor Corridor, up the Royal West Tower Stairway, up, up, up to a room at the top of the tower, where there were a desk and a chair and ink and parchment and a quill pen and nothing else. King Humphrey IV left Tansy there, and the prince sat at the desk and began to write.

Parsley focused her spyglass on the parchment and saw—

> *I will never again rip the Royal Robe.*
> *I will never again rip the Royal Robe.*
> *I will never again rip the Royal Robe.*
> *I will never again rip the Royal Robe.*
> *I will never again rip the Royal Robe.*

A tear fell on the parchment and blurred three lines of *never again*. Parsley felt like crying too.

Five

By the time Parsley was fifteen, she had watched Randolph and Rudolph get Tansy in trouble for scores of things he hadn't done— denting the Royal Armor, laming the Royal Steed, breaking the hand off the marble statue of King Humphrey I, and releasing the flea big enough to fill a teacup from the Royal Museum of Quest Souvenirs.

The flea was the worst. It bit King Humphrey IV, and his cheek swelled as big as a teakettle. Tansy spent a whole week in the Royal West Tower that time.

Parsley despised Randolph and Rudolph. She half wanted Tansy to punch each of them in their Royal Noses, but she admired him no end for his forbear-ance. Whenever she saw him in the spyglass, she smiled and smiled.

One day, Bombina saw her smiling and was instantly jealous. "What's so special out there?" she roared.

"Nothing," Parsley said nervously. "Just the roses in Biddle Castle's garden." Bombina hadn't turned anyone into a toad since she'd promised not to nine years ago, but Parsley knew she still could. She smiled at the fairy. "Our roses are better, though."

Bombina relaxed. She marveled, as she often did, that she had given up her hobby—her art—for this lass. Bombina had felt dreadfully deprived at first, but then she'd discovered that *not* turning people into toads gave her a delightful sense of power. Since she never used up her yearly limit, she could always turn someone into a toad if she wanted to. And she still turned objects into toads, so her skills hadn't gotten rusty.

The next day Tansy accompanied his brothers on a ride to Snettering-on-Snoakes, and Parsley watched them in her spyglass.

They were young men now. Parsley admired how tall and straight Tansy sat in his saddle. Randolph and Rudolph looked squat and awkward by comparison.

As the horses ambled along, Randolph and Rudolph argued over what color the Royal Steed should be.

"The Royal Steed must be brown," Randolph declared. "And anyone who doesn't agree is a ninny."

"Wrong!" Rudolph yelled. "The Royal Steed must be black, and you're a ninny nincompoop."

"I think," Tansy said, "that—"

"Tell him, Tansy," Randolph said. "You know I'm right."

"Tell him I'm right," Rudolph said.

"I think the Royal Steed must be taller than—"

In her spyglass Parsley saw Randolph and Rudolph turn on Tansy.

They both shouted, "You're a nitwit ninny nincompoop, and you'll never ride the Royal Steed."

I'm not a nitwit, Tansy thought. The Royal Steed can be any color, but it has to be tall, so subjects can find their sovereign. And rattles have to be tied to its knees, which will also help people locate the king. Why don't Randolph and Rudolph ever think about their subjects?

The three princes rode on in silence.

Parsley kept watching them. Turn! she thought. Come closer. Come this way. Please come.

They turned onto Rosella Lane. Parsley rushed downstairs to the library, where she threw open a window and leaned out.

She could see them, actually see them, without the spyglass! They were walking their horses down the lane. Tansy looked even nicer than he did in the spyglass, and his freckles didn't stand out quite so much. She smiled a warm, friendly smile.

Randolph and Rudolph didn't notice Parsley, but Tansy did. She seemed to be smiling at him. It was such a kind smile too, a beautiful smile, even if her teeth were as green as grass. Tansy didn't remember anyone smiling at him like that ever before.

The princes reined in their horses only a few yards from Parsley.

"The fairy Bombina lives here," Randolph announced. "A king must invite nearby fairies to a banquet every year."

"Every other year," Rudolph said. "That's quite enough."

Tansy smiled back at Parsley.

She liked his smile. Hers broadened into the loveliest, most rapturous smile ever.

Bombina came into the library carrying a bouquet of peonies from the garden. She saw Parsley's smile and became wildly jealous. Who was getting that smile? She ran to the window.

Noblemen!

Not for long. Toads!

Parsley heard Bombina and turned, a frown replacing her smile.

If Parsley had smiled at Bombina—if she hadn't frowned—

But she did frown.

Bombina decided to do the one who wasn't a twin first. She shifted her weight to her left foot, stared hard at him, and lowered her chin, still staring.

Oh no! Parsley thought. "Don't!" She leaped in front of the fairy.

Bombina found herself staring straight at Parsley.

Aaaa! Bombina tried to stop casting the spell, but it was too late.

Six

What?!! Parsley felt trapped by Bombina's gaze. She tried to squirm away from it, but she couldn't. Wind rushed by her ears, and Bombina's eyes grew bigger and bigger.

Parsley's skin pinched. Something was squeezing her harder and harder, squeezing her insides and outsides, her face and her feet and her bones and her stomach. Her ears rang and boomed.

Then it was over. Whew! She wondered if she'd looked funny while it was going on, wondered if Tansy had noticed. She turned to see.

Where was he?

Where was she?

She faced a wall that hadn't been there a second ago. It looked familiar, though. She recognized the wallpaper lily pads, but they were much too big.

Then she knew. She looked down at herself. She was chartreuse! She was a Biddlebum Toad!

She looked way way up and saw Bombina's horrified face.

See what your transformations got you, Parsley thought angrily. She wanted to scream and wail. But she didn't make a sound. She didn't know what she'd do if a croak came out of her.

Oh no! Bombina thought, feeling dizzy. Parsley will never smile at me again.

Bombina saw the three princes gawking at her, so she pulled the window shut. Then she drew the drapes, being careful not to step on poor Parsley.

Her darling was so tiny and ugly. Bombina couldn't stand to look at her. Sadly, even tragically, the fairy hiccuped twice.

Parsley vanished.

In Rosella Lane Tansy shook his head to clear it. Where had the smiling maiden gone? What had the fairy done with her?

Bombina flew to the fairy queen's palace and begged an audience with her. As soon as she saw Anura, she began to weep, although she'd never wept in all her three thousand seven hundred and fourteen years. Between sobs she blurted out the whole tale.

"Please do something. You can punish me. You can lock me up. Only let me see Parsley's human smile once more." She wiped her tears. "Toads don't have lips or teeth. Did I ever tell you what beautiful green teeth my Parsley had?"

"My poor Bombina," Anura said. "You have reaped the bitter rewards of your folly."

Bombina nodded, tears streaming.

"It would give me the greatest pleasure to help you.

But you know that the only way dear Bayleaf can—"

"Her name is Parsley," Bombina wailed.

"Yes, of course. But there is only one way your Paprika—"

"Parsley!"

"Sorry! But there is just one way your little, er, maiden can resume her human shape. And that is if some other human proposes marriage to her."

Bombina smiled through her tears. How could she have forgotten? All she had to do—

"No, my poor wretched Bombina. You cannot force a young man to propose, and the little toad cannot reveal what happened to her and what the remedy is. The proposal must be of the man's free will, or it will not transform anything."

Parsley discovered that toads could cry. Or once-human toads could, anyway.

Oh, why had Bombina broken her promise?

She wept for a full hour. Then she looked around. She was on the bank of a wide stream. A few yards away a rotting bridge crossed the water. Ferns and a weeping willow grew along the stream bank. Beyond them was a field of tall grasses. If Parsley had been at her human height, she would have seen goats grazing in the distance.

Parsley wondered what she'd eat here. There was no parsley.

Her tongue whipped out and caught a fly. She blinked and swallowed.

Ugh! she thought. I ate an insect! It tasted sweet. She started crying again. I won't do that twice. I'll starve first.

Her tongue snaked out and snagged a mosquito. She blinked and swallowed.

The mosquito was salty. Parsley stopped crying. Maybe she had been wrong to limit herself to parsley for all those years. She wondered how an ant would taste.

Seven

When the twins and Tansy returned to Biddle Castle from Snettering-on-Snoakes, King Humphrey IV sent for them. He rose from his throne and hugged Randolph. Or maybe it was Rudolph. He could never tell them apart. He knew about the difference in the size of their nostrils, but he could never remember which big nostril belonged to which twin.

He didn't hug Tansy.

"Lads!" He beamed at the twins and frowned at Tansy, hoping the boy wouldn't break anything just by standing still. "We were thinking about which of you should be our heir."

Randolph and Rudolph glared at each other. Tansy's heart started to pound.

"We have two stalwart sons to choose between."

Tansy's heart stopped pounding.

"So we have contrived a contest. The son who fetches us one hundred yards of linen fine enough to go through our Royal Ring"—King Humphrey IV took a ring off his pinky—"will wear this medallion." He reached into the pocket of his new Royal Ceremonial Robe and pulled out a golden medallion on which was inscribed *His Highness's Heir*. This was the cleverest part of the plan. Soon he'd know which twin was which. "The winner will rule when we are gone, and all Biddle will do his bidding."

Tansy's heart started to pound again. The contest meant trouble! Rudolph wouldn't stand for it if Randolph won, and Randolph wouldn't stand for it if Rudolph won. Whoever won, there would be trouble in Biddle.

"Father?"

King Humphrey IV scowled at Tansy. "Yes?"

"Can I seek the linen too?"

King Humphrey IV considered how peaceful home would be if Tansy were away. "You may." But he'd never let the lad rule Biddle, not even if Tansy's linen could pass through a ream of pinky rings.

Parsley spent an enjoyable afternoon sampling insects. Fleas were spicy. Ticks were sour. Midges tickled pleasantly as they went down, and caterpillars happened to taste a lot like parsley.

Late in the day a goatherd drove her goats across the stream. Parsley hid under the bridge, terrified of being trampled.

When the goats had all crossed, the goatherd sat on the far bank and dangled her feet in the stream.

Was I ever that big? Parsley wondered. She hopped

backward, feeling nervous. She could be squashed so easily.

The goatherd saw the movement. She waded across the stream and groped through the ferns under the bridge. "A toad!" She picked Parsley up and placed her on her enormous palm. "Perhaps more than a toad. Kind sir, speak to me!" She waited. "Perhaps you can't talk. But you can hear my sad tale. I am not truly a goatherd." She sighed, and the wind from the sigh almost knocked Parsley off her perch. "I have been transformed."

You too? Parsley thought. Were you once a toad?

"In my true form I am a princess, Princess Alyssatissaprincissa."

To Parsley's horror Princess Alyssatissaprincissa brought her huge face right up to Parsley. Parsley's right eye looked at a pimple as big as a bumblebee. Then Princess Alyssatissaprincissa kissed Parsley's side. The suction of the kiss pulled her skin away from her ribs.

After the kiss Princess Alyssatissaprincissa waited a moment and then dropped Parsley. She slogged back across the stream, muttering about the scarcity of frog princes.

The ferns cushioned Parsley's fall. She lay still, catching her breath.

Bombina spent the day knocking her knees together to enhance her vision and her hearing. She finally saw Parsley crouching under a fern and looking like any

"I AM NOT TRULY A GOATHERD."

other chartreuse Biddlebum Toad, except for a faint sparkle that only a fairy could detect.

It was too sad to bear. Bombina had to look away. I'll never be jealous again and I'll never turn anything into a toad again, she thought, not even so much as a needle or a beetle. That will be my punishment.

Early the next morning King Humphrey IV saw his sons off. "Return in a week," he said.

Randolph and Rudolph each climbed into his own Royal Carriage. Tansy mounted his mare, Bhogs, whose name stood for Brown Horse of Good Speed.

When they reached Snettering-on-Snoakes, the villagers lined the road to see them off, and Bombina watched from her palace. She recognized the princes and itched to turn them into toads. If it hadn't been for them, Parsley would still be human. But she kept her promise and let them go by.

A mile beyond the village the road forked. The Royal Road continued to the left and wound through the principal towns of Biddle on its way to Kulornia. The right fork was Biddle Byway, which meandered through tiny villages and hamlets and never arrived anywhere.

Randolph and Rudolph took the left fork. Tansy started to follow them. But then he pulled Bhogs up short and turned her onto Biddle Byway.

If I stick with them, he thought, and we find the perfect length of linen, who'll get it? No—who won't get it? Me.

Eight

y the end of her first day as a toad, Parsley had eaten seven fleas, twelve ticks, two spiders, a worm, a caterpillar, four gnats, and eleven midges. Then she'd gone to sleep. When she woke up late the next morning, she was surprised all over again that she was a toad. She stayed still and thought about the advantages and disadvantages of her new state.

On the plus side was diet. Bugs were scrumptious! But that was about it for the plus side.

On the minus side was the goatherd Princess Alyssatissa whatever the rest of her name was. Also on the minus side were the loss of her spyglass and the loss of Tansy in her spyglass.

And she missed Bombina. She remembered Bombina's magic tricks and how exciting it had been, especially when she was little, to live with a fairy. She remembered being disappointed when Bombina had said that only magical creatures could make magic.

Parsley's pulse quickened. She was a magical creature now.

What could she try?

Bombina began all her spells by standing on her left foot, so Parsley tried to do the same. But balancing on one foot was hard. Her shape was all wrong for it. She struggled for twenty minutes before she finally managed it and stood, wobbling a little for ten whole seconds. Then she started to go over, and she had to hop three times, while her head nodded and wagged, before she got steady again.

A silver lady's comb appeared in the air before her and fell into the moss at her feet.

She'd done it! Accidentally, but she'd done it. Too bad she had no hair.

She started to topple again. She frowned and hopped back two steps, stumbled, and got back onto her left foot.

A crock of brown boot polish landed next to the comb.

Parsley meant to laugh, but it came out as a croak, her first croak. It was a warm and melodious sound. She liked it and croaked again. She extended her four legs and stood tall and croaked again. The pitch was a trifle lower that way. She sat back to try to raise the pitch, but before she could open her mouth again, she found herself rising into the air, eighteen inches at least. She flew across the stream and crash-landed on the opposite bank.

She lay still. Gadzooks! Making magic was fun!

On the first morning of the contest, Tansy passed through the hamlets of Harglepool, Flambow-under-

"... AND CRASH-LANDED ON THE OPPOSITE BANK."

Gree, Lower Vudwich, and Craugh-over Pughtughlouch. In the afternoon he passed through Snug Podcoomb, Woolly Podcoomb, Podcoomb-upon-Hare, Upper Squeak, Lower Squeak, Popping Squeak, and Swinn-out-of-Crubble.

Wherever he went, Tansy asked Biddlers how they thought Biddle should be ruled, and he looked at linen. Each hamlet had its own master weaver, but not one of them could weave linen fine enough to squeeze through a bracelet, let alone a ring. Tansy worried that he would have found better cloth if he'd taken the Royal Road with his brothers.

Meanwhile, Randolph and Rudolph passed through towns with important-sounding short names like Ooth, Looth, Quibly, Eels, Hork, and Moowich. In Ooth the twins stopped at the first master weaver's shop they saw. The weaver pulled down his finest bolts of linen to show them.

"Hmm," Randolph said, "that one might do." He picked up a corner of cloth.

"Yes, it might." Rudolph picked up the other corner and glared at his brother.

"I saw it first." Randolph pulled the linen away from Rudolph.

"No, you didn't." Rudolph grabbed his corner again and yanked.

The linen tore down the middle.

"What have you done?" the weaver yelled. He wouldn't let the twins leave his store until one of them bought the ruined fabric, even though it didn't come close to fitting through a pinky ring. Randolph wound up paying, since he had touched the cloth first. His footman loaded it into his carriage.

There were fourteen master weavers in Ooth, and by the time the twins' carriages rolled out of town, seven bolts of torn linen were in each carriage. And not one square foot of cloth was fine enough to go through a pinky ring.

Parsley spent the afternoon learning to make magic. She made mistakes at first and created a big pile of objects that a toad didn't need, like a frying pan, a bow and arrows, and a bass fiddle.

But finally, she figured out how to make blue and pink and yellow balloons appear over the stream. They were a lovely sight, dozens of them, drifting over the water in friendly flocks.

By sundown she'd learned how to make almost anything she wanted, including a sprig of parsley, which had tasted awful. She'd taught herself how to make things vanish too. It was simple. All she had to do was hiccup twice, just as Bombina used to. She'd also perfected her flying, and even more important, she'd discovered how to land. She'd learned to knock her knees into her belly in order to see or hear anywhere in Biddle. She looked at Biddle Castle immediately, but she couldn't find Tansy or his horrible brothers there.

There was one bit of magic she couldn't perform, though. No matter what she tried, she couldn't turn herself back into a human.

Nine

ombina peeked at Parsley while Parsley was making magic. She hadn't known that her toads could do that. Hah! she thought proudly. I bet Parsley is the only one smart enough to figure it out.

At dusk Princess Alyssatissaprincissa came by with her goats. "Oh, Sir Toad," she called, "Your Royal Highness, where are you?"

Uh-oh! Parsley decided to fly out of danger. She stood tall and croaked. But before she could finish the spell, Princess Alyssatissaprincissa picked her up.

"I apologize, Your Majesty. I didn't know the right way before. Now I'll turn you back into a prince in no time." She hurled Parsley into the side of the bridge.

Oof! Parsley landed in a patch of dirt. *Yow!* She wondered if her back was broken. She lay still and tried not to cry.

Princess Alyssatissaprincissa waded into the stream. Just a toad, she thought, just a stupid toad.

After Princess Alyssatissaprincissa had gone, Parsley sat up carefully. Her back wasn't broken, but she was sore all over. For the first time she understood why Bombina turned people into toads.

Days passed. Randolph and Rudolph fought over linen in twenty towns. They hired extra carriages to carry all the cloth they had to buy. But none of it would pass through a pinky ring.

Tansy had no better luck. In Woolly Podcoomb he bought the best bolt of linen he saw, hoping it was better than anything his brothers had found.

The sixth day of the contest dawned sunny and hot. Tansy purchased an apple in the hamlet of Whither Prockington and looked at linen. In Thither Prockington he looked at more linen. He was surprised, two miles farther along, to come upon Hither Prockington, which wasn't on any of the maps in the Royal Library. But Hither Prockington didn't have any fine linen either.

He rode on. After an hour he came to a stream.

Parsley saw the horse and rider coming and hopped under the bridge. Tansy let Bhogs drink and slipped off her back to stretch his legs.

"It's you!" Parsley cried—and discovered that she could speak.

Tansy thought he'd heard a voice, but he didn't see anyone.

Parsley hopped toward him. "Prince Tansy! Your Highness!" She wished she could hop faster. He was only a few yards away, but that was a fair distance now. She thought of flying, but she didn't want to startle him more than he was about to be startled.

Tansy was sure a maiden was calling him. Was she hiding under the bridge? He started toward it.

"Pray watch your feet."

He stood still.

"Look down, Your Highness."

A chartreuse Biddlebum Toad blinked up at him. A talking toad! Was he bewitched?

"I'm so glad to see you." Parsley tried to curtsy and almost toppled. "Especially without your wicked brothers."

Tansy gasped and fell back a step.

"They're lying snitching stinkers."

It's the heat, Tansy thought. I'm hearing things. He rushed to the stream and dunked his head. The cold water felt good.

Parsley hopped down to the stream.

Tansy stood up. He felt his mind clear. He wouldn't hear any talking animals now.

"In truth, I hate your brothers."

The toad again! He *was* bewitched.

"In truth, I admire you. I admire you so."

There she was, chartreuse and warty and smiling at him. Such a nice smile. Something in his heart fluttered.

Bombina saw Tansy with Parsley. It was that prince again! She began to feel jealous, but she stopped herself. She had sworn not to, and she'd keep her oaths from now on.

"There she was, chartreuse and warty
and smiling at him."

Maybe the prince would be good for something. After all, her Parsley's smile was still the sweetest most adorable sight there was. Maybe . . .

Tansy sat on the riverbank and moaned. "I'm bewitched."

"No, you're not." Parsley opened her mouth to tell him about her transformation, but the words wouldn't come. She croaked to clear her throat and tried again, but she still couldn't. She stood on her left leg, spun around, and hopped twice, hoping to get some magic going, but nothing happened.

He watched her. He'd never seen a toad spin before.

She gave up. "You're not bewitched, Your Highness. I'm a talking toad." Maybe this would convince him. "If you were bewitched, you'd hear your horse speak too, wouldn't you?"

Perhaps she was right. He went to Bhogs, who was grazing near the weeping willow. "Bhogs, speak to me. Am I bewitched?"

Bhogs switched her tail and went on grazing, which meant either she couldn't speak or she didn't have anything to say. Either way, he could still be bewitched.

"If you were bewitched, the fish would be talking to you, and so would the dragonflies and the caterpillars and the"—Parsley's tongue snaked out. She snagged a gnat and swallowed it—"and the gnats and the . . ."

Maybe he was only a little bewitched, just enough to understand Toad.

Parsley decided to change the subject. "What brings you here, Prince Tansy?"

He didn't want to be rude and not answer, even if he was only imagining that the toad was speaking. If there really was a toad.

He sat again. "My father has set a contest for my brothers and me." He told her about the test and the prize. "The linen I bought isn't nearly good enough."

"I can help you!" Oh, it was wonderful to be a magical creature! "I can give you linen fine enough to go through the eye of a needle."

"If only you really could." He sighed.

Parsley felt irritated. How could she prove herself? She couldn't. He wouldn't believe the linen she made was real, no matter what. But maybe he'd believe it when his father gave him that golden medallion.

She had an idea. "Close your eyes, Your Highness."

Tansy closed his eyes, certain that when he opened them, he'd see a length of perfect linen. Perfect, but imaginary.

Parsley balanced on her left foot, feeling nervous. She had to get this just right. She tapped her nose with the fourth and last finger or toe of her right hand or front foot. Then she bent over and tapped her chin on the ground. Next she croaked at the highest pitch she could manage. And it worked.

"You can open your eyes."

Tansy did, and there, on the ground near his knee, was about three inches of coarse dirty linen.

Ten

arsley tried not to laugh at Tansy's astonished face. "Put the linen in your saddlebag, Your Highness, and be sure it doesn't fall out."

"Thank you." Feeling silly, Tansy put the useless cloth on top of the bolt he'd purchased. "I must be going." He mounted Bhogs and galloped off without looking back.

"Farewell, dear Prince Tansy."

He shuddered and rode on. When he reached Biddle Castle, servants were unloading bolt after bolt of fabric from Randolph's and Rudolph's carriages. He took his saddlebag and followed the servants to the throne room.

King Humphrey IV was surrounded by a sea of cloth. He didn't know why the lads had carried so much home and why all of it was torn, and why none of it was nice enough to wipe his nose on.

"I have better linen somewhere, Father," Randolph said desperately. "I don't know where it's gotten to."

"I have better linen too," Rudolph said. "I don't know where mine has gotten to."

As soon as he saw the torn cloth, Tansy knew that his brothers had fought over every bolt. But most of it still looked better than the stuff he had.

King Humphrey IV said, "You lads are disappointing duffers."

"Father?" Tansy said. "I have linen too." He knelt before the throne and opened his saddlebag.

And the softest, creamiest linen he'd ever seen billowed out.

What? Tansy thought. Where's the scrap the toad gave me? Am I imagining this cloth? His fingers trembled as he drew it out.

"Let us see." Frowning, King Humphrey IV reached for the cloth. He didn't want Tansy to win, but the fabric was the finest he had ever touched. "Superb, son. Sublime."

There *had* been a toad! A magical talking toad.

"It will pass through the eye of a needle, Sire," Tansy said. He'd won! He was going to be king. King of Biddle!

"There's my cloth," Randolph said, "the cloth that I was searching for."

"There's *my* cloth," Rudolph said.

Together they said, "Tansy stole it."

Parsley saw and heard it all, and she hopped up and down in fury. But she dared not fly to Tansy's aid. No one would believe a toad, and Randolph or Rudolph would step on her.

⚓ ⚓ ⚓

"I didn't steal anything!" Tansy said. "I wouldn't."

King Humphrey IV was confused. Tansy probably had filched the fabric. But from which brother? The king looked back and forth from one twin to the other until he was dizzy, but he couldn't tell.

"We shall have another contest." King Humphrey IV paced, threading his way between the mountains of material. Hmm . . . What should it be? he wondered. Hmm . . .

He had it! His grandfather, King Humphrey III, had failed at this quest and had brought home that frightful flea instead.

"Whoever brings us a dog small enough to fit in a walnut shell shall win the throne." There.

Tansy kept protesting that he'd already won until King Humphrey IV said that if he didn't shut up, he wouldn't be allowed to take part in the new contest.

He did shut up, and he set out again with his brothers the next morning. Even though he was angry at his father and the twins, he was glad to be going back to the toad. He wanted to thank her and to apologize for not believing in her. And, of course, he wanted to ask for her help again, to beg for it, if he had to.

At the fork in the road outside Snettering-on-Snoakes, Randolph's carriage and Rudolph's carriage followed Bhogs onto the Biddle Byway.

They mustn't follow me! Tansy thought. One of them might step on the toad and squash her. Or they'd fight over the little dog and hurt it, or one of them would grab it and race home.

Tansy and the twins reached Harglepool. Tansy was trying to figure out how to slip away when he saw puppies playing outside a rickety shed. He made out the shapes of more puppies inside, and he saw a sign— *Best Barkers in Biddle. Ten pence per puppy.*

Some of the pups were tiny. Maybe Randolph and Rudolph could find their dogs here and stop following him.

He tied Bhogs up outside the shed. The carriages rumbled to a stop. Tansy began to go into the shed, but Randolph and then Rudolph pushed past him. He went in behind them.

A woman was sitting on a stool and combing a small dog in her lap.

Randolph said, "Harrumph—"

Rudolph said, "Harrumph, my fine woman—"

Randolph said, "Show me your smallest dog."

Rudolph said, "Show *me* your smallest dog." He glared at Randolph and stamped his foot. The whole shed shook.

Randolph glared at Rudolph.

Tansy tiptoed out of the shed.

Eleven

ansy galloped along the Biddle Byway and finally reached Parsley's stream. He tied Bhogs to the willow and walked slowly and carefully toward the bridge. "Oh, Mistress Toad," he called.

When he came close, Parsley said, "Here I am, Your Highness."

Tansy knelt down. "I apologize for not believing in you. Thank you for helping me, Mistress Toad."

"My name is Parsley, Highness. You're welcome, but I didn't help as much as I'd hoped. You've been most unfairly treated."

"You know!"

"Certainly. You won the contest, and you have to win the next one too. For Biddle's sake." She beamed up at him. "You'd be our best king ever."

That ravishing smile! His heart fluttered again. He blushed and mumbled, "I'd try to be, Parsley."

"You *would* be. If you finally win—"

"I don't think I'll win, unless you help me again. I need—"

"A dog small enough to fit in a walnut." Parsley nodded. "I'll be happy to help."

She had him close his eyes while she made the most charming teensy-weensy dog—curly brown fur with a black patch on its back. Then she hid it.

"Open your eyes."

Tansy saw a coconut in the tall grass.

"Crack it carefully when you get home. The dog's name is Tefaw, which stands for Tiny Enough for a Walnut."

Tansy placed the coconut in his saddle-bag and thanked Parsley at least a dozen times.

She was embarrassed and changed the subject. "If you won and became king, what would you do?"

Tansy sat down. She squatted next to his right hand and never took her eyes off his face.

"I would build small Royal Glass Hills all over Biddle for children to slide down. I'd breed thousands of fireflies and release them for light on dark nights. And every year I'd give a Best Biddler Award in three categories: interesting dreams, knowledge of Biddle history, and acrobatics."

Parsley loved Tansy's plans, and she had some ideas of her own, like letting subjects go on quests and putting their discoveries in the Royal Museum of Quest Souvenirs, or like having the Royal Army build chicken coops for people's chickens during peacetime.

Parsley and Tansy talked for hours. When the

goatherd Princess Alyssatissaprincissa came by, Parsley made a big haystack and hid herself and Tansy inside it.

Bombina watched them talk. Keep smiling, Parsley, she thought. Smile, my love.

Tansy liked Parsley's smile more and more, until he believed that toads were the most beautiful creatures in Biddle. And the smartest and the friendliest.

For her part Parsley admired Tansy more and more. And when he said he'd make toads the Royal Animal and make people pay a fine for squashing them, her heart almost burst with love.

Night came. Tansy stretched out under the bridge, and Parsley settled down a yard or two away, in case he rolled over in his sleep.

They talked the whole next day and the day after that and the day after that, for six days, until Tansy had to return to Biddle Castle.

While he saddled Bhogs, he tried to say how much it had meant to him to talk to her, but he couldn't find the words. He mounted Bhogs and looked down at Parsley. "Thank you, and farewell." He rode off, turning to wave until he could no longer distinguish her from the grass.

Twelve

ansy heard barking as soon as he crossed the Royal Drawbridge. In the throne room puppies were chewing on the Royal Drapes, making messes on the Royal Rug, leaping at Royal Chair Legs and Royal Table Legs and the Royal Legs of Randolph and Rudolph. King Humphrey IV was standing on his throne, lifting his new Royal Ceremonial Robe out of reach.

None of the puppies was small enough to fit in a walnut shell.

"I had a smaller dog somewhere, Father," Randolph said.

"I had a smaller dog too," Rudolph said.

"Remove these puppies," King Humphrey IV roared.

Royal Servants shooed the dogs from the room. King Humphrey IV descended and sat on his throne.

Tansy knelt down. "I have a dog too." He took out the coconut. Using his hunting knife, he cracked it carefully and found a walnut shell inside. He began to smile as he cracked the walnut shell—and found a peanut shell. That Parsley! Grinning broadly, he

"I HAVE A DOG TOO."

cracked the peanut shell and found a pistachio shell, and inside the pistachio shell was Tefaw. The dog pranced around on Tansy's hand and barked an astonishingly deep bark for such a tiny creature.

"There it is," Randolph said. "There's my dog."

"There's *my* dog," Rudolph said.

Together they said, "Tansy stole it."

"I did not steal it!" Tansy yelled. "I got it my—"

"Did too steal it," Randolph hollered.

"Did too steal it," Rudolph screamed.

King Humphrey IV was puzzled. The twins had never lied before. But Tansy did look truthful, and they hadn't said a word about a coconut.

There was only one thing to do. "We will have a final contest. The son who brings home the most beautiful bride will be our heir." The twins would hardly be able to say they'd misplaced a maiden.

Parsley was angrier than she'd ever been before. Tansy won, she thought, fuming. Fair and square.

Bombina wondered why Parsley looked so angry. The fairy watched and waited.

Randolph and Rudolph didn't try to follow Tansy this time. Their carriages turned onto the Royal Road and sped on.

Tansy kicked Bhogs into a gallop. He didn't know what to do. He didn't want to pick a bride just because she was pretty.

Bhogs streaked through Harglepool.

The kindest queen in Biddle history was Queen Lorelei, and her nose had been a bit too big. And although Queen Sonora had been beautiful, she was remembered for her wisdom.

Bhogs dashed through Lower Vudwich.

Besides, no matter how pretty his choice was, his father would probably say Randolph's or Rudolph's choice was prettier.

Bhogs flew though Podcoomb-upon-Hare.

And what if he won and had to marry a maiden he didn't like?

Bhogs tore through Popping Squeak.

He didn't know what to do. The only thing he knew was that he wanted to discuss it with Parsley.

If only he could find a maiden as smart as she was— as smart and sweet and understanding, with a smile that was even half as heartwarming.

There was her stream. He slid off Bhogs's back. "Parsley, where are you?"

She was so happy to see him. She put all her happiness into her smile.

As soon as Tansy saw the smile, he knew. He couldn't marry anyone but Parsley, even if she was a toad. He had to marry his love, if she'd have him.

He dropped to his knees. "Parsley, will you marry me?"

Bombina whooped and yelled, "He did it! My precious Parsley! I love that prince!"

For a moment Parsley just blinked up at Tansy. Her smile froze. Wind rushed by her ears. She'd felt this wind before. What???

Oh no oh no. Her skin was expanding. She was pulsing all over, her insides, her head. *Boom! Boom!* It hurt! And her blood was rushing, swooshing, flooding.

Tansy's dear face, coming closer, looking frightened. And now she was above his head, rising higher. Oh oh oh!

It was over.

Parsley panted, her hand pressed to her chest.

Her hand! She had a hand?

She looked down at herself. She was human again!

It's the maiden from the fairy's palace, Tansy thought, the one with green teeth.

Tansy saved me! Parsley thought. She smiled down at him. "Of course I'll marry you, if you still want me."

"I do!" He could see his beloved toad in her smile and in her eyes.

She said, "Do you like parsley?"

Thirteen

andolph and Rudolph each decided that it didn't matter who they thought was the most beautiful maiden. It only mattered what their father thought.

On the outskirts of Ooth Randolph saw a pretty maiden picking roses in her garden. He stopped his carriage and got out.

Rudolph got out of his carriage.

"I say," Randolph said, "will you marry me if my father the king chooses me to be his heir and chooses you as the most beautiful bride?"

Rudolph said, "Will you marry *me* if the king chooses me to be his heir and chooses you as the most beautiful bride?"

"I asked her first," Randolph yelled.

"I asked her second," Rudolph shouted.

The maiden giggled. She pointed to each of them in turn and said:

"Which son?
Either one.
Pink, gold, blue.
I choose you!"

She pointed at Randolph.

He smirked at Rudolph and climbed back into his carriage. The maiden climbed in after him. The carriages rolled on.

Whenever Randolph and Rudolph passed a pretty maiden, they stopped their carriages and each asked her to marry him if King Humphrey IV chose him as heir and chose her as most beautiful.

Some maidens picked Randolph. Some picked Rudolph. Some refused them both and said:

"Which son?
Neither one.
Pink, gold, gray.
I say nay!"

By the time they reached Moowich, each twin had ten carriages full of maidens.

Tansy and Parsley and Bhogs ambled down the Biddle Byway. At the end of the week they reached Biddle Castle. As soon as she saw it, Parsley felt nervous. She wanted to win the throne for Tansy, but she didn't think she was pretty enough.

In the throne room Randolph's maidens were

milling about on the right side of the room, and Rudolph's were milling about on the left. There were scores of them. King Humphrey IV was glad to see so many winsome wenches, but what kind of kings would the twins be if they couldn't make up their minds about which maiden to marry?

Tansy entered holding Parsley's hand. He led her to the throne, and they both knelt down.

"Father, this is Parsley, the most beautiful maiden in Biddle, the maiden I wish to marry."

"Let us look at you, lass."

Parsley blushed and smiled at King Humphrey IV.

"She's hideous!" Randolph screamed. "Look at her teeth."

"Look at her teeth!" Rudolph shrieked. "She's horrendous!"

No one saw Bombina materialize behind Rudolph's maidens. Luckily for the twins, she didn't hear what they'd just said.

King Humphrey IV noticed the color of the damsel's teeth, but he paid more attention to the loveliness of her smile. With such a smile her teeth could be sprouting fur and he wouldn't mind.

"Sire!" Randolph hissed. "Think of your ripped Royal Robe."

"Sire!" Rudolph hissed. "Think of your broken scepter."

King Humphrey IV frowned. He looked over at Randolph's lasses and beckoned to one of them. He beckoned to a beauty of Rudolph's too. They

approached, and each of them was at least as pretty as
Parsley.

"Oh no you don't!" Bombina belowed. She marched
to the throne. She wouldn't turn the king into a toad,
but she'd turn him into something.

A fairy! King Humphrey IV trembled. He stood
and bowed. Randolph and Rudolph trembled. They
bowed too.

Tansy gasped. She was the one who'd turned
Parsley into a toad! Well, she wasn't going to do it
again. He drew his sword.

Parsley ran into Bombina's arms. "I missed you!"
She smiled up at the fairy.

Tansy sheathed his sword.

Bombina felt dizzy. Her Parsley was smiling at her
again. She began to weep happy tears. "Oh my dear!"

King Humphrey IV thought, The damsel is dear
to a fairy? A fairy's friend would make a fine future
queen. He cleared his throat. "Tansy shall be our heir."

Tansy could hardly believe it. He was going to be
king, and he was going to marry his love. He felt overjoyed, overjoyed in a solemn way. He'd be a fair and
kind king, and he'd make sure his subjects always had
enough bathwater and mittens and—

Randolph screeched, "But I have to be king!"

Rudolph screeched, "But I have to be king!"

Randolph yelled, "Tansy broke the scepter and he
tore—"

Parsley said, "He did not! You both did it and
blamed him."

"They did?" King Humphrey IV looked at the twins. Could this be true? The fairy would know. "Did they?"

Tansy held his breath.

Bombina stared at each twin in turn and used her fairy powers to find out. She nodded. "They did." She felt a thrill. Randolph and Rudolph would make superb toads. She stared at Randolph.

"No!" Parsley yelled.

Bombina stopped staring. "No?"

Parsley considered. Randolph and Rudolph deserved to be toads if anyone did. But Princess Alyssatissaprincissa might propose to one of them, and then he would be a prince all over again. She had an idea. She whispered it to Bombina, who nodded.

The fairy flapped her wings twice, and howled *wee- joon zowowow ay yay ay.*

Epilogue

andolph and Rudolph spun around faster and faster, so fast that they created a tornado in the throne room, and all the pretty maidens wept and whimpered.

At last the twins stopped spinning, and two goatherds stood glaring at each other. Bombina hiccuped twice, and they vanished, one appearing in a meadow just north of Princess Alyssatissaprincissa and the other appearing in a meadow just east of Princess Alyssatissaprincissa.

Parsley and Tansy were married the next day. King Humphrey IV conducted the ceremony, and Bombina gave away the bride. Zeke and Nelly were there, along with Parsley's younger brother, Pepper.

Eventually Randolph married Princess Alyssatissaprincissa, and Rudolph married the princess's sister, Countess Marianabanessacontessa, who was also a goatherd. Having their own separate herds of goats pleased the twins, and they came to like each other.

Bombina never turned anyone into a toad again,

but she performed thousands of other magic tricks for Tansy and Parsley's children, who all inherited their mother's captivating smile.

Tansy was a wonderful king. He put his subjects first, and he rode a tall horse so they were always able to find him. His subjects loved having their own souvenirs in the Royal Museum of Quest Souvenirs, and his subjects' chickens loved the coops the Royal Army built for them.

Bombina's cook taught Parsley's favorite parsley recipes to the Royal Cook, and the Royal Cook invented a few of her own. Parsley's smile grew greener and greener, and she never ate another insect.

And they all, monarchs and subjects and goatherds and fairies, lived happily ever after.

The
Fairy's Return

Love to Betsy and Ben and Amy and Sean

and their animal pals.

—G.C.L.

One

nce upon a time in the kingdom of Biddle a baker's son and a princess fell in love. This is how it came about—

Robin, the baker's son, rode to Biddle Castle in the back of the bakery cart. His older brothers, Nat and Matt, sat on the driver's bench with their father, Jake, who was a poet as well as a baker.

Robin began a joke. "What's a dwarf's—"

"Son," Jake said,

> *"A joker is a fool,*
> *Who never went to a place of learning."*

Nat said, "Jokers are dottydaftish." He had a knack for inventing words.

Matt said, "Jokes are dumdopety." He had a knack for inventing words too.

Robin hated being thought stupid. "Jokes aren't dumb or dopey, and I'm not dotty or daft. If you'd ever listen to a whole joke, you'd see." If they did, they'd realize that jokers were just as smart as poets and word inventors.

Jake just shook his head. Robin was the first moron in family history. Not only did he make up jokes, he also gave things away. Why only a week ago, on the lad's eleventh birthday to be exact, Robin had given a roll to a beggar. For free!

Generosity was against family policy. Jake had told his sons repeatedly never to give anyone something for nothing. He had learned this from his own father, a genius who could make up three poems at once.

The bakery cart rumbled across the Biddle Castle drawbridge. At the door to the Royal Kitchen, Jake reined in their nag, Horsteed, who had been named by Nat.

When all the bread had been carried into the kitchen, Jake began to chat with the Royal Chief Cook. As Jake often said,

> *"A nice customer chat*
> *Puts a coin in your bonnet."*

Nat chatted with the Royal First Assistant Cook, and Matt chatted with the Royal Second Assistant Cook.

Robin began to tell his dwarf joke to the Royal Third Assistant Cook, but the Royal Third Assistant Cook interrupted with his recipe for pickled goose feet with jellied turnips.

Robin disliked jellied anything, so after he'd heard the recipe three times, he said, "How interesting. Please excuse me." He slipped out the Royal Kitchen Door and into the Royal Garden, where commoners weren't allowed.

But he didn't know that.

Two

Dame Cloris, the Royal Governess, sat primly upright on a bench in a small meadow in the garden. Her lace cap had slipped over her face, and it fluttered as she breathed. She was fast asleep.

Princess Lark sat on the grass nearby, her favorite ball a few feet away. She wished she had someone to play with.

Yesterday had been her eleventh birthday, and her birthday party had been awful, just like every other party she'd ever had. The guests had been children of the castle nobility, and the party had begun with a game of hide-and-seek. Lark had taken the first turn as It. While she counted, she wished with all her might that this time her guests would really play with her.

But when she opened her eyes, she saw that no one had hidden. Oh, they were pretending to hide. Aldrich, the Earl of Pildenue's son, was standing next to a tree, with one foot concealed behind it. And his sister, Cornelia, had stationed herself behind a bush that only came up to her waist.

The children wouldn't hide because they were afraid Lark would fail to find them. And not one of them dared to let a princess fail at anything.

She had told them she wouldn't mind. She had also said she wouldn't mind being It forever. But it didn't matter what she said.

The next activity, baseball, was even worse. When Lark was at bat, if she hit the ball at all—a yard, a foot, half an inch—no one tried to catch it. They thought it would be disrespectful to make a princess out, so Lark had to dash around the bases for a home run she hadn't earned.

When the other team was at bat, they tried not to hit the ball, because it would never do for their team to beat Lark's.

Lark declared the game over after one inning and declared the party over too. She ate her birthday cake alone—the single bite she was able to get down before she ran to her room, sobbing.

And now here she was, in the garden with her ball and a sleeping governess. She watched idly as Robin approached. She noticed that his jerkin was plain brown, without even the tiniest jewel. How unusual. And there was a hole in his breeches.

She sat up straight. His feet were bare. He was a commoner!

Lark had never spoken to a commoner. Maybe he'd be different.

Robin had no idea who the old lady and the lass

were. He only knew the lass looked sad. Maybe a joke would cheer her up, if she'd let him tell it.

"Hello," he said. "What's a dwarf's . . ." She wasn't interrupting. He began to feel nervous. ". . . favorite food?"

She smiled up at him. He hadn't bowed, which was wonderful. But she had no idea what the answer was. The king of the dwarfs had visited Biddle last year, but she couldn't remember what he'd eaten. "Potatoes?"

Robin's heart started to pound. She was going to listen to the punch line! "No. Strawberry shortcake." He waited.

"Why straw—" Then she knew. She started laughing. A dwarf! Strawberry *shortcake*!

Robin laughed too, for sheer delight. She liked the joke! He sat down next to her and tried another one. "Which rank of nobility is best at math?"

Was this another joke? "The earl?"

"No. He's earl-y and catches the worm."

She pictured Aldrich's father grubbing for worms. That was so funny.

Robin thought she had the best laugh, gurgly and tinkly. "It's the count."

Numbers! A count! She laughed harder.

Robin thought, She has a superb sense of humor.

Dame Cloris, the governess, snored, a long rattle followed by two snorts. Robin and Lark giggled.

"Why is a king like a yardstick?"

Lark tried to guess. Her father didn't look anything like a yardstick, not with his bad posture. She gave up and shrugged.

"They're both rulers."

She laughed. Rulers! The king would love it. "I can't wait to tell Father."

Robin frowned. "You're lucky. My father hates jokes. Is your father a Royal Servant?"

He didn't know? Oh, no! As soon as she told him, he'd turn stiff and uncomfortable, just like everybody else. She thought of lying, but she didn't like to lie, and he was too nice to lie to anyway. "No. He's the king."

He blinked. "Then you're—"

She nodded. "I'm Princess Lark."

Three

obin jumped up and bowed. A princess liked his jokes! Bowing wasn't enough. He took her hand and pumped it up and down.

Lark was delighted. Most people were afraid to touch her. "What's your name?"

"Robin."

"We both have bird names!" It was amazing.

"I wouldn't like to be named Spoonbill." He grinned. "Or Swallow. Good morning, Master Swallow. How did your breakfast go down?"

"Or my name could be Vulture. Good morning, Princess Vulture. I hate to think what you had for breakfast." She stood up. "Why doesn't your father like your jokes?"

"I don't know why."

He looks sad, Lark thought. "They're terrific jokes. How do you think of them?"

"I don't know." He blushed. "I just do."

"All the time?"

"Except when I'm unhappy or angry. Then I can't

make up any. I can't even remember my old ones." He changed the subject. He didn't like to think about being jokeless. "Why is a bakery—"

Dame Cloris moaned in her sleep.

"Who's she?"

"She's Dame Cloris, my governess." Lark giggled. "She's a deep sleeper. Why is a bakery what?"

"Oh. Why is a bakery like a garden?"

Lark tried to figure it out. One was outdoors and one was indoors. That wasn't it. She stopped trying. It was more fun to let him surprise her. "I give up."

"They're both flowery." Or floury, he thought.

She chuckled. "You're clever."

That wasn't what his father and brothers thought. "My father's a baker. You should visit our bakery. It's in Snettering-on-Snoakes. You could come tomorrow." If she came, he wouldn't have to wait a week to see her again. "Or the next day." And maybe she'd make Jake and Nat and Matt listen to a joke.

"I'd like to come."

"When you do, could you order me to tell you a joke, a whole one, all the way through?"

She nodded. Nobody had ever asked for her help before. They just wanted to do things for her.

Robin could hardly wait. Everything would change when his family heard a whole joke. He loved Lark!

He was so happy, he had to do something. He picked up her ball and gave it to her. "Want to play catch?"

Did she! She threw him the ball. He threw it back.

He threw hard. He didn't seem to care if she failed to catch it. This was what she'd always wanted. This was heavenly.

She was terrible at catch, since she'd never had a chance to practice. But she was happy to chase the ball and throw it back as well as she could.

Sometimes when she missed the ball, it wasn't her fault, though. He kept telling jokes and timing them so that she was laughing when he threw the ball. He was playing tricks to *make* her miss. She loved him!

The ball bounced off her arm. She and Robin ran after it, but—

Oh no! It hit Dame Cloris's skirts, right below the knee.

Dame Cloris yelped and opened her eyes. A commoner! With Princess Lark! She screamed, and then she fainted.

Lark and Robin rushed to her. Two Royal Garden Guards came on the run. One waved smelling salts under Dame Cloris's nose. The other picked Robin up by his collar and carried him away.

Robin yelled, "Don't forget! Come to the bakery."

"I'll be there."

The guard dumped Robin at the Royal Kitchen Door. "Stay out of the garden," he growled, and marched off. Robin slipped into the kitchen, where Jake and Nat and Matt were ending their customer chats.

On the way back to Snettering-on-Snoakes Robin

"A COMMONER! WITH PRINCESS LARK!"

announced, "While you were talking, I played catch with Princess Lark, and—"

"You falsfibbulator!" Nat started laughing. "That's the sillfooliest thing I ever heard!"

Matt laughed too. "It's nutcrazical!"

Jake stopped the cart. "Matt! Natt! I mean Nat! Matt! Don't make fun of Robin just because he isn't as brilliant as we are. He only *wishes* he could meet a princess and play—"

"I don't only—"

"But it's a bad wish." Jake was proud to be a commoner and wouldn't have wanted to play catch with a king.

"Royalty and commoners must never mix.
Remember this, or you will be in a predicament."

"She's going to come to the bakery." So there.

Jake was shocked. Robin truly believed he'd met the princess. He was too stupid to know what was real and what wasn't. He was an imbecile.

Robin repeated, "She's coming. And she likes my jokes. You'll see."

Four

n the Royal Dining Hall that evening, Lark said, "Father . . ."

"Harrumph?"

"Today I played with the lad I want to marry someday." She laughed, remembering the ruler joke.

The king smiled. His daughter had a lovely laugh, and he didn't hear it often enough. "Well, harrumph?" Meaning, *Well, who?* King Humphrey V was known far and wide as King Harrumphrey.

"He's Robin, the baker's son. He told—"

King Harrumphrey's face turned red. "You're not harrumphying any harrumpher's son!"

"I will so harrumphy him, I mean, marry him!"

"Harrumph!"

The next morning Lark told Dame Cloris that she wanted to go to Snettering-on-Snoakes.

Dame Cloris yawned. "I'm feeling too sleepy, Your Highness. I can't go with you . . . and you can't go without me."

The following day Dame Cloris said she was still

too sleepy. The day after that she was too tired, and the next day she was too sleepy again.

Lark appealed to her father. "It would be educational for me," she said. "I'd meet our subjects."

King Harrumphrey frowned. Was the baker's son behind this? "You don't have to meet any harrumphs. When the Royal Chief Councillor puts our golden harrumph on your head someday, you'll harrumph all you need in an instant."

"But Father, what if I don't harru—know all I need?"

"Sweetharrumph, trust us, commoners are harrumph. Even worse, they're harrumph."

"Please, can't I go? I won't stay long."

"No, you can't. Not for all the harrumph in Kulornia."

Robin was miserable when Lark didn't come to the bakery the next day or the next. He couldn't even cheer himself up with jokes, because he was too upset to think of any. And it didn't help that Nat kept calling him His Hikingness, and that Matt kept saying, "Where's your prinroycess?"

It crossed Robin's mind that Lark had only pretended to like his jokes. After all, nobody else liked them.

But she *had* liked them. He was sure of it. And she had liked him. He couldn't have imagined it.

Maybe she'd hurt herself and couldn't come. Or maybe that snooty Dame wouldn't let her come. That must have been it. He felt better and made up three jokes.

The next time they delivered bread, he'd find out what had happened. He'd tell the new jokes, and he'd get proof that they'd met. Maybe she'd write on Royal Stationery that she thought he was clever and his jokes were funny.

Most important of all, when he saw her, he'd tell her he loved her.

But Jake wouldn't take him to the castle anymore. He said,

> *"To the castle you could come*
> *If you weren't so darn moronic."*

That made Robin mad. He wasn't moronic! And if his father wouldn't take him, he'd go on his own.

Every afternoon one of the brothers went to Snoakes Forest to chop wood for the bakery oven. Whoever it was packed a picnic lunch, took the family's ax, and set off.

When it was his turn, Robin chopped the wood as fast as he could. Then he hiked past the Sleep In Inn, through fields and low hills, and on to Biddle Castle.

On the way he thought of a dozen more jokes. The seventh was his favorite: Why do noblemen like to stare? Because they're peers.

He pictured Lark's reaction. First surprise, and then her musical laugh, which would make him feel prouder than a prince and smarter than anyone in his whole family tree.

But when Robin reached the castle, he couldn't get past the Royal Drawbridge Guard.

He tried again on his next seven turns chopping wood. Sometimes the Royal Drawbridge Guard stopped him. He got past that guard a few times, only to be stopped by the Royal Castle Door Guard or the Royal Garden Gate Guard. Once, he managed to enter the castle, but the moment he put his foot on the Royal Grand Staircase, the Royal Grand Staircase Guard rushed at him and tossed him out as if he were a sack of flour.

Oh, Lark! Oh, love! He might never see her again, the one person in Biddle who appreciated a good joke.

Five

wo years passed, but Lark didn't forget Robin. How could she, when he was the only one who'd ever treated her as a normal person? How could she, when the last time she'd laughed had been with him?

King Harrumphrey tried to make her laugh. He'd sneak up on her and tickle her. But she'd stopped being ticklish long ago. He'd make funny faces. They might have made her laugh, if it hadn't been his fault she couldn't visit Robin. So she'd scowl instead.

The king often sent the Royal Jester to amuse her. But the jester was as afraid of offending her as everybody else. So he'd just turn cartwheels and never tell jokes. And his cartwheels weren't that funny.

Two more years passed. Nat became betrothed to Holly, the oldest of the Sleep In innkeeper's three daughters. Matt became betrothed to the middle sister, Molly.

Robin had stopped thinking of Lark a hundred times a day. Whenever he did remember her, he concentrated on something else to keep from feeling bad.

He still hadn't succeeded in telling his family a complete joke. He would have given up, but jokes are meant to be told, and they'd pop out in spite of himself.

And he still hadn't convinced his family that he wasn't simpleminded. One day, in desperation, he gave in and tried word inventing. He said, "I may not be brillbrainiant, but I'm smarquick enough."

But Nat said, "Stupidated people always think they're keenwittish."

And Matt said, "Your words are the flimflawsiest I've ever heard."

Jake, however, thought Robin's invented words were a good sign. He began to hope that his youngest boy was finally catching up to the rest of the family.

That is, until the day Robin gave an entire muffin to the tailor. Robin was at the front of the bakery, taking coins and making change from the cash box. The tailor, who was the poorest person in Snettering-on-Snoakes, stepped forward with a halfpenny for the leg of a gingerbread man. Robin saw him look hungrily at a blueberry muffin.

Robin glanced around. Nat was taking scones out of the oven. Matt was in the storeroom. And Jake was looking down as he rolled out dough.

Robin grabbed a blueberry muffin just as Jake raised his head. The baker watched, appalled, as Robin passed the muffin to the tailor.

"Stop!" Jake shouted.

"'Stop!' Jake shouted."

The tailor ran out of the shop.

Jake's hopes for Robin collapsed. The lad didn't understand proper behavior. Jake repeated his rule slowly.

"Never ever give anything away for free,
As my father said. Listen to him and to I."

From then on Jake wouldn't let Robin do anything except knead dough, the most boring job in the bakery. Robin hated it, and he despaired of ever proving he wasn't thickheaded.

A week later Golly, the youngest of the innkeeper's daughters, sat herself down on the bench next to Robin's kneading table. She said, "Dearie, I fear you're worrying about me."

Why? he wondered. Was something wrong with her? She looked healthy.

"You're fretting that I won't marry you."

He stopped kneading.

She went on. "Some wenches may not want a stupid husband, dearie, but I do. I'm bossy, so when we're wed, I'll run the Sleep In and I'll run you."

Robin gulped. "I'm not marrying anybody." Lark flashed into his mind. Once he would have liked to marry her.

Golly poked his arm and laughed. "At the inn, your job will be fluffing up the pillows. That's like kneading, dearie."

Jake left his cake batter and came to them.

"*Son, Golly will make a fine wife,*
Since your mind's not sharp as a dagger."

"I'm not marrying anybody."
Jake laughed along with Golly.

Six

olly sat with Robin all morning, and she didn't stop talking for a second. She told him who would be invited to their wedding and which songs would be sung and which dances danced. She told him what jerkin to wear on the wedding day and which side to part his hair on.

He didn't knead the dough that morning. He punched it and squashed it and strangled it.

Eventually Golly left to have her lunch at the inn. Robin packed his own lunch in a basket and left too. It was his turn to chop wood, but first he needed to walk off the hours with Golly. He circled around the Sleep In so she wouldn't see him and headed for the hills and fields south of Biddle Castle.

He wasn't far from the castle when he heard someone singing in the distance. He stood still. He'd heard that voice before. He heard a deeper sound. It was familiar too. He ran toward the sounds.

When he got closer, he could hear the words to the song.

"O alas. O alack.
O woe is me.
I've lost my true love,
And I'll never fly free."

As he ran, he thought, That's odd. *Me* rhymes with free.

Almost a mile from Robin, Lark was sitting on the bank of Snoakes Stream. She'd pulled her skirts up to her knees and had taken off her slippers and her hose. Her feet dangled in the stream. She was feeding the ducks and singing her heart out.

"My love's not a widgeon,
Nor a pigeon."

Those are birds! Robin thought. He ran faster.

"My love's not a macaw,
Nor a jackdaw."

The voice was farther away than he'd thought. He was getting near the castle.

"My love's not a waterfowl,
Nor a tawny owl.
O alas. O alack.
O woe is me.
I've lost my Robin . . ."

A robin! Me? He was out of breath, but he managed one last burst of speed.

There they were. An elderly lady with a lace cap over her face was snoring on a blanket. And Lark was on the stream bank.

"And we'll never fly free."

He rushed to her. "Lark!"

She turned. "Robin?" She stood, almost losing her footing on the slippery stones in the stream. Her skirts trailed in the water. She smiled radiantly. "Robin!"

He thought of a joke. "What does the postal coach driver wear in cold weather?"

A joke! Lark hadn't felt so happy in years. "I don't know. What?"

He'd missed her so. He hadn't realized how much till now. He forgot about the joke and just smiled at her.

Dame Cloris stirred on the blanket. In her dream King Harrumphrey was making her a countess.

Lark prompted Robin. "What?"

What what? Oh, the joke. "When it's cold out, the postal coach driver wears a coat of mail."

She thought for a second, then laughed. A coat of mail! A coat of letters!

He'd never stopped loving her, not for a minute, whether he'd known it or not.

She began to climb out of the stream, but she lost

her balance. "Oh, no!" She reached out to Robin. Before he could grab her, she fell backward into the water with a big splash.

In the governess's dream, the king's sword clanged. He touched it to her forehead. "I harrumph you a Royal Harrumphess."

Robin thought Lark might be hurt. He waded in. She laughed and splashed him.

He splashed her back. She was delighted. No one else would have splashed her. She held out her hands as if she wanted him to help her up, but when he took them, she pulled him down.

Water got in his nose. He snorted and shook the hair out of his eyes. He splashed Lark again.

She laughed.

Dame Cloris's snore changed pitch. She dreamed there was a commotion at the door of the Royal Throne Room.

Lark brushed the water out of her eyes. "I missed you," she said. "I tried to go to your bakery, but nobody would let me."

She did try! "I went to the castle to find you."

"You did?"

Dame Cloris whimpered. In her dream, seven commoners strode into the throne room.

Robin said, "But I couldn't get to you. The guards kept stopping me." He took a deep breath. "I love you."

"I love you. Will you marry me?"

Robin knelt in the water. "Yes, I'll marry you. I'm

honored. I'm . . ." He leaned over to kiss her hand.

In the dream the commoners chanted, "No count-esses for governesses! No governesses for countesses!" Dame Cloris woke up. She opened her eyes and saw Lark and Robin in the water. She screamed.

Seven

A Royal Drawbridge Guard, his sword drawn, raced to Dame Cloris's aid.

Robin surged out of the stream and ran, calling behind him, "I love you."

Lark called back, "I love you. Remember, we're betrothed."

Dame Cloris fainted. The guard picked her up along with Lark's slippers and hose. He escorted Lark to the Royal Throne Room, where she stood in her bare feet, dripping on the Royal Tile Floor. He placed Dame Cloris on a chair. She revived and told the king what she'd witnessed.

King Harrumphrey yelled *"Harrumph!"* for a full five minutes. Lark just looked defiant.

Finally, his anger collapsed. "Larkie, why do you want to harrumphy him?"

"He makes me laugh." And he treated her like she was an ordinary person. And she loved to be with him.

The king thought about it. There was nothing

wrong with laughter. But laughing with a commoner was vulgar. Laughing with a prince was excellent.

Hmm . . . He summoned the Royal Chief Scribe.

"We wish to harrumph a proclamation."

The scribe unrolled a scroll and dipped her pen in ink.

"Hear harrumph. Hear harrumph."

Hear ye. Hear ye, the scribe wrote.

"Insofar and inasharrumph that we have a harrumphter . . ."

Insofar and inasmuch as we have a scepter . . .

"Not this harrumphter." The king raised his scepter. "That harrumphter." He pointed at Lark.

. . . daughter . . .

King Harrumphrey continued.

Lark listened, horror-struck.

"And said harrumphter, Princess Harrumph, is old harrumph to marry—"

"Father!"

He ignored her and went on.

The scribe wrote, *. . . and said daughter, Princess Lark, is old enough to marry, then let it be known that we will bestow her hand upon any . . .* She was stuck again. She thought for a moment and wrote, *. . . man who . . . .*

King Harrumphrey tapped the scroll. "Not that 'any harrumph.'"

The scribe wrote *noble* in tiny letters to the left of *man.*

The king was getting annoyed. "Not 'any harrumphman.' 'Any harrumph.'"

"He means 'any baker's son,'" Lark said.

King Harrumphrey frowned, and the scribe knew better than to write *baker's son*.

The king roared, "Harrumph! Any prince who can make said princess harrumph."

. . . *any prince who can make said princess harrumph.* The scribe crossed out *harrumph*. Happy! Must be. She wrote, *happy*.

"Not 'harrumphy.'" King Harrumphrey paused. He wanted Lark to be happy. And she would be. The proclamation would make sure of it. "Not 'harrumphy.' 'Harrumph.'"

In turn the scribe tried *wise, good at checkers, able to speak six languages, say harrumph more often, live a long time*. The scroll was getting messy, and she was going to have to copy it all over, if she ever figured out what it was supposed to say.

At last, the king shook his belly and said, "Har har har harrumph."

She got it.

Hear ye. Hear ye. Insofar and inasmuch as we have a daughter, and said daughter, Princess Lark, is old enough to marry, then let it be known that we will bestow her hand upon any prince who can make said princess laugh.

After he finished chopping wood, Robin returned to the bakery and started kneading again. He felt so joyful that new jokes were coming to him as fast as he could think.

Nat said, "Father has splenthrillous news, Robin."

"The king roared, 'Harrumph!'"

Today's a good day for good news, Robin thought, smiling.

Jake cleared his throat and announced that Nat, Matt, and Robin would wed Holly, Molly, and Golly in two weeks. He added, "From then on,

> *"Nat and Matt will roll dough for the pie tin,*
> *While Robin fluffs up pillows at the hotel."*

Robin's jokes stopped coming, and he almost screamed. Golly was the last person he wanted for a wife. She didn't have a bit of Lark's sweetness, Lark's sense of humor, Lark's complete lovableness.

He took a deep breath. He was going to marry Lark. She'd tell her father about their betrothal, and then she'd come to him or send for him, or whatever royalty would do.

But what if the king didn't want him to marry her?

Well, maybe he wouldn't at first. But she'd persuade him. She'd tell him how much they loved each other. He'd understand.

Eight

ark couldn't sleep all night. What if a real prince made her laugh? What if he told a joke almost as good as one of Robin's, and she laughed before she caught herself? She wouldn't love the prince, but she'd be stuck with him.

She worried about it till dawn. Finally she decided that she had to make herself sad, so sad there'd be no chance of a laugh, no matter what any ridiculous prince said.

While she dressed, she thought of the calamities that befell people every day. They stubbed their toes, lost their favorite hat feathers, put spoiled raspberries into their mouths, were stung by bees, misspelled words, dropped their candy in the dirt. The list was endless.

A tear trickled down her cheek.

While she waited for the first prince to come, she read tragedies in the Royal Library. Within a few days she was weeping steadily. She cried herself to sleep at night and woke up crying in the morning.

King Harrumphrey hated to see her cry. It made him feel like crying too. He would have done almost anything to make his Larkie happy. Anything but let her marry a commoner.

A week before Robin's wedding to Golly, the first prince arrived at Biddle Castle. He was taken to the Royal Tournament Arena to perform before an audience of Lark, King Harrumphrey, Dame Cloris, the Royal Councillors, and any Royal Nobles who wanted to come. No commoners allowed.

The prince juggled cheeses while a mouse stood on his head. The councillors and the courtiers and the king laughed and slapped their knees. Lark wept.

In the next five days, more princes came and performed. A prince told shepherd jokes. His best joke was *Why is a bandit like a shepherd's staff?* The punch line was *They're both crooks.* The audience hooted with laughter. Lark rolled her eyes and wished for Robin. Then she wept.

A prince talked to his foot and pretended it was answering him. Lark recited under her breath, "Suffering, tribulation, death, drought, plague . . ." She wept.

After each performance she asked for permission to marry Robin, but the king always harrumphed no.

Two days remained before the wedding. Robin had heard nothing from Lark, and he was desperate to know what had happened. While he kneaded bread, he worried that the king had refused to let her marry

"The prince juggled cheeses while a
mouse stood on his head."

him. He also feared she had decided his jokes weren't any good and had changed her mind about loving him.

Golly, standing at his elbow, talked about going to Ooth Town for their honeymoon to see the roundest clock in Biddle. Then she left to try on her wedding dress.

Someone in the bakery said the word *princess*.

Robin's head shot up. He stopped kneading.

"What seems to be the princess's troublicament?" Nat asked the schoolteacher.

"She never stops crying. Give me six scones."

Oh, no! Robin tried not to shout. "Why is she cry-ing?"

"I'm not sure, but the king is going to marry her off to the first person who makes her laugh." The schoolteacher didn't know the person had to be a prince. "The contest is being held in the tournament arena."

Robin knocked over the kneading table and rushed out of the bakery. He had to think.

Back inside, Matt said, "The lad is flipliddified and madaddlated."

Robin paced up and down in the bakery yard. When the schoolteacher had said that Lark was weep-ing, Robin had thought it meant the king had refused to let them marry. And then, for one glorious moment, when the schoolteacher had described the contest, he'd thought it was for him, that it was Lark's way of bringing them together. But if it was, then why was she crying?

Something terrible must have happened.

He started striding to the castle. He'd tell the guards he wanted to compete in the contest, so they'd let him in. He had to find out what was going on, although he wouldn't be able to compete. He was much too upset to make up jokes.

But the Royal Drawbridge Guard wouldn't let him pass. The guard didn't even let him say what he was there for.

Robin was beside himself. He'd have to marry Golly, or he'd have to run away, far from Lark. Either way, he'd lose his love. On his way home, he broke down and cried.

Golly thought a weeping Robin was the funniest thing she'd ever seen. Jake gave her towels to dry off the dough as Robin kneaded it. She wiped and laughed for an hour or two. Then she went back to the Sleep In, to monogram an extra dozen handkerchiefs for her trousseau.

Through his tears Robin watched her go. He wished Golly were a princess and that Lark were an innkeeper's daughter. He wished the guard had let him in. He wished Lark were here right this second. He wished.

Nine

ate that night the fairy Ethelinda flew over Biddle. She'd been flying for seven years, ever since she'd left the court of Anura, the fairy queen. Anura had scolded her for not giving a single reward or punishment to a human in centuries. Ethelinda had explained that she was afraid to because she'd bungled it the last time.

"Conquer your fear!" Anura had commanded. "Mingle with humans. Reward and punish. Do not disobey me!"

Ethelinda hadn't obeyed, but she hadn't disobeyed either. She'd just stayed in the air. But now she had to land. Seven years of flying were too much, even for a fairy. She was exhausted. She looked for a secluded spot where humans were unlikely to come. Ah. There.

She landed in a clearing in Snoakes Forest and stretched out under a pine tree, where she fell fast asleep.

The next morning, Jake packed a breakfast for Nat

and sent him off early to chop wood. There was a lot to do today, and he wanted his two smart sons there to help him. He had to bake the usual quantities of bread, muffins, and scones, and he had to make the wedding cake for tomorrow.

Nat entered Snoakes Forest and went straight to the clearing where Ethelinda lay sleeping.

His footsteps woke her. She jumped up and took the shape of an old woman. She hoped whoever was coming wouldn't do anything that required a reward or a punishment.

Nat entered the clearing. Ethelinda frowned at his basket, hoping he didn't have food in there. "Good day," she said in a voice that wavered.

"Good day." Nat smiled and bowed. He opened the basket and took out a jug of blackberry juice, three hard-boiled partridge eggs, and two fig-and-almond scones.

The dreaded meal! Ethelinda thought. The fairy rules were very clear. She had to ask the human to share. If he did share, she had to reward him. If he did not, she had to punish him.

"Kind sir," she said, "would you share your victuals with me?"

Nat knew Jake's rule. "No, Mistress. I am enorm-vastically sorry, but our family doesn't give our edibles or sippables to anyone."

She had to punish him! "So be it," she said. So be what? What should she do? She was shaking like a leaf.

Nat ate his breakfast.

Ethelinda thought of making him choke on a bone. But eggs and scones don't have bones. She didn't want to make snakes and insects come out of his mouth, because that hadn't been a great success the last time.

Nat patted his mouth with his napkin and stood up. "Please excusion me. Time to get to work." He picked up his ax and went to an oak tree.

She got it! She waved her wand, which was invisible because of her disguise.

Nat swung the ax. It slammed into the air six inches from the tree and stopped. It wouldn't go an inch closer no matter how hard he pushed.

"Huh? What—" He swung again. The ax stopped again.

He examined the ax. The blade was as sharpcuttable as ever. Something was protecting the tree. He reached out, expecting the something to stop his hand. But nothing did. He swung again. The ax slammed into the air and stopped again.

He frowned at the old lady. Did she cause this?

But she was leaning back against an elm tree with her eyes closed. Besides, what could she have done?

It must have been that tree. He went to a pine tree and swung the ax. It stopped six inches from the bark.

He ran from tree to tree, trying to chop down one after another. But he couldn't, not a single one. He screamed, not an invented word, not a word at all, only a scream. He ran out of the clearing, still screaming.

Ethelinda resumed her fairy shape. She'd done it. Anura should be satisfied. Ethelinda flapped her wings—and barely got off the ground. She was still exhausted. She landed in a heap and stayed there.

When Nat got home from the forest, he was muttering to himself and swinging the ax wildly. Matt feared that he might have become as goofdoltish as Robin, and Jake agreed. They pinned Nat to the ground and took the ax.

Robin didn't notice. Tomorrow was the wedding. It would be the end of everything.

Matt packed a brunch. If Nat couldn't cut down a tree, he, Matt, certainly would be able to. Hadn't he been axchopperizing trees since he was seven years old? He set off while Jake mixed batter for three dozen muffin tins.

As soon as Ethelinda heard Matt coming, she turned herself back into the old lady. When he too refused to share his meal, she punished him exactly as she'd punished Nat.

Jake became seriously worried when Matt returned in the same state as Nat. Jake thought,

> *Now all my sons have lost their wits,*
> *And Nat and Matt are having conniptions.*

Jake couldn't go to the forest himself. He had twenty-seven loaves of bread in the oven plus all those muffins and no sane son to watch them. Robin would have to go. Jake packed a lunch and put the ax in Robin's hand. He watched Robin go and then got to work on the wedding cake.

Ethelinda was delighted to see Robin. This punishment was terrific. She couldn't wait to use it again.

Robin put down his basket. It didn't occur to him to eat. He wasn't thinking at all. His mind was just bleating *Lark! Lark!* again and again. He staggered to a maple tree and raised his ax.

"Wait, kind sir!" Ethelinda went to him and stopped his hand. "Don't you want your lunch?"

What was she saying? Something about his lunch? He mumbled, "Don't want it."

"Oh, kind sir, may I have some?"

Lark! Lark! He raised the ax again.

"Kind sir!" Ethelinda shrieked. She grabbed the ax and wrestled it away from Robin. She faced him, panting. "May I eat some of your lunch?"

Lark! Lark! "Go ahead."

Go ahead?

Oh no! She handed the ax back to him. Now she had to reward him, which was where she'd made her biggest mistake the last time.

She opened his basket and took out a wedge of Snetter cheese and a poppy-seed roll. What could she give him? She couldn't think of a single foolproof reward.

Robin began to chop down the maple.

Then Ethelinda remembered a reward the fairy queen, Anura, had told her about. It was a bit odd, but Anura said she'd used it hundreds of times and it had always worked.

Robin raised the ax again. One more chop and the

maple would go over.

Ethelinda raised her invisible wand.

Robin swung the ax.

Ethelinda waved the wand.

The tree went over.

Honk! A golden goose stood on the stump, ruffling her golden feathers.

"HONK!"

Ten

obin didn't notice the goose. He began to hack off the maple's branches.

"Oh," Ethelinda said, "what a beautiful golden goose!"

Robin felt a stab of exasperation. "You can have her."

Ethelinda stared in shock at him. And saw how unhappy he looked. "Why, what's the trouble, kind sir?"

He shook his head and chopped the maple into logs.

She made her voice sympathetic and comforting. "You can tell me. I'll understand."

The sweetness of her voice reached him. He looked up. Ethelinda made her expression kindly and patient.

He found himself talking. "I love Princess Lark and I hate . . ." He told the whole story. It was a relief to tell someone.

Ethelinda wasn't sure what good the goose would do, but she had faith in Anura. "Pick up the goose," she said. "Take her to the castle."

"I won't be able to get past the guards." He didn't move.

"Pick up the goose!" Ethelinda bellowed.

He began to pick up the logs.

"With that goose, no one will stop you." Ethelinda didn't know if this was true, but she'd make it true.

He dropped the logs and picked up the goose.

Honk!

He didn't believe no one would stop him, but he'd try anyway.

Ethelinda asked where he was going, just to make sure.

"To the princess."

At last. "The goose is sticky, so you may need these words: *Loose, goose.* Don't forget them."

The goose was sticky? What did that mean? Robin picked up a fallen leaf and touched it to the goose's feathers. It stuck. He said, "Loose, goose." The leaf fluttered to the ground.

Hmm. He had an idea. He left the clearing, walking fast.

Ethelinda brushed grass off her skirts. She felt rested, refreshed. She hurried after Robin. "I'll come too, kind sir. I may be able to help if anything goes wrong."

When he got near the Sleep In, Robin slowed to a saunter. If Golly didn't see him, he'd bang on the door. If he had to, he'd shove the goose up against her.

Upstairs in the inn, Golly was embroidering and

looking out the window. Huh! she thought. There was Robin, with a goose in his arms and an old woman at his side. Golly squinted. What a fine golden goose. She frowned. Why wasn't he bringing the goose to her?

Because he was her dim-witted dearie. She laughed. "Look!"

Holly and Molly came to the window.

"We could cook the goose and share the feathers," Golly said.

The three of them ran downstairs and crowded out of the inn. Robin pretended not to see them and hurried off again.

"Dearie," Golly called, laughing. "Wait for me."

He kept going. They ran after him. Golly reached him first. She grabbed the goose's tail and pulled.

Honk!

Golly laughed. "Dearie!"

Robin heard her, but he didn't turn around. He hoped Holly and Molly would touch the goose too, and he hoped they'd stick too. Otherwise Golly had better look very funny, because she was all he'd have to make Lark laugh.

The goose pecked Golly's arm.

Yow! Golly tried to let go, but she couldn't. She stopped laughing. She was beginning to be annoyed.

Molly had almost reached the goose.

Golly yelled, "Don't touch the—"

"What?" Molly grasped Golly's elbow and didn't touch the goose.

"I'm stuck. Pull me off."

Molly pulled.

Honk!

But Golly stayed stuck.

"Help me, Holly!" Molly called, and held out her hand. "Pull!"

Holly took the hand and pulled.

Honk!

But Golly stayed stuck.

The three of them trotted after the goose. In a few minutes, Molly got tired. "I'm going home." She tried to let go of Golly's elbow. She yanked and tugged.

Honk!

She was stuck.

Holly tried to let go of Molly's hand, but she was stuck too.

Eleven

Hmm . . . Robin thought, glancing back. Whoever touches the goose becomes sticky. And the next person and the next become sticky too! He wondered how long a chain he could make. They did look funny, the three of them.

Golly was angry. "Dearie, stop this instant!"

Ethelinda didn't care a bit for Golly. Now *there* was a human who could use punishing.

Robin saw a mule and wagon in the distance, coming back from Biddle Castle.

It was the Snettering-on-Snoakes chandler. He wondered where Robin was going with that goose and why Golly, Holly, and Molly were traipsing after him. And who was the old lady?

"Whoa, Jenny," he called to his mule.

Holly, Molly, and Golly yelled to the chandler to set them loose. When he understood what they wanted, he tied a rope to Jenny's harness and threw the rope over Holly.

Oh, no! Robin thought. The goose can't be stronger than a mule.

"Pull, Jenny. Pull."

Jenny tried, but she couldn't. She got pulled instead.

The goose *is* stronger! Robin thought.

The chandler tried to jump down from his cart to see what was wrong, but he couldn't. He was stuck to his bench.

Robin glanced back and almost laughed. The beginning of a joke came to him. Why does a king always seem glum? But he was still too upset to think of the punch line.

The chandler and his cart and mule followed Robin and the golden goose. Holly and Molly kept hollering that Jenny should try harder. Golly kept screaming at Robin to stop, to listen, to behave himself . . . dearie.

The Royal Drawbridge Guard saw a strange parade, heading for Biddle Castle. He frowned. There was the chandler. But the chandler had left only a little while ago. Who were the others with him?

The chandler looked flustered. Could be trouble. The guard got his pike ready.

They came closer. The guard wondered why the chandler and his mule and wagon and three wenches were following a lad with a golden goose. Why were the wenches shouting? Why did the mule look so confused? And who was the old lady?

Then the guard understood. The lad was really a prince! A contestant! The guard started laughing and put down his pike. This was so funny. It was sure to win. He bowed as Robin approached.

Robin thought, He's letting me in! The old lady is right! Maybe he'd like to come along too. He called, "Help yourself to a feather."

The guard lunged at the goose.

Honk!

The guard was stuck.

Robin was going by the Royal Kitchen Door just as the Royal Third Assistant Cook stepped outside.

My, the cook thought, that's a fine pair of goose feet, perfect for pickling. He reached out and grabbed the goose's right foot.

Honk!

In the Royal Tournament Arena Lark wept on. So far seventy-five princes had tried to make her laugh. The king and the Royal Nobles were merrier than ever before. But Lark's eyes hurt from crying so much. Two Royal Laundresses worked day and night to keep her in fresh hankies.

Right now a prince was saying "Fififferall" over and over. At first no one had laughed, but after a few minutes a Royal Baroness had begun to giggle, and then the Royal Chief Councillor had joined in, and soon everyone was laughing heartily.

Except Lark, of course.

A commotion at the arena's entrance drowned out the prince. Heads turned. Lark didn't look up.

Robin, Holly, Molly, Golly, the Royal Drawbridge

Guard, and the Royal Third Assistant Cook jogged into the arena. Behind them, the chandler, Jenny, and the cart clattered along. Ethelinda skipped and leaped and waved her arms in the air, to add to the silliness.

Robin saw Lark. There she was. Weeping! Her sweet face was unutterably sad. She was wiping her eyes and staring at her lap. She hadn't even seen him.

He broke into a run. *Lark! Oh, Lark!*

Twelve

King Harrumphrey and the courtiers saw the goose parade and roared with laughter. Even the prince saying "Fiffifferall" laughed. The Earl of Pildenue fell out of his seat, laughing. Dame Cloris woke up and started laughing. King Harrumphrey rocked back and forth on his throne.

Lark wept and never looked up. Where was her love now? Did he miss her?

Robin moaned. Whatever had happened to Lark must have been—must still be—awful. He began to cry in sympathy.

Under the laughter and the shrieks, Lark heard a new sound. She closed her eyes to hear better. Someone else was weeping.

Robin ran across the arena. He shouted, "Oh, Lark! Oh, my love! Oh, don't cry!"

She opened her eyes. Robin? Here? Yes! She smiled rapturously at him. Just at him—because she didn't notice the guard, the cook, Ethelinda, Golly, Molly, Holly, the chandler, Jenny, the cart, or the goose.

She's smiling! Robin thought. He smiled back at her through his tears.

Lark jumped up, knocking over her outdoor throne. Then she saw the spectacle behind Robin. They were so funny! She ran down the arena steps, laughing as she ran.

Ethelinda laughed too. Giving a successful reward was its own reward.

Robin thought of the punch line for the joke about why a king seems glum. He laughed. His laughter shook the goose.

Honk!

Golly shrieked, "Dearie! Get away from that princess."

Robin said, "Loose, goose."

Holly, Molly, Golly, the chandler, the mule, the cart, the Royal Drawbridge Guard, and the Royal Third Assistant Cook were released from their hold on the goose and each other.

Royal Nobles poured onto the field. They surrounded Robin and bowed to him and shouted, "Congratulations!" Ethelinda stood at the edge of the crowd. She was sure she'd never have trouble with rewards again, now that she'd found the goose.

"Harrumph."

The crowd parted for King Harrumphrey.

He was delighted to see Larkie laughing again. And this young prince had done it cleverly. Dressing like a commoner—very smart. He'd make a fine son-in-law. "We are pleased to make your harrumphance, Your

Highness." He put his arm around Robin's shoulder. "What kingdom do you harrumph from?"

Highness? Kingdom? Who did the king think he was? Robin knelt. "I live in Snettering-on-Snoakes, Sire. I'm Robin, the baker's son."

He *is* a commoner! the king thought. He's that blasted baker's son.

"I want to marry him," Lark said.

King Harrumphrey wanted to throw him into the Royal Dungeon. But he couldn't, not with Larkie smiling at the boy in that demented way.

Golly opened her mouth to say that she was marrying Robin.

"Son," the king said, "only a prince could win the harrumph."

Golly shut her mouth.

Robin thought, So that's why Lark was weeping. He thought of weeping again himself, but he couldn't stop smiling at her.

King Harrumphrey turned to his daughter. "You don't want to harrumphy him, honeyharrumph. We'll give him a harrumphdred golden coins instead."

Ethelinda was furious. She hated a snob. Couldn't the king tell what a fine lad Robin was?

"No, Father. He doesn't want a gift."

"A harrumphdred golden coins and a golden cage for that golden harrumph."

"No thank you, Your Majesty."

"Father, I'm going to cry again."

"Don't harrumph. We hate it when you harrumph.

Let us think." He couldn't let her marry a commoner. What would his Royal Forebears have done? Well, King Humphrey IV would have devised a test. What kind of test? Hmm . . .

"We will consent to the harrumphage," he said, "if the lad can pass three harrumphs. For the first harrumph he must find someone who can drink a whole cellar full of harrumph." He saw Lark's expression. "Very fine harrumph. Only the best."

Golly laughed. Her dearie would never pass the test.

Who could drink so much? Robin wondered. And what's harrumph? Beet juice? Bat's milk?

I can do it, Ethelinda thought. I can drink anything.

"The second harrumph is to find someone who can eat a hill of harrumphs as tall as our Royal Glass Hill."

Now what's harrumph? Robin thought. Skunk sausages?

"And the third harrumph . . ." The king paused for effect. ". . . is to come to Biddle Castle on a ship that harrumphs on land or water."

Lark frowned. "What?"

"A harrumph that sails on land or harrumph." No commoner can pass these tests, King Harrumphrey thought. But if this upstart does, we'll dream up three more tests, and then three more. As many as it takes.

Thirteen

The third test might be hard, Ethelinda thought.

Robin couldn't imagine how he'd pass any of them. He was going to lose Lark all over again.

"The tests are impossible," Lark wailed.

"Sweetie, this harrumph has already made you laugh, and you and we thought that was imharrumph-ible."

But that was because he's my love, she thought. And because he's funnier than anyone else.

Robin remembered that the old lady had said she might be able to help him some more. He turned her way, and she winked at him—although she still wasn't sure about the last test.

Robin began to have a suspicion about her. "I'll try," he told the king. He bowed. "Farewell." Farewell, my love.

"Farewell." Lark smiled bravely.

Robin picked up the goose and started out of the arena. Ethelinda walked at his side. Golly began to go with them, but the fairy waved her invisible wand.

Golly's feet wouldn't move, no matter how hard she tried. "Dearie, I want to come with you."

He kept walking.

"Get back here and help me, dearie."

He walked faster.

When they were out of sight of the castle, Robin said, "You're a fairy, aren't you?"

Smart human! Ethelinda resumed her normal form.

Honk!

Robin staggered back. She was gigantic! And those wings! Pink, fleshy, and vast.

He thought it might be a good idea to bow, so he did. "Will you help me?"

She turned herself into a hungry-and-thirsty-looking beggar. "This is the right shape for the first two tests, don't you think?"

He nodded. They waited a half hour so it would seem as if he had spent some time searching for someone. Then they started back to the tournament arena.

Meanwhile, King Harrumphrey was annoyed because he'd used up seven hundred kegs of cider flooding the basement of the Royal Museum of Quest Souvenirs. Worse, he had no idea how he was going to un-flood it when Robin's person failed to drink it dry.

But in case whoever it was succeeded, the king had ordered the Royal Kitchen to cook thousands of meatballs for the second test. Most likely everybody at the castle was going to be eating meatballs till meatballs came out of their eyeballs.

Lark felt a little hope when she saw the beggar, who was as skinny as one of the goose's legs. His cracked and chapped tongue hung out, for certain the driest tongue in Biddle. King Harrumphrey started to worry.

Holly, Molly, the chandler, the guard, and the cook had left. Golly had stayed, although the spell on her feet had worn off.

At the museum a Royal Servant opened the trap-door to the cellar. Cider lapped against the ceiling. Robin put the goose down and stood next to Lark to watch.

Ethelinda used her fairy powers to discover if anything was in the cellar besides cider. Seventeen rats, drinking and swimming. She made them vanish. She didn't want their whiskers anywhere near her mouth, and she didn't want King Harrumphrey to claim that she'd had help drinking a single sip.

The servant handed her a ladle.

A ladle! It would take years with a ladle. Ethelinda waved it aside and lowered her head into the cellar.

She began to drink. The first seventy gallons were delicious, but after that she wished someone had thought to add cinnamon. When a hundred kegs were gone, she could no longer reach low enough to drink. The servant went for a ladder.

While they waited, Ethelinda said, "Thank you, Sire. I would have perished of thirst if not for you. I only hope there's enough here to satisfy me."

King Harrumphrey nodded and tried to look

"TILL MEATBALLS CAME OUT OF THEIR EYEBALLS."

gracious. Lark and Robin held hands while he whispered jokes into her ear. Her favorite was Why are elves delicious? She thought the answer was hysterical: Because they're brownies.

Golly glared at Lark, Robin, the goose, and the beggar. She swore to give that beggar a kick if he ever showed up at her inn.

The king thought up two additional tests, in case he needed them. He'd make Robin find someone who could play twenty musical instruments at once and someone who could go up the Royal Grand Staircase on his head.

The servant returned with a ladder. Ethelinda descended two rungs and drank.

In an hour the cellar was dry. King Harrumphrey inspected it carefully, hoping against hope that he'd find at least a drop of cider, but he didn't.

It took Ethelinda one and a half hours to finish the meatballs. When she was done, she bowed to the king and burped.

King Harrumphrey said, "Robin, you must harrumph back here in two hours with a harrumph that can sail on land or sea."

Lark said, "You didn't say there was a time limit."

"Two harrumphs and no longer. By Royal Harrumph!"

Fourteen

In a field beyond the castle, Robin patted the goose and waited for Ethelinda to create the ship. Instead, she sat on the ground and put her head in her hands.

He cleared his throat uneasily. "Is there a problem?"

"I'm thinking." She could make a beautiful ship, one that could weather any storm. But on shore it wouldn't budge. She could make a wonderful carriage that would go anywhere on land, even without a road. But in water it would sink.

Robin said, "What if the sails turn into wings when the boat reaches the shore?"

"Then the king would say it's a bird on land and not a boat."

The minutes ticked by. An hour passed. The sky began to get dark.

An hour and a half passed. The stars came out.

Maybe the lad was on the right track with the wings idea, Ethelinda thought.

Fifteen more minutes passed.

What if she filled the hold with wings? Not birds, just wings. When the ship was on land, the wings would fly up against the ceiling of the hold and lift the ship off the ground.

That was the way to do it. She waved her wand.

Robin gasped. The boat was beautiful, painted yellow with blue trim. The sails were blindingly white. If it could move on land, it would pass the test.

But King Harrumphrey probably still wouldn't let him marry Lark. The king would think of more and more tests, until the fairy got sick of tests and left him.

I have to think of a way to make this the last one, Robin thought. He stared at the ship. It needed something, something to show what kind of ship it was. It needed a pennant.

A pennant! That was it.

"Is there any empty land far from here where I could be prince?" he asked.

Ethelinda thought for a moment. "You could be Prince of the Briny Isles. This ship will get you there in seven years. You'll starve to death, though, unless you like anchovies."

"That doesn't matter." If he actually had to go there, his idea would have failed. "Would you make a pennant that says 'Prince Robin of the Briny Isles'?"

She did, and she dressed him as a prince, in a red satin robe and a doublet with diamond buttons. On his head she placed a silver crown set with rubies.

They mounted a plank onto the ship. It set sail across the field. The boat was a glorious sight, skimming a foot above the ground, its sails bellying out in the breeze.

When the boat reached the castle, it descended into the moat, to prove that it could sail on water too. Then it rose again and stopped a few yards from Lark, the king, and Golly, who were standing near the castle drawbridge. Ethelinda, disguised as a nobleman, threw a ladder over the side. Robin and the nobleman climbed down and bowed. The goose remained on deck, strutting up and down and honking.

Lark curtsied and said, "Your Highness."

King Harrumphrey scowled. The lad looked better, but a baker's son in prince's clothing was still a baker's son.

Golly gasped. Robin had passed every test. He was going to marry the princess! How dared he? She screamed, "Dearie, I wouldn't marry you if you were the stupidest lad in Biddle. You led me—"

"Be silent," Robin said. "I command it."

Golly was so surprised, she fell silent.

He sounds princely, King Harrumphrey thought, but still . . .

Ethelinda said, "I am the Duke of Halibutia and the envoy of the King of the Briny Isles. He sent me here to find an heir worthy to rule after his death, and I have found him. Prince Robin has more natural royalty than anyone I've ever encountered."

"Sire," Robin said, "I have passed your tests. Give

me your daughter's hand in marriage."

"Do, Father. Please."

Robin continued. "Then we shall depart for my kingdom, which is seven years' sailing from here." He held his breath, hoping.

King Harrumphrey frowned. Since the envoy—a duke!—had chosen Robin, then the lad had truly become a prince. But seven years! Even if they turned around and came back as soon as they got there, the king still wouldn't see his Larkie for fourteen years.

He couldn't live for fourteen years without the sight of her. "Harrumph. Er, we admit that you are a prince, but can't you stay here? Can't those Briny Harrumphs do without you?"

"If I stay here, I'll just be a baker's son."

"Father . . ."

King Harrumphrey looked at his daughter. She was half smiling. He knew what would turn that smile into a laugh. And he knew what would turn it into a frown and tears.

There had been enough tears. "No, you will not be a baker's harrumph. You will be a Harrumph Prince of Biddle."

Lark and Robin hugged each other. They danced across the Royal Drawbridge and back again.

Robin was so happy, he decided to try out a joke on King Harrumphrey. He said, "Why does a king always seem glum?"

King Harrumphrey frowned. What was the fellow talking about?

Lark was thrilled. Now Father would see what Robin was really like. "Why?" she said.

"Because he's . . ." Robin sighed dramatically. ". . . a sire."

The king stared. Then he got it. A sire. A sigh-er! He started laughing. "Har har harrumph." It was the funniest joke he'd ever heard. "A harrumph-er!" This commoner-turned-prince would liven up the castle. "Har harrumph har. Harrumph har har."

Lark preferred the yardstick-ruler joke. But if Father loved this one, that was all that mattered.

Epilogue

ake was as opposed to the match between Robin and Lark as King Harrumphrey had been. He said,

"I forbid the marriage with Princess Lark.
I would rather see the boy wed a barracuda."

King Harrumphrey offered to elevate Jake to the rank of earl and to knight Nat and Matt, who had finally recovered from Ethelinda's spell.

The three of them refused to become nobles. However, Jake agreed to the wedding when the king named him Royal Chief Poet and named Nat and Matt Royal Co-Chief Dictionarians in charge of adding new words to Biddlish.

Robin and Lark were married within a week, and the whole population of Snettering-on-Snoakes was invited, even though every one of them was a commoner.

King Harrumphrey performed the wedding cere- mony, although Lark and Robin weren't sure if the harrumphiage they were entering into was their marriage or their carriage.

Dame Cloris snored straight through the king's speech. Golly stayed awake. She sat next to the chandler and decided he was the man for her. If she couldn't boss him around, she'd boss Jenny the mule.

After the ceremony Robin told a joke:

"Why is a horse like a wedding?"

He waited, but not one of the guests could think of the answer, so he told them, "They both need a groom."

Lark laughed and laughed. She felt so proud of Robin, the funniest prince in Biddle history.

Jake wasn't sure he got the joke. His own Horsteed had never had a groom in his life. But he smiled and waited for the laughter to subside, so he could recite a poem to Robin.

> *"I thought to maiden Golly you'd be wed,*
> *But you married Princess Lark in place of her."*

Robin and Lark thanked Ethelinda over and over for her help. Their gratitude went a long way toward restoring her confidence, and she was certain she'd never make another mistake.

The party after the ceremony was held on the bank of Snoakes Stream. Robin and Lark waded right in and pulled courtiers and commoners in after them for a Royal Splashfest. The golden goose waddled in too and splashed and honked at everybody. Lark was in

heaven, splashing dukes and counts, and having them
splash her right back.

And they all lived happily ever after.

Harrumph!

Honk!

Gail Carson Levine grew up in New York City and has been writing all her life. Her first book for children, *Ella Enchanted*, was a 1998 Newbery Honor Book. Levine's other books include *Fairest*; *Dave at Night*, an ALA Notable Book and Best Book for Young Adults; *The Wish*; *The Two Princesses of Bamarre*; and the six Princess Tales books: *The Princess Test*, *The Fairy's Mistake*, *Princess Sonora and the Long Sleep*, *Cinderellis and the Glass Hill*, *The Fairy's Return*, and *For Biddle's Sake*. She is also the author of the picture book *Betsy Who Cried Wolf*, illustrated by Scott Nash. Gail, her husband, David, and their Airedale, Baxter, live in a two-hundred-year-old farmhouse in the Hudson River Valley of New York State.